Cowboy Lullaby

Kadian Tracey

Disclaimer:

Cowboy Lullaby
Edited by: Kato Rayne
Proofread: Lottie
Formatted by: Kendra Mei Chailyn
Cover by: Kendra Mei Chailyn
Copyright © 2025 by SusuKhaa
ISBN: 978-0-9869550-1-3

Prologue

The rain had stopped pounding against the glass. The old tree just to the right of her window hadn't crashed into the side of the house for a good ten minutes.

And the smash of thunder followed by the sizzle of lightning hadn't scared the hell out of her for some time. Still, those thoughts seemed almost trivial to what was happening inside Jennifer Cozel's mind.

Her heart had been busy slamming inside her chest as though it wanted to hop out and run away. Jennifer wouldn't blame it.

Another loud bang sounded from somewhere in the house and she jumped. Her eyes caught the chest behind the door then lifted to see if the handle would twist to the right then to the left. When nothing happened but another loud bang, she shifted slightly to alleviate the pain her legs.

What day is it?

Jennifer trembled at her father's footsteps storming through the house. He'd been on another one of his binges. Those always put him in a mood.

Two days of a steady intake of alcohol with no food always made him more than cranky.

Each morning after he disappeared to wherever it was he went in the day time, she would lug the bag of liquor bottles to the recycle bin at the back of the house. Lately, she'd made more than two trips.

That couldn't be healthy.

How could one person drink so much? And how could he drink so much and was able to function? How was that a possibility?

The nights when his favorite baseball team lost were the worst. The mornings were even harder.

A long time ago, she'd learned to stay out of his way after a bender. Her father was a miserable human being to begin with. The alcohol only pushed forth the really mean side of him.

Jennifer couldn't remember a time when her father was sober. She couldn't remember a time when he'd been much of a father—one who cared or tried making her happy. She couldn't remember ever being his little girl or feeling as if he cared.

How sad was that?

Her father's abuse of alcohol had always been a thing.

He drank to wake up.

Drank to fall asleep.

Drank to silence the demons inside his head.

Often, she would hear him yelling at them when he wasn't screaming at her. Mostly, they had to do with the death of her mother. The sympathy she felt for him losing the love of his life had died like her mother, years ago.

She was very young when her mother passed, and he didn't once stopped to think Jennifer had lost someone too. Instead, her father had fallen into his feels, dangerously, and had taken it out on her every chance he got while smelling like a brewery on fire.

He drank when he was happy, when he was sad but most importantly, he drank whenever he took a good look at Jennifer.

After years of taking the abuse, no matter what she did, Jennifer knew she reminded him of his dead wife—a twitch of her shoulder, a tilt of her head.

The abuse became worse as she grew older.

She would stare at pictures of her mother, holding them up beside her head in the mirror.

Her eyes, her hair, the flatness of her nose, the pudginess of her cheeks—each time she did that, it was her mother's eyes looking back at her.

Her father couldn't escape his dead wife. Each time he walked into the house and laid eye son Jennifer, it only brought the ghost with her—and the beatings grew worse.

Hence the drinking.

Sometimes a scent in the air reminded him of her. Since that was obviously Jennifer's fault, the first time he shoved her to the ground and punched her into unconsciousness.

Afterward, he'd fill a bucket with cold water and toss it in her face.

That was a horrid way to wake anyone up. The chock of the water had her jerking upright, screaming then clawing at her neck. The cold water against her body left her gasping for breath.

Jennifer would never get used to that.

She was in her final semester in high school and was pretty sure she was going to fail. He had forbidden her to go back to school. She wasn't sure the reason.

Maybe it was because School made her happy. He'd told her once that if he couldn't be content, she would never be. Then again, it could be because he couldn't touch her while she was at school and every fibre of him hated that. When she out of his hatred, Jennifer was someone—people knew who she was, and they asked her thoughts on things.

It could also be because he knew the moment she was finished school she'd leave. If she failed no one would hire her.

Who would hire a high school drop out?

Then she'd be stuck with him—forever.

After she turned eighteen, the county no longer required her to go to school.

Which made no sense to her for that was when they should have been pushing her the last few steps, so she'd finish.

No one came looking for her—not even her best friend. She was legally an adult and that was the law. She held out no hope anyone would save her. But the one thought that kept her awake at nights, was that her father could kill her in the house and no one would wound be the wiser.

Her father had to go out for more booze. That was the only peace she'd gotten over the past few weeks. Whenever the car left, Jennifer would peer out her window and watch until it was long gone before tiptoeing out of her room to get something to eat. But she couldn't take anything he would miss.

Luckily, she'd stashed a couple of Jamaican buns with a tin of cheese in her room. All she really needed was water.

If she didn't open the cheese, she could keep it hidden in her room for as long as she needed.

Filling her traveler's mug with cold water she drank the whole thing and refilled it. After checking to ensure she hadn't moved anything else, Jennifer hurried to the bathroom. She took a quick shower, used the bathroom, then darted back to her prison.

Before she got too comfortable, she locked the door and shoved the heavy chest behind it. That didn't keep her father out when he was on a rampage—but it slowed him down, bought her some time to brace herself.

After getting dressed, she went about something to eat.

The buns she'd bought were getting smaller and she wasn't sure how much longer they would last. When it was all gone, she would be out of money, out of food and out of luck.

Sometimes, before he demanded she become a shut-in, her best friend would sneak something over and she would quickly eat it. Gale was good for Jennifer and gave her some happiness in an otherwise dark world.

Breaking off a piece of the bun, Jennifer shoved it into her mouth. The sweet of it flooded her senses, causing her to moan and rest helplessly against the bed.

Her eyes caught the scars on her leg when she stretched them before her. Swallowing the lump in her throat, Jennifer used her free hand and tugged her dress down to cover them. When it didn't cover her ankles, she curled her legs beneath her bum and took a breath.

Suddenly she wasn't hungry anymore.

In a state of heightened fear, she sat in the same position until her legs cramped, throbbed then went numb.

Still, she didn't dare move.

The darkness flowed in through the window and still she didn't move. Her eyes burned and from time to time she forced herself to blink. Though she yearned for sleep, she couldn't. Every time her eyes closed, she remembered her father then jerked awake.

He'd be drinking that evening.

She wouldn't be getting any sleep.

Time passed, slowly. Jennifer only knew that because the room was now black except for the periodic dance of someone's headlights going around the corner by the house. The hushed silence was only interrupted by the rumble of engines only to die in the distance and returned to solitude.

A loud bang on the front door pulled her upward. She grabbed the bun she'd still have out, wrapped it up and shoved it into her bag. She pushed it under her bed and pulled the sheets down over it. Out of habit she looked around to ensure she had no contraband.

Jennifer took a breath and rose. Her legs trembled, weak by the position they'd been in for such a long time. That caused her to slump forward, and she caught herself on the edge of the bed.

Shaking her legs, Jennifer tried working out the numbness. When she finally had some feeling back into her legs, she was going to sit again but curiosity kept her up.

The knock came again.

The fact she'd missed a car pulling into the driveway scared her. But she was exhausted—yes, that explained it.

5

The knock sounded once more and by this time, Jennifer sucked in enough courage to leave her room. She pulled the chest from before the door and stuck her head out. The hallway was spotless, silent. The walls were devoid of pictures. The halls empty of any kind of fixture except a solitary light bulb on at the end of the hall on the centre wall.

On the tips of her toes, she scurried from her room and peered over the balcony before hurrying down the stairs. She peeked into the scantily furnished room.

Marshal wasn't there.

When she got to the front door, she pulled her sleeves down over her arms, took a breath and pulled the door open.

To her shock and relief her father wasn't standing there. Instead, two police officers faced her.

"May—may I help you?" Jennifer asked softly, ensuring not to meet their eyes.

"Hi, your name?" one asked.

Jennifer glanced upward quickly then casted her stare to his belt buckle. In that quick glimpse, he gave her a grim smile, one she'd recognize anywhere.

Jennifer was used to sadness.

"Jennifer, Jennifer Cozel."

"What is your relationship to Marshal Cozel?"

Jennifer couldn't speak for the lump in her throat just wouldn't allow the words to come out. Clearing her throat, she tried again. "He's my father."

"I'm afraid we have some bad news." The other officer spoke up. "Your father was killed a little earlier in an accident."

Jennifer stood before the police officers with her arms wrapped around herself. If her father was dead, it was no accident. He was probably too wasted or too hung over to see where he was going and crashed into a tree.

"Did you hear me ma'am?" the cop asked. "Your father is dead. He ran a red light and was struck by a drunk driver going the other way."

I knew it.

Eighteen year old Jennifer blinked, then nodded. "I heard you. He was drinking."

"We figured. There was a bottle of Jack Daniels in the car after they managed to cut him out with the Jaws of Life."

"Did anyone else get hurt?" she whispered.

"Yes. The driver in the other car but nothing life threatening."

"That's good."

"What's good?

"My father is always drinking." A sinking feeling pulsed through her, leaving her feeling empty. Still, she was left with a profound sense of something urgent, something on the point of breaking inside. "If he was going to crash I'm glad no one else died. Thank you for informing me officers." Jennifer squeaked. "Where can I...can I..."

"His body is at the morgue." One of the cops handed her a card. "You can go there and identify it."

She wrapped her fingers around the card and nodded again.

"We're really sorry for your loss."

She smiled tightly, backed into the house and closed the door. She pressed her back to it, breathing quickly. The card was digging into her flesh for she held it too tightly, but she couldn't seem to stop herself and release it.

Marshal Cozel is dead.

What did that mean?

Freedom?

Blessed freedom?

Should she be happy or sad? Should she be doing back flips? What was she supposed to feel for the death of the man who'd stomped her into the ground?

Jennifer wasn't sure how long she stood there or when she'd even moved. When she shook her head, she was sitting in the living room on the old sofa. The card the police officer had given her was on the seat beside her.

Perhaps it was a joke.

It had to be a rouse. Marshal was testing her to see if she would do anything foolish. He wanted to see if she'd eat any of his food or use anything he bought. She wouldn't fall for it and she had no intention of going into a morgue to feed his sick sense of perversion.

Though she didn't touch any of the food in the house, Jennifer did went back to school. Most of the teachers took pity on her at the news of her father's demise and allowed to catch up on the days she'd missed. One even gave her an extra credit assignment.

If he was going to kick her ass for breaking his rules, she was going to make the ass-kicking be for something that would help her after she could use once she had backbone enough to leave.

Her drama teacher was the only one who gave her a hard time.

Jennifer merely ignored the woman—she didn't need the class to graduate.

It was to fill a spare period she hadn't wanted to use. She didn't see Gail, her best friend. Jennifer figured the girl was busy, and merely buckled down to bring her grades back up. Jennifer found out a day later that Gale was away with her mother on some conference her mother had to do for work.

Another week slipped by and each day she arrived home to voicemails from the morgue. After three weeks, a letter arrived.

She ignored it.

A month later, her father still didn't surface. She kept expecting him to crawl out of some dark corner, but he never did.

Finally, on a bright afternoon, Jennifer left school and took the bus going in the opposite direction from her house. She'd never done that before—she never dared.

Her father would wait for her after school to see if she was home on time.

If she wasn't, he would beat her until all she did was curl into a ball on the floor and wait for it to be over.

Sometimes it wasn't her fault.

The bus would be late, or the first bus would be too full. Then she would have to wait for a second or a third. She would walk but she would have gotten a beaten anyways because the distance was too far to make it on time.

In front of the police station, Jennifer took a breath and climbed the stairs. In through a set of glass doors, she stopped at a front desk and managed a smile. "I'm here about my father."

"Your father?"

"Y-yes. He is in the morgue?"

"Oh, you mean the unclaimed body. Good thing you came today."

"Why is that?"

"They've already kept him longer than they should." The man replied, perusing something on his computer screen. "He was about to be cremated today."

"Oh."

"Hold on. I'll get someone to escort you down."

Jennifer nodded and sat on one of the chairs in what looked to be a makeshift waiting room. The walls had posters of Mothers

Against Drunk Driving instead of paintings, but she didn't care. Jennifer had a shiver inside her as though someone was walking over her grave.

The irony of it all wasn't lost on her. Marshall had been a drunk all her life and for him to be killed in the manner he'd died was the biggest irony of them all.

She managed a small chuckled then. "How fitting."

"Did you say something?" The officer asked, leaning half his body out to look at her.

Jennifer blushed but shook her head. She clasped her hands in her lap and kept her head down.

"Hi, you're here about the body?"

Jennifer whipped around and rose. The woman standing there was older. She wore a black lab coat with the name "Silverman" stitched against the right breast in neat, white letters. Though her hair was thinning, she was still put together immaculately. "Yes. I'm Jennifer Cozel."

"His daughter?"

"Yes, ma'am." A bad taste rose in Jennifer's mouth.

Claiming Marshal left a bitter taste in her mouth.

"I'm Doctor Silverman. Please, come this way."

Jennifer followed the woman down a corridor to the elevator and down two floors. In the basement, they walked a long a creepy hallway then into a room that smelt eerily like a hospital. There were shiny tables set out in the centre of the room and on the far wall was what looked like lockers.

She shivered.

Dr. Silverman walked over to the lockers and turned to face her. Jennifer stood just on the other side, facing her.

"Are you ready?"

"I think so."

"Keep in mind, he's been on ice for quite some time, so his skin colour might not be what you are used to."

Jennifer nodded.

Dr. Silverman hesitated, her lips in a thin line. For a second, it seemed she wanted to say something to Jennifer, but changed her mind and opened the small, silver door. A small gust of white smoke puffed out.

The room was suddenly freezing. The locker's door creaked before she reached in and grabbed something and pulled.

Pushing air out her mouth, she kept her eyes fastened on the bulge in the black bag even as Dr. Silverman's long fingers, with the unpainted nails, pulled the zipper down. Finally, it was open, and Dr. Silverman pushed the flaps aside.

Jennifer lifted onto her tip toes and looked down into the corpse' face.

He was a strange, light purple colour.

Streams of steam lifted from his flesh—she remembered what that was. After being frozen, oxygen caused the small puffs of smoke to rise upward.

She gasped.

"Is this your father?" Dr. Silverman's voice echoed in the silent room.

Jennifer tilted her head looking at him. She marveled at how helpless he seemed in that moment. She'd been so terrified of him for all her life, afraid of his mouth, his temper, his gaze. Now, he laid there, frozen in death and all she could think of was why God taken so long to answer her prayers.

"Is this your father?" Dr. Silverman repeated, a little louder this time.

She lifted her eyes to the Doctor and nodded. "Yes. That's him."

"We need to make arrangements for you to take the body."

"Take it?" Jennifer asked. "I don't want it."

"Umm…" She seemed shocked. "Surely, you want to do what his last wishes were."

"Last wishes?" Jennifer shook her head. "Lady, this man hasn't been sober in years to do anything much less tell anyone what his last wishes were."

"So—"

"I can't. I don't know the first thing about making arrangements for a funeral." I sniffled. "I'm still in high school."

"If you don't, the county will have to cremate him."

"Then, that's what will have to happen. I'm sorry. I have to go." Jennifer took off running. A sign pointed her in the direction of the stairs and she shoved through the heavy doors.

Taking the steps two at a time, she reached the main floor, huffing and puffing.

Her lungs hurt as though starved for air.

Outside, she doubled over and hurled into a bed of flowers to the left of the railing.

Repeatedly, her body heaved.

11

She threw up until her throat burned and even then, her body dry heaved.

Finally, she straightened her back and flopped to the low wall.

That night she spent a few hours sitting in front of the fridge on a chair. What did she know about running a house? With her luck her father probably hadn't paid the bills in a while, so she would have to move out.

But she hadn't gotten anything in the mail to tell her that. With a shrug. Jennifer set to work cleaning out the fridge.

Once that was over, she turned her attention to the liquor cabinet. After grabbing a box from the kitchen, she stacked every, single bottle in it. She had no used for the stuff and she'd be damned if she became her father.

With it full, she tugged it across the floor to the front door and set it on the front porch. It would have to wait there until garbage day.

Next to go were all the veggies her father didn't want her to eat. They had rotted long before his death—he just hadn't bothered throwing them out.

Once the cleaning was done, a brilliant idea materialised in her head.

Even though she couldn't take care of the house, she was pretty sure she could sell it. Jennifer spent the next few days digging through her father's possessions until she found the deed. It was in her mother's name.

Since she had the death certificate for her mother in her room, she was sure it wouldn't be a big deal to get the deed changed over to her name.

That would make the sale easier. She'd have to search for it on the internet then talked to Gale once her friend returned from her small trip away.

She lay on the bed with her mother's death certificate beside her along with the deed.

There was a sound at the window.

Jennifer turned her eyes then darted for it. She flung the window open and peered down into the late evening light.

"You can use the door." Jennifer called to her only friend.

"Where's your father?" Gale Dumas replied.

"I'll come down and get you."

Pulling her body in, she pulled the window close and hurried down the stairs. She opened the door and Gale stuck her head in the door.

"Where's your dad?"

"He died."

"The hell you say?" Gale stood akimbo. "You're messing with me."

"Nope. He died in a car crash almost two months ago. I'm just trying to figure out what I'm going to do with myself and this place."

"You can't stay here." The two walked into the kitchen and flopped into a chair. "There will be too many bills to pay and you're not working."

Jennifer boldly went to the fridge and pulled out a plastic bag with pita wraps. She then found cheese and some chicken sticks in the freezer. She dumped them into a foil tin and stuck it in the oven before pouring two glasses of milk and sitting down with her friend.

"I know all that. I don't know the first thing about keeping a house. I want to sell it and get a small apartment with the money. Do you think your mom could help me out?"

"I'm sure she can. You want to pack up some things and come stay with us? I don't want you in this house alone. It creeps me out."

Jennifer took a drink from her glass and inhaled deeply. She was never able to sleep over before. She figured it would a treat. With a smile she hugged Gale tightly. "Thank you."

"For what?"

"For being there for me. For helping me as much as you could even though he wasn't very nice to you."

"Girl, please. He wasn't nice to anyone. I just wished I could have done more. Now." Gale eased back. "Let's take that food to go. You go pack while I make sure everything is turned off down here."

Jennifer hugged her again and rushed up the stairs. She was eighteen years old and for the first time she would be going out on a Friday night.

Not only that, but she would be having her first sleep over.

What should she pack? Not wanting to look foolish, Jennifer packed the essentials—nightgown, toothbrush and a few changes of clothes.

She also dug through her drawer and hauled out, her best under-wears she set aside for special occasions. The day she went on her first and only date, she wore the pink one with the bow on the back.

It wasn't because she thought anyone would see it but because it made her feel like a woman.

He never called her afterward. He saw the scar on her shoulder and ran so fast in the other direction, Jennifer swore she still had whiplash. Her father never knew about Kevin.

"Jenny! Pull the lead out! Let's go! Mom wants the car back." Gale yelled from down the stairs before Jennifer heard her footsteps on the step. "You coming?"

"I'm coming." Jennifer made a face. "I just—I've never slept over before. I don't know what I'm doing."

"Don't worry about it. Whatever you forget, we'll hook you up. Let's go."

Gale grabbed the bag from the bed and headed for the door.

Jennifer followed but ran back to grab her house keys and the stuffed teddy bear that had long since lost an eye and a couple buttons from where it sat on her bed. She then ran after her best friend.

The moment they were in the car, Gale peeled from the side street by her house and south on Campow Road.

"I'm so jealous of you. I can't drive." Jennifer sighed.

"That can be changed. Your tyrant is dead. There's a whole world out there for you right now."

"Seriously, Gale. Thank you!"

"Don't mention it. You want to thank me? Let's get your life off the ground."

Jennifer didn't reply to that. She simply clutched her teddy bear to her chest with one hand and stuck the other out the window to enjoy the wind blowing through her fingers.

One

Heavenly—there was no other word to describe the cool, clear water flowing over his skin.

Swimming was his backup plan. What Rone would rather be doing was pounding the pavement in a good jog. Sure, his doctor told him the running was hell on his aging knees, but Rone enjoy it. Sure, he could use a treadmill, but there was something seriously heart-breaking about walking and not really going anywhere.

Besides, a run would have been a lot more invigorating and would have given him a chance to be by himself and clear his mind. But that plan was quickly shelved when his best friend's little girl found out he would be leaving.

The moment she was told the news, Anne he wouldn't let him out of her sight.

She spent most of the morning clinging to him. Even when she napped, she did so in his lap, with her ear over his heart and her hand tangled in his shirt.

Eventually he convinced her he wasn't going to leave without saying good-bye and she allowed him to go for a swim. But as much as he loved the water, he couldn't hide away in it all day.

With that thought firmly in mind, Rone pushed from the swimming pool and looked around him.

His friends and fellow Team Alpha members were busy. Some were fussing around with a football.

His best friend, Chance, was turning burgers on the grill while the rest chased Anne around.

It was hilarious to him watching those men—those large, muscular men who strike fear in the hearts of hardened criminals be so tender and playful with a little girl.

Grabbing a towel, he walked over to where Chance was and peered over his shoulder.

"You're burning my hot dog."

Chance laughed. "Sorry bro. I love you and all, but I don't swing that way."

Rone laughed. "Only you would let your mind go there."

Chance crinkled his nose and waved the large fork at him. "You've known me for years—you signed up for this."

Rone groaned but grinned.

"I can't believe you're leaving. I don't know if there's anyone else I want to do this job with."

Rone hung his head and rubbed the back of his neck with the towel. "Sorry man. I'm burnt out. Cap'n says if I ever wanted to come back, I can. But this job...it takes a toll, you know? I want to be able to let go before it seeps deeper. If I don't, I fear I will one day lose my mind."

"I know this isn't easy for you."

"No. It's not. I love this job. I love this team."

"But your sanity is priority."

Rone nodded. Before he could say anything else, Anne squealed his name.

He turned in time to feel her darting around his legs in her attempt at hiding from the other two officers.

"Save me." She giggled.

Bending over he tossed his towel over his shoulder and scooped her up. "Don't worry princess! I, your knight, shall protect you!"

She giggled and tightened her arms around his neck. Rone looked by her head at his friend.

Chance was a single father. Anne's mother worked with the DEA and had been killed on duty a mere four weeks after returning to the force from maternity leave.

"I was thinking of ending it too." Chance spoke. "For her."

Rone kissed Anne's cheek then handed her to one of the female officers. Chance was in line to replace him but Rone knew he couldn't argue with Chance's logic—not when it came to Anne.

"If you're going to leave, you should talk to the brass before they put you in charge of the team." Rone spoke. He knew Chance had to be thinking about it.

"I know. It's something that's been going through my mind since she was born. Her mom's death was an even bigger push."

Silence.

"I can't let her grow up with a father who's never there for her or a dead one." Chance started again. "Then again, I don't want her to lose all of this."

Chance motioned around them and then over to where one of their team members were tickling Anne.

She was laughing and flailing.

Rone chuckled. "She'll never lose all of this, Chance. We love Anne like she's our own and will always protect her. That should never be a worry for you. We will always step up whether we're on this team or not. I'm Uncle Rone and that means the world to me. You know that, right?"

Chance nodded. "I'm thinking of moving somewhere small—someplace she can be safe and have a normal life. I don't want her growing up, worrying if I'm coming home. ''No little girl should have to."

"Remember when I told you I have the ranch in Barley with a guest house? If you want a place, you got it. All you have to do, is say the word."

"I don't want to impose..."

"Chance." Rone stepped closer to his friend and closed the grill ensuring he had Chance's full attention. "We're brothers, right? And brothers do for each other. Besides, do you see that beautiful child? She deserves your world. I would do anything for her and so would you. If you want a house, that's already there you're welcome to it. Its three bedrooms, bathroom and everything. It's on my property so no worries about rent or any of that garbage. It'll give you time to get on your feet. So, I repeat—all you have to do, is say the word."

"She would love living so close to you and the horses."

Rone laughed.

"Look," he said. "Don't make any decisions today. And you don't even have to make them tomorrow. Today is for something completely different."

"Saying goodbye."

"Nah." Rone patted Chance on the shoulder. "It's for family."

Their talk seemed to leave them both at a good place so Rone went inside to shower, dry off and change.

At some point, Anne must have noticed he was gone for she stuck her head into his bedroom a while later calling his name. With a smile, Rone lifted her to the center of the large bed, kissed her head before digging through his bag for a shirt.

"Are you leaving forever, Uncle Rone?" Anne asked.

"When you say forever—are you afraid you won't ever see me again?"

She nodded.

"Well, my darling, you can always visit," he said. "I will always come back. And when you're having a bad day all you have to do is pick up the phone."

"You promise?" She asked, sticking her pinky finger out toward him.

Rone smiled and hooked his pinky with hers. "I promise."

After dressing, he scooped her into his arms and carried her back downstairs to a rousing game of tag with their sniper and explosive expert.

Rone watched for a little then went to help Chance get everything done.

They finished making the food and soon, everyone found a place around the makeshift table in the backyard.

It was by no means perfect, but Rone couldn't remember feeling more loved—well except when Anne wrapped her arms around his neck and looked at him like he was Superman.

They laughed and ate and Rone never felt happier. By the time the sun began setting, they'd cleaned up and the others had said their goodbyes.

Rone sat with Anne, cuddled in his arms, fast asleep.

He remained in the silence of his friend and the music of the city around them. Detroit was slowly going to sleep, and he could hear teenagers passing down the street laughing and shouting to each other.

Rone kissed Anne's head while wondering if he would feel the same way about his kid—if he ever got around to it.

"I know why you're hesitant to come to Barley."

Chance inhaled long and hard. "Really? And why, o-great-reader-of-minds, do you think I'm hesitant?"

"You're worried about living so close to someone else."

"You're not even close. Detroit is the only home my baby has ever known. I'm just worried about taking her away from all that."

"Are you sure?"

"Positive. But Barley seems like a place I'd enjoy." He sighed. "The kind of place where I'll go to work and come home at a normal time to spend time with Anne—where I can put her to bed. I want her to be able to play in the backyard, and not have to worry about her being in danger. I'll think about it."

They sat together in the music of Detroit, long after the sun was gone, and the moon rose in the sky.

The automatic outdoor lights at the back of the house flickered on and moths floated in to buzz around it. Finally, Rone stood and lifted Anne to his shoulder.

He carried her into the house with Chance behind him and laid her on her bed. He removed her shoes, untangled her hair from the ponytail and covered her gently.

Kissing her forehead, he remained where he was for a while. It would be the last time in a long time since he'd be tucking her in.

"You're going to miss her."

Rone smiled and swallowed the lump in his throat. "This is as close as I'll ever come to having a little girl. I don't want to lose that."

"You won't."

"She's growing up, Chance." Rone turned to look down at Anne. "One day she's going to be too old to remember who I am. She won't be calling me Uncle Rone anymore and I think that day will break me more than any other."

"Don't be silly. I won't let her forget."

Rone said nothing. He knew if he had, his voice would crack.

"You'll have your own one day." Chance said, softly. "And you're not losing Anne. You're moving to another city not outer space."

Rone managed a small smile while fussing with the blanket over Anne.

Chance would never understand.

There was something a lot deeper to it all than just losing Anne. The sadness in him pushed to the surface and to keep from crying, Rone stroked a hand over her head and stood. He rubbed his palms against his thighs then walked by Chance.

"Remember to tell her I love her. I don't ever want her to forget."

Chance nodded. "She won't."

"I mean it."

"I know, Rone. I'll tell her." Chance exhaled. "Or you can call her when you miss her and tell her yourself."

Rone's eyes burned and after a quick hug, he left the house behind, riding his motorcycle through the streets that had become so familiar to him.

How did he get so far away from the small town he grew up in?

The dream was never an elite taskforce. It was to make his father proud of him—to show Raymond that he did turn out better than people in the town thought he would. Somewhere along that journey, he wound up in Detroit.

When he parked in front of his house—what used to be his house, Rone felt as though a part of him would always be there.

It was already sold, and they gave him two weeks to leave, but he didn't need all that.

Most of his things had already been shipped to Barley. Next to go was his motorcycle. It would be on a truck the next day. He needed the time to clear his mind.

Before going into the house, he removed the plate from the cycle and carried it inside. He gathered all the papers he needed for when the truck got there first thing in the morning and placed them on the floor by the door.

There wasn't much else to do. Instead of worrying about that, he called his friend and stood by the window watching the moon.

"Hello?"

"Justin? It's Rone."

"Well, hey you! You ready for your long drive back?"

Rone laughed. "Not by a long shot. You know if Chris is on his way?"

"Yeah. His flight leaves in about twenty minutes. Not sure why he chose such a late flight. Not like he had anything else doing today."

"You know Chris. He likes last minute. Anyway, I just wanted to call and see how my stuff got there."

"Fine. Your father and I moved it all into the main house. We didn't know where to put your bed, so we place it in one of the rooms in the guest house." Justin paused to cough. "I mean the main house already has a few."

"Damn, I forgot. Thanks man." Rone thought about it. "On second thought, donate the bed to the shelter. They'll come and pick it up at the house. Also, give them the dresser. Just make sure there's nothing in the drawers."

"That's a good idea—it's better than throwing them out. You be safe on this road trip, eh? And don't let Chris drive."

Rone laughed and hung up.

He plugged the cell in and placed it on the floor before pulling his shirt over his head.

He folded it and dropped it beside the phone. He got his air mattress out, activated the automatic pump and left it to fill while he took a shower.

As the water flowed over his body, he braced his left arm against the wall and rubbed his other hand against the elaborate tattoo against his right side. He closed his eyes and pushed his head beneath the downpour.

Water cleansed everything. Wasn't that what they said? Water was forgiving. It could wash you clean and give you a fresh start. Rone needed a fresh start—he needed a way to live his life without missing Anne and Chance so much.

He wanted a way to take the US Marshals out of his blood and give him a new point of view for his new job. He prayed then they were right about the water.

With his only towel left unpacked wrapped around his waist, he turned off the automatic pump and sat on the air mattress.

His life was about to change. Not only was he leaving Detroit. Rone was going from being the commanding officer of a US Marshal team, to being the sheriff in a small town. That alone terrified him enough to reconsider. But he had no choice—life went on and he had to move with it.

His mind drifted back to the things that mattered—friendship, love, family. All of that he'd found with the Alphas and little Anne.

Thinking about the beautiful, bright-eyed girl made him wonder for the millionth time what kind of father he would be. Sure, he was good with Anne, she made it easy. But what would happen if he had his own kids?

Checking his phone, he eased back against the mattress and stared up at the ceiling. He folded an arm behind his head as a pillow and inhaled deeply.

Perhaps it was the impending road trip home, or the move away from all he knew but he couldn't sleep.

He pushed from the bed and walked to the door where he'd placed his guitar and sat on the bed again. Inside the guitar bag was a notepad and pen.

As always when he couldn't turn off his brain, he opened the book to the same page as always—to a page with a song he'd been writing since he was about seventeen years old.

No matter what he did or how long it had been, he just couldn't finish the song.

Two

Jennifer stood in the bedroom and looked around at the few pieces of furniture that adorned it. She walked out the door, down the hall and entered the living room.

It wasn't any better, but it was just as clean as the bedroom. She smiled proudly, grabbing her purse from the sofa and going through it. Finding the piece of paper she wanted, she unfolded it and looked again at her signature on the dotted line.

She was the proud owner of her own apartment.

Falling to the sofa, she kicked her legs out before her excitedly, closed her eyes and squealed. Who would have thought she could save up enough money working two dead end jobs for so many years to get her own place and a little car in Barley?

Sure, it wasn't much of anything to some people—but to Jennifer, what she owned was everything.

Things were beginning to look up for Jennifer Cozel years after her father's death. She stood and walked from the living room into the kitchen and grabbed a chocolate cupcake from the fridge.

The table in the small dining room was second hand. She'd tackled the garage sales in Barley, snagging everything she could find, from the beautiful paintings on the walls to the table and the chairs as well as the laundry basket in the bathroom that looked like something from a horror flick. She didn't mind. It served its purpose.

The ringing phone pulled her from the smooth, velvet of the chocolate cake and into the kitchen. She snagged the phone off the wall and dropped it between her head and shoulder. "Hello?"

"Hi, I'm calling for Jennifer Cozel."

"Er, speaking."

"Jennifer, it's Datsun from the diner?"

"Oh!" She exclaimed, putting what was left of her cake on the counter. Her heart was suddenly racing like never before. "How are you?"

"I'm doing well. Listen, the reason I'm calling is to offer you a job."

Jennifer fought the urge to scream but couldn't get rid of the need to fist pump, so she indulged silently while jumping up and down. "Thank you so much! When do I start?"

"Well, our waitress Kelly still has two weeks, so you can start in a week. I need her to train you before she leaves."

"That's fine. Thanks again."

"You're very welcome. Come on in first thing Monday morning and we can do the paperwork. That way we won't have to worry about them when you start. Is that cool?"

"It's perfect!"

A ringing bell caused Jennifer to look up. For a moment she couldn't remember where she was or why there would be a bell.

Crap—at work.

Why did she keep zoning out at the most inappropriate times? Frowning, she tilted her neck one way, then the next, took a deep breath and lifted her chin.

"Order up, Jenny!"

"Oh...right!"

Jennifer dropped the mop and hurried behind the counter. She washed her hands, dried them in her apron and rushed to the back counter.

She balanced the three plates piled high with eggs, bacon, toast and a side of home fries, and walked over to her regular breakfast crowd. She prayed when she was that age she could be as happy as they seemed to be.

She wanted to be able to smile and not have to worry about anything—not money, not lovers, nothing.

"Jenny!" Raymond Jennings greeted her. He'd come in late and hadn't ordered. "How are you this morning?"

Jennifer placed the food in front of the other three and smiled at the old man. "I'm good." She snagged a bottle of ketchup from another table and placed it in the center of the three.

"You found a good man yet?" Mrs. Robb questioned. "We all want to go to your wedding and dance."

Every morning Ms. Robb asked the same thing, and each time Jennifer felt her heart drop. She managed to place the usual smile on her face. "Not since the last time you asked, my dear." Jennifer told her.

"You know, my son is single." Raymond Jennings offered again. "Fine man. Ex-US Marshal, new sheriff."

"Raymond." Jennifer took a breath.

"I don't know why he is still single at his age. When I was his age, I was married with him crawling around in the daytime and keeping me awake at nights."

Jennifer blushed. "I'm pretty sure your son can find his own woman. He just isn't ready yet."

"He's thirty six?" Beatrice questioned. "I think he still has some time."

"It doesn't matter! He's old enough to be married with children. It ain't normal!" Raymond frowned. "He sure is taking his sweet, damn time...sorry. I shouldn't swear in front of a lady, but I would like to see my grandkids before I die."

Jennifer laughed. "Have you told him that?"

"Of course. I've told him."

"Well, maybe he's gay," Beatrice spoke up. She was normally the quiet, contemplative one. "Have you ever stopped to think of that?

Mrs. Robb who was swallowing a mouth full of orange juice burst out laughing, sending a spray of juice everywhere. Mr. Jennings pushed back, pressing into the booth's seat while Beatrice frowned.

"Sorry." Mrs. Robb apologized. "But you can't say things like that when I'm drinking."

"My son is not gay." Raymond sputtered. "How dare you even mention that?"

"Mr. Jennings I'm sure your son isn't gay." Jennifer patted the old sheriff on the shoulder. "He's just not ready or just haven't found what he's into yet. And even if he is, you will still go to his wedding and dance, right?"

Raymond sighed.

"Of course. It would mean he would be settled down and living."

"To top it all off, this town isn't really conducive to a healthy dating life." Jennifer pointed out. "Have you noticed the dating pool around here isn't what it used to be? And these days you can't really jump into anything. Don't worry, Mr. Jennings. You'll hold your grandkids. Just give it some time."

"How many times have I told you to call me Raymond?" Raymond asked. "I only mentioned it because you would make a good woman for him."

Jennifer took a breath. "I should get back to work. What do you want to eat today Raymond? Usual?"

"Boring." Beatrice teased.

"Boring?" Raymond huffed. "I'm not boring."

"It's either that or old." Mrs. Robb pushed. "Pick one."

"You know what. I'll have the BLT with a side of home fries and scrambled eggs." Raymond ordered. "And add some of them sausages."

"All right, coming right up!" Jennifer smiled. She walked the order to the chef then returned to the floor.

It wasn't a part of her job description, but she liked it when the diner was spotless.

Datsun always frowned at her when he saw her doing any maintenance stuff. He always said he didn't pay her enough for that, but she didn't mind.

If she kept her hands busy, her mind doesn't wander to the fact she was twenty-nine and still had nothing or anyone in her life.

Rolling her shoulders at the thought, she eyed a patch of dirt close to the door and ran into the back to get the *wet floor* sign.

She finished wiping the floor then set up her sign and by the time she washed her hands, Raymond's breakfast was ready.

Breakfast morphed into lunch and just after four, the evening waitress who happened to be Jennifer's her best friend wandered in.

The diner would be opened for another six hours before closing.

By the time Darlene hugged her to take over the reigns, Jennifer's body was one big ache. She didn't bother sitting down to cash the till out.

She finished it, signed the receipt and brought it into Datsun's office.

The routine was the same—drop all the cash into the safe except one hundred then returned the till to the cash register.

It was only then that she signed out, removed her apron and stuck it in her little bag.

Like she usually did, Jennifer hurried into the staff bathroom to wash her face. Staring at her reflection in the mirror, she could barely recognize her mother or herself.

She was reminded then she wasn't any man's definition of a woman. She had no makeup on, nothing to cover the bags under her eyes or the slight indents of wrinkles she knew would be coming in soon.

Sighing, she bowed to flash water on her face, then patting it dry with a piece of paper towel.

Maybe the age lines was time, maybe they were caused by the stress of being a waitress. Once she'd gotten the job a year ago, she never thought she'd still be

Being a waitress was supposed to be a temporary thing—something to keep her from depleting her savings.

While working part-time to become a teacher, the struggled had been real. But soon, part-time work wasn't cutting it anymore and it was time for her to move out from living with Gale.

School quickly became unimportant and she dropped out a year shy of graduation.

The truth was, Jennifer did not have any prospects.

All she had was a scantily furnished apartment in a small town. Mr. Raymond Jennings saw her sitting in the diner and promptly informed her that his friend who owned the diner was looking for a waitress.

She had no experience but still Datsun hired her. After a few broken dishes, dropped meals and spilled coffee, Jennifer finally got the hang of carrying six plates at a time by balancing them on her arms without dropping a single one.

Straightening her clothes, she headed back to the front. "Hey, Datsun, I'm heading out."

"See you in the morning, Jenny." He waved. "I'm getting ready to leave soon too. Is Darlene here?"

"Er...she's..."

"Right here!" Darlene walked behind the counter while tying her apron strings behind her. She pressed a kiss to Jennifer's cheek. "Hello again, beautiful."

Jennifer smiled and hugged the young woman who'd become the closest thing to a real friend she had in Barley. "You be safe. If you need a ride home after work call me."

"I'll be fine. But if I don't wanna walk all the way home I'll call you." Darlene snickered. "Are we on for Saturday?"

"What were we supposed to be doing again?" Jennifer couldn't remember.

"Junk food and girl's night? You said you were going to think about it."

It hit her then and she laughed. "Sure. I'll have the wine and you bring the junk food. I think I have some chicken in the freezer. I could fry some."

"I love your fried chicken! So, I'm totally there!" Darlene smiled.

"See you later."

Jennifer exited the diner after waving to a few customers and hurried across the street to her second-hand car. It wasn't anything much but it got her from point A to point B and it was hers.

She stopped a moment to enjoy the late afternoon sun glowing against her face. The sound of a car getting close caused her to open her eyes and looked around.

It was the Sheriff's car.

Without stopping to see who was actually in it, she climbed into her own and started the ignition. She reversed from the spot and pulled into the street leading away from the center of town and toward the only apartment building in Barley.

She was running from the Sheriff and she hadn't even met the guy.

Perhaps she should take a look at him—not because she thought anything could come of it, but because Raymond was so hell bent on her hooking up with the man.

Each time he saw her, he was sure to point out his son was single. She chuckled at that, and made the left turn into the parking lot to the small, two floor building.

The climb to her apartment was hard. It wasn't that many stairs but after standing all day, she felt like sitting on one of the steps and stay there.

Still, she persisted and soon was able to flop into the worn sofa in the living room. With a quick glance at the clock, she reached for the phone to call Gale.

The two of them were trying to plan time to get together but with Gale's life and her non-life, they couldn't seem to figure out a time.

"Gale Stanley."

"Hey Gale. It's Jenny."

"I know, sweetie. How are you? How's Barley?"

"Barley is Barley." Jennifer sighed. "Gale, can I ask you a question?"

"Sure."

"Do you think I'm due for a husband?"

"I've been telling you for years you need to find a good man." Gale chuckled. "You've been ignoring me. What brought this on?"

"Well, one of the locals, Raymond, remember me telling you about him?" Jennifer pulled her body from the sofa and moaned. She then walked into the kitchen and peered into the fridge.

"Yeah."

"His son is the sheriff and every time he sees me, he makes it a point to remind me the sheriff, is single. This morning at breakfast someone asked if I found a man yet and he once again pointed it out."

Gale laughed. She laughed until she snorted.

Jennifer pulled a bottle of spaghetti sauce out of the fridge along with some green and red peppers and placed them on the counter. "What? I didn't think it was so funny. I wanted the ground to open and swallow me whole."

"Jenny, you're a beautiful woman. You're the only one who doesn't see it. Every father, except yours, wants what's best for his kids. And if this man is trying to nudge you toward his son, it's very obvious he thinks you can be good for his boy."

"I think he's a tad old—the son I mean."

"Even better."

"And what about what I think?" She washed the peppers and placed them to drain on a chopping board while she set a pot on to boil for the pasta.

"I know what you think, and I don't like it. You can't stay alone for the rest of your life. Come on, Jenny. Step out there. Not all men are like your father. And so this man is older? So what?"

Jennifer took a breath and rolled her eyes before rummaging for some cooked chicken from the night before. She spent time chopping it up into smaller, bite-sized pieces.

"And how comes you haven't met this son yet? How big is this town?"

"Not very. But he's only been Sheriff for about five months. Before that he was a US Marshal somewhere in Detroit."

"You know a lot about this man."

"His father has been telling me his life story. I called to find out when you can come by here," Jennifer said. She was changing the subject. The one about her love life was becoming slightly irritating.

"Changing the subject—fine." Gale sighed. "Okay I have some time off in a week and a half. Not this weekend but next weekend after that. What about you?"

"Good." Jennifer replied. "This weekend wouldn't be good. I have plans. Next weekend, I work in the mornings, but I'm off on the Sunday. If you don't mind spending a few hours by yourself."

"I don't mind." Gale replied. "I'll send you more info once I figure out what time and all that."

"Thanks. It'll be good to see you after eight months."

"I hear that. All right,. I have a meeting. But I'll call you first thing tomorrow. What time you heading to work?"

"Seven-thirty. I have to leave here by then to get to work on time and get prepared. Call me after five in the evening instead."

After Gale agreed to the plan, Jennifer hung up and pressed her back to the counter.

It wasn't like she was trying to stay alone forever. She just wasn't ready. Deep down she knew that was an excuse. The last time she dated she was twenty-one and thought there was such a thing as true love. But that hadn't ended well, and she just didn't want to put herself out there again.

The bubbling of the water caught her attention, and she dropped some pasta in. While that cooked, she walked to the window and stared out into the falling of the night.

Three

Rone sat on the fence and strummed his fingers over the guitar strings.

After his run it was too early to make his way through town, so he simply sat there, playing around with a line that popped into his head in the shower.

Perhaps it was the call he'd ignored coming in from Nashville. He hadn't picked up because he knew who it was, and he wouldn't break a promise he made when he was twenty.

Matt called three times before Rone finally took the phone off the hook and rolled over to face the wall. He just knew he wouldn't get any sleep.

Pressing his palm over the strings, Rone gave up and brought the instrument back to his bedroom and placed it on the stand.

He then climbed behind the wheel of his truck and pulled from the front yard.

The drive through the town would have been a relatively short one but Rone took his own time.

He stopped in a few places to check on where the young ones would hang out to make sure nothing was out of place. He also stopped at the diner, but they weren't open yet.

Still, Datsun the owner got him some coffee before he finally made his way into the station.

Rone picked up the ringing telephone and dropped it between his shoulder and head. He hadn't even checked the caller display. "Yeah?" he said while flipping through a file folder.

"Uncle Rone?"

"Anne! My darling, how are you?"

"Am good. I miss you."

"I miss you too, princess. How's school going?"

"I don't wanna go. But dad says I gatta."

Rone laughed softly. "You know how you always wanted to own your own horse?"

"Yah-huh."

"Well, if you go to school and get good grades, one day you can buy as many horses as you wish. How does that sound?"

She giggled. There was a rustle on the other end of the line before Chance's laughter filled the phone.

"Even over the phone you make her laugh." Chance spoke. "How are you?"

Rone dropped the file on the desk before stretching the cord to the cabinet and opening it. He flicked through the letters until he found the one he wanted and lifted it out.

"Been better. I'm exhausted."

"I hear that. I gave them my notice today."

Rone dropped the file into the spot marked "R" and turned to sit on the edge of his desk. "What did they say?"

"The chief wasn't happy especially since you left and now I'm leaving but the truth is I can't let them make my decision for me. Anne is getting older. A move now would be less traumatic than when she's a teenager."

"Can't complain with that logic. So, where you're moving to?"

"Well, uncle Rone did promise he had a guest house we could use."

Rone grinned. The joy that surged through him was unlike anything else. He laughed softly. "And uncle Rone still has that offer out there. If you want me to come by and drive you guys here or..."

"Nah. We'll back up and hit the road. She's old enough now to remember things. I want her to have that memory of us together, on the road."

"That's a good idea."

"It'll be like a mini vacation, make it a road trip. She's never stayed at a hotel before. It would be a treat for her. So after we ship everything we'll make it fun. You looking for a deputy?"

"You couldn't be my deputy if you tried." I scoffed. "But the fire department is looking for a head. I know the pay is somewhat the same as you're making now. But with this, you'll have more time for your baby and to write that book you've been pushing around inside your head."

"Really? I don't even know if I'd qualify. It's been too long." Chance sighed. "But I should follow my heart with that book—be an example to Anne."

"With a recommendation from the captain and your old firehouse you got it in the bag." I encouraged him. "Just contact them and find out."

Chance promised he would. "It was pretty easy switching from fire to cop. I guess I'll find out how easy it will be to switch back."

"Don't think of it that way." Rone advised. "Think of it as a transition."

The two made other plans about the move and after they hung up, Rone sat for a moment on his desk trying to think of what was about to happen.

But he had to wait until his friend and god-daughter were actually in Barley before he started thinking of presents to bombard her with.

Chuckling at that thought, he gathered his things and exited the office.

When Rone walked into the house, he could hear his friends slamming the dominoes into the table. He rolled his eyes and dumped his keys into a bowl by the door. He'd forgotten he had plans for them to swing by.

All Rone had been looking forward to was a shower and a cold beer.

But when he heard them having so much fun, he didn't have the heart to say hello and go to bed. Sticking his hat on the holder, he removed his shoes, hung up his jacket and walked into the room where Justin and Chris were engrossed into the game.

They barely looked up to say hello.

Rone didn't take it personally.

He knew what happened when his friends got together.

In the living room, Rone pushed the sofa from the wall and hunched down. He put in his code and the safe's door beeped before popping open. He pulled his gun out of his holster along with the badge and stuck them in the safe. After closing the door, he eased the sofa back in place.

It'd been a long day and spending time at lunch with his father hadn't helped his mood any.

Once again Raymond was going on and on about not having grandkids and how he didn't want to die before seeing any.

Sometimes Rone would get up and walk away.

Sometimes he just zoned out. Other times he wondered why he even bothered doing anything at all.

Pushing his hair from his face, Rone tried not to get upset about his dad. A part of him could understand why Raymond was so pushy about him getting married. His father wanted grandchildren Rone understood that. In the same breath, he wasn't about to jump into bed with the first woman who came along.

Besides, the pool of women in Barley wasn't the most extensive.

After his return to the small town, most of the people his age had either moved away or were married. It wasn't like he didn't want to get married, but some things you just couldn't—shouldn't—rush.

"You look like crap." Chris Asher pointed out. He handed Rone his beer. "You need this more than I do."

"Thanks." Rone muttered.

Rone took a drink from his friend's beer but handed the bottle back and entered the kitchen to get one of his own. He took a drink from the bottle. "I'm exhausted. Who thought for a town with not much crime, there is so much damn paperwork?"

The others laughed. "Yeah. It's all politics here my friend," Justin Kitting said, shuffling the dominos to set up a new game. He drew a hand and held them up to peer at them. "It'll pick up. Wait a little."

"No thank you." Rone told him.

"You saw the Cap'n today didn't you?" Chris wanted to know. "How did that go?"

"The same old. I left the place feeling like I wanted to bash my head in with a Louisville Slugger." Rone groaned.

"He means well." Justin placed a domino down and looked at his hand with a frown. "I do *not* like this hand."

"It has nothing to do with your crappy playing." Chris teased. "Stand up and take it like a man!" He dropped a domino to block the game so he could play again.

"Hurry up and lose so I can play." Rone patted Chris' on the shoulder.

They laughed and Rone rose and walked into the kitchen to see that Chris had gotten to it.

There was a large pot of curried chicken sitting on the stove along with another with rice.

He grabbed a plate and dished himself out some then walked to the balcony and sat out there. He placed the beer bottle by his foot and dug in.

For some reason he was thinking about the woman he saw leaning against her car. She had her face turned up to the sun with a peace he hadn't seen in someone in a long time. He didn't know anyone who took that much pleasure in feeling the sun.

It's been a while since he even took any notice in the sun.

For a moment he was transfixed on her, just staring. He wasn't even sure why he was so drawn to her. She was unlike anyone he'd ever been interested in before. She was shorter than him—perhaps five three and voluptuous. Hair was pulled back into a short ponytail and no jewelry.

"Rone!" Justin hollered. "Chris lost! This is awesome! I don't care how it happened. I'm glad it did."

"I lost? How'd I lose?" Chris sounded perplexed.

"I'm going to savour this moment," Justin pushed. "Put it on a t-shirt—maybe even a coffee mug or two. A tattoo! That's what I'll get!"

"A tattoo?" Chris questioned. "Really? Jerk."

Rone laughed, picked up his beer from whereby his foot and walked his half empty plate to where his friends were. Justin was doing a weird, sort of, pelvic thrust while Chris was staring at the board like he thought the meaning to life was on it.

"I don't get it." Chris shook his head. "I just don't get it."

Rone placed his plate on the table and dragged up another chair. The three started playing.

"Your old man on you about dating again?" Justin asked.

"When is he not on me about that? You pass Chris." Rone grinned and placed another domino down.

The next morning Rone went for a jog and returned to his place.

He checked the time and groaned.

He had just enough time to shower and run out the door to meet his father for breakfast.

For some reason, Raymond insisted on it. To appease his father and to change the subject from the dangerous territory of his dating life, Rone had agreed.

Now, all he wanted to do was put his hand in a fire pit rather than sit through another session of *are you gay?* with his father.

After a fast shower, he grabbed his gun and badge.

Stuffing his head into his hat, he was out the door while shoving his arms into his light jacket and pulling it around his gun and badge.

There was no traffic in Barley like there was in Detroit, so he was at the diner in time to watch his father walk in with Beatrice.

For a moment, he sat in the car, just to get a second of peace. Finally, he took a breath and climbed from behind the wheel. He jogged across the street and let himself in the front doors. Tiny bells chimed above his head and he had to smile about that.

"Morning sheriff!" Mrs. Robb called. "Your father is waiting for you."

"Mornin'. Thanks. Morning Beatrice." Rone removed his hat.

"Hello handsome." Beatrice waved her hanky at him. "If I was a few years younger..."

"And had your own teeth." Mrs. Robb chimed in.

Beatrice growled at her and Rone laughed, pressing a kiss to Beatrice's cheek. "It's good to see you Bea."

She smiled and he walked to fall into the booth across from his father. "Morning." He placed the black hat on the table toward the corner and pulled off his jacket to bunch behind him on the seat.

"Morning, son. How was your night?"

"Same old. Played a couple of games with the boys..."

"Good...you hungry then?"

"Starving." Rone replied. "It's like we forget to eat when we play."

Raymond was waving at someone while Rone glanced at the menu.

"Hello Raymond." A feminine voice greeted. "You having your same this morning?"

"Why not?" Raymond's voice was happy. "I'm feeling particularly good today.."

"What are you up to Raymond Jennings?" She wanted to know.

Raymond laughed softly. It'd been a while since Rone heard his father laugh, truly laughed. But with this woman, his father lit up.

Rone looked up to see the woman who brought out such joy in his father and his breath was caught in his throat. It was the woman from the day before. He smiled and extended his hand to her. "Rone Jennings."

She looked down at his hand for a moment and Rone thought she wouldn't take it. When she wrapped a soft hand around his and shook she said nothing.

"Don't you have a name?" He questioned.

"Yes. I do."

"Want to share?"

"Share? With whom?"

"With me."

She eyed him with suspicion. He'd been a cop far too long to miss that look. Her shoulders heaved slightly then fell. "Jennifer Cozel."

"It's very nice to meet you."

She smiled but the moment it spread her beautiful lips, the mirth was gone.

She moved her brown eyes to his father and all of a sudden Rone felt as though the sun disappeared behind a cloud.

The irrational mind in him was jealous of his father for a brief moment. Rone shook his head. That was the stupidest thing he'd ever allowed to swim through his mind at any moment ever in his life. Frowning at the silliness of that thought, he picked up the menu again.

After she took his father's order, he ordered some pancakes and coffee. He felt it the moment she left and couldn't meet his father's gaze. He'd just flirted with a woman in front of his father and didn't even realize he was doing so until she left.

"So?" Raymond asked.

"So what?"

"Do you like our Jenny?"

Rone groaned wanting to bang his head into the table. "Dad." It was always strange talking to his father about women. No matter Rone's age, he didn't think he'd ever get used to it.

"Stop playing Cupid."

"Cupid?" Raymond laughed softly. "Me? I saw the way you looked at her. It wasn't like a man who isn't a little bit interested. You are more than interested. You pried her name out of her."

"I was being nice." Rone sat back and folded his arms.

"Right. Sure, you were. If you were being nice you wouldn't have tried so hard. You'd have just let her walk away. And besides, you already knew her name."

"I did not!"

"Whatever." Raymond rolled his shoulders.

Rone chuckled. "I did, didn't I? But let me handle this, okay? You led the horse to water, now let me drink if I want to."

"Strange way of putting it." Raymond laughed. "But, fine."

Rone looked over his shoulder to watch the way she interacted with Beatrice and Mrs. Robb. She had a lovely spirit about her. Shaking his head, he looked at his father again. He could never hide anything from his father so he wasn't about to start at thirty-six.

Nodding, he took a sip from his father's glass of water. "Do you know anything about her?"

"Not the deep stuff." Raymond shrugged. "She's always been good to me. Though, I think she's a little shy. I'm not going to introduce you two and get to know her for you. That's your job. I know you think I'm superman, but I'm not as young as I used to be."

Rone laughed. "Seriously, do you think she'd be a good match for me?"

"Well, I see the women you normally date. I mean—she's nothing like any of them. But for some reason I don't think she'd let you get away with anything."

"Get away with something? Oh, father why must you torture me?"

"Now who's being a drama-king?" Raymond winked at him.

Rone grinned. "There's something about her that I find myself being so attracted to."

"Are you sure it's not the fact she didn't fall all over you?"

Rone shook his head.

"She's a beautiful woman, Rone."

"I know that." Rone replied. "I can see that. But that's not it. I can't put my finger on it. Anyway, let's change the subject. I wanted to talk to you about Chance."

"What about him?"

"I told him he and Anne could have the guest house if he decided to move to Barley." Rone explained softly. "He wants to get away from the city, get Anne away from the noise and the drama."

"Sounds like a good idea. Is he willing to give up the Marshals?"

"For his baby, yes."

"Now, that is a father—there's nothing better than a father's love."

Rone nodded.

"Okay gentlemen." Jennifer interrupted. "Breakfast is served."

Rone stood and helped her with the plates she was balancing quite expertly. Their fingers brushed and he trembled slightly hoping she didn't see. He sat once the plates were settled on the table and she handed his father a bottle of ketchup. After she walked away, Rone glanced at his father.

"Go," Raymond said."

"Where?"

"Don't be dumb, kid. Go!"

Rone shove a piece of toast into his mouth and took a breath. Giving his father one final look, he pushed from the seat and approached the bar where she was busy wiping it down. "Hi."

"Hi. Did you want something for your table?" Jennifer asked.

"No, not that. Can I talk to you for a second?"

"About?"

"What are you doing tonight?"

She eyed him, the same doe-eyed expression, laced with suspicion she'd looked at him with earlier. She didn't trust him and he couldn't say he blamed her.

"I go home, read a book. Go to bed."

"Can I interest you in dinner?"

Jennifer glanced over his shoulder toward Raymond and knew precisely what she was thinking. "This has nothing to do with him. I saw you yesterday. I wanted to speak with you, but you left before I could park."

"Sure, you did." Jennifer sighed. "Okay, I may look the way I do but I'm not desperate for a man. I know your dad means well, but no thank you."

She turned to walk away. Desperation bubbled inside Rone's body and he forced himself not to reach across the counter and grab her arm. "Jennifer."

She stopped and looked at him. He could see she was slowly losing her patience. Her head slipped to one side and she sighed dramatically.

"Forget about my father for a second."

"Very well. Raymond forgotten."

"I'll make you a deal?"

Jennifer folded her arms across her wonderful breasts. Those things could make a grown man fall to his knees and cry. Licking his lips, he was careful not to stare at the way her cleavage bubbled at the top of her shirt.

"I take you to dinner. If you don't have a good time we never have to talk about it again. We'll just become good friends."

"You're serious?"

"Very serious."

"All right, Mr. Jennings..."

Rone laughed. "That's my father. You can call me Rone."

"All right Rone. But you have to pick me up," Jennifer said, softly. "I live in the Bethune Apartments."

She stared at him intently.

Rone shrugged. "I'll be there at eight? That's not too late, right?"

"No."

Rone smiled and eased from the stool. He waved at her and hurried back to the table.

"So?"

He smiled at his father. "We have dinner tonight."

Four

Her bedroom only had her bed, a dresser she picked up at a second-hand store, one bedside table from a garage sale and a standing lamp.

The lamp and bed were the only new furniture in the room. The curtains were material she bought and stitched herself and they came out quite well if she was to be completely honest. She didn't have the money for the finer things but Jennifer was pretty happy with how the room turned out.

The first thing she did after arriving home was made her bed. The morning rush had her charging out the door without getting much of anything done.

With that out of the way, Jennifer emptied the garbage then paid a few bills.

When she finally had nothing to do, it dawned on her she had a date coming up that night.

Her heart fluttered painfully within her chest.

For about two years after her father died, Gale's mother had to repeatedly rush Jennifer to the hospital because of the same ache in her chest.

The doctors finally told her she was experiencing panic attacks and taught her ways to control them.

She exhaled through her mouth before inhaling and holding the air in. Counting to ten forward then backward, she exhaled and inhaled again.

She continued the slow, methodical routine until the pain and the tightness in her chest subsided.

Jennifer sat on the edge of her bed, staring into her very limited closet. There was another thing to have a slight panic attack over.

The door had fallen off and she didn't have the money to fix it. It wasn't for lack of trying to do it herself. It was a matter that she wasn't a handywoman and failed miserably each time she tried reattaching the door to its hinges.

The door suddenly fell to the back of her mind and Rone with his beautiful eyes and luscious lips swam to the forefront. She was utterly and completely out of her depths. Rone Jennings was out of her league.

She looked at him and all she could see was every sexy, cowboy from every romance novel she'd ever read.

Then he'd smiled at her, those lips tugging upward exposing perfectly lined, white teeth.

His silver eyes shimmered when he asked her to share her name.

As he sat on the barstool asking her out, his dark hair fell into his eyes leaving him looking so dangerous. She wanted him then and that feeling scared her more than actually going out on the date. Jennifer spent so much time building up the walls, keeping all feelings of softness for a man out.

When she watched him enter the diner, he had a poise and surety about him that left her hiding the hardness of her nipples by pressing a pile of menu to her chest.

He didn't look like the man to deserve a virgin. Rone looked like the kind of man who knew precisely what he wanted and any woman he chose would have to be equally as confident.

Jennifer never bothered learning what lead up to actually going out with a man.

Looking fabulous was of the upmost importance for her dinner with the sheriff. But what should she wear?

She had never been on a date with a man like Rone before and that compounded by the fact she didn't go out—period— meant she didn't have anything fancy. Help would be needed for this—lots and lots of help—and maybe a miracle or two.

Frustrated, she fell to her back on the bed and reached for the telephone. Jennifer thought of calling Gale but what was Gale going to really do from so far away?

Besides, Gale was probably jet setting around the globe.

Her friend would squeal then tried giving her some advice like *give this man a break—be calm. Don't freak out.*

Then what?

Jennifer would still be left sitting on the side of her bed silently having her second panic attack in the same day; either that or go on the date naked.

Oh right—that wouldn't freak him out at all.

She rolled her eyes. What she needed was someone to hold her hand. She needed someone to show her what to do to entice a man like Rone Jennings who looked so damn good in a pair of jeans and a cowboy hat.

She called Darlene.

The phone rang. It was the longest few seconds of her life. Jennifer tapped her fingers against her thigh. "Come on, pick up. Please be home."

Ring.

"Hello?"

"Hey Darlene. It's Jenny."

"Hi, my dear. How are you?"

"Are you busy right now?"

"Nope. I was trying to figure out a crossword puzzle and its driving me nuts. What's a seven letter word for trash?"

"Garbage."

"Are you sure?" Darlene questioned. She went silent for a second then gasped. "You're right!"

Jennifer laughed.

"I really need to get out more. What's up?"

"You have to get to my place as soon as you can. I need your help with something."

"Er..." Darlene trailed off. "You're starting to worry me, Jenny. What's going on?"

"I feel weird talking about this over the phone. Can you please come over? I would really appreciate it."

"Jenny..."

"I'll tell you when you get here. Please, hurry."

Hanging up, she went through her closet. She pulled a few dresses she thought would go well.

Even though she didn't know where he was taking her or if he was even serious, she took down a blue dress, a black one and a light pink one.

The light pink one she'd only worn once to some dinner Gale had at work.

No one really saw it for she spent the night alone at a table, clutching a glass of flat sofa.

There was no other reason to wear it. She hung that dress up with the other two before digging again.

When she heard the doorbell, she took a moment to pull down a skirt suit, a pants suit and another dress she didn't remember she had. It still had the tag on it.

After setting them on the bed Jennifer hurried for the front door. Darlene hurried in, kicked off her shoes and turned to face her.

"Okay, what is going on?" Darlene demanded.

"I'm going out to dinner tonight," Jennifer said in a soft voice. She was embarrassed. At twenty nine she shouldn't be going through such pressure and uncertainty. "I really don't know what to wear."

"You're going out to dinner? It's not with Raymond is it?"

"Of course not."

"Good."

"Raymond is my breakfast date."

"Oi." Darlene laughed. "Who with then?"

"Rone Jennings."

"Rone Jennings...as in Sheriff Rone Jennings?"

"The one and only."

Darlene blinked at her with a blank expression on her face. The silence between them was unbearable. She walked around her friend and entered the kitchen.

A part of her expected Darlene to burst out laughing. Everyone else would when they saw the two of them walking into a restaurant or anything like that.

A new fear gripped her inside and she quickly looked for something to drink, eat or throw across the room. Jennifer settled for a bottle of water, wrung the cap off and drank half the contents before Darlene entered.

"Are you joking? You asked a man out?"

"You should know better than that. I didn't ask. He did. I think his father put him up to it even though he said Raymond had nothing to do with it."

"So?" Darlene sat on the edge of one of the chairs. "Maybe he doesn't have anything to do with it."

"And I'm Fred Astaire. Raymond is trying to get grandkids and at this point I don't think he cares who their mother turns out to be—even me."

"Why you gatta be so cynical?"

"Because I have no reason whatsoever to think this will end in anything but tears, *my* tears. I mean life can be cruel sometimes for everyone else and most times for me."

"Stop thinking like that. Even if his father told him to ask you out, your foot is in the door. Now it's up to you to be your fabulous self with that beautiful smile and sweep this man off his feet. You're going to be so sexy and engaging he won't know what hit him."

Jennifer laughed. "I'm just...ugh."

"Well, ugh is a good way to express yourself. I totally understand ugh."

Jennifer drank the rest of the water, dumped the bottle in her makeshift recycle can—a box she took from the restaurant after they unpacked all the cans of lemonade mix from it—and turned to look at her friend.

"I don't mean to be so cynical." She huffed. "I promise. Sometimes I think I'm just one big negative. But every man I've ever gotten close to in my life turned out to be just like my father or just plain old jackasses. I have nothing but bad to draw from."

"And yet you still put yourself out there. What does that say about you?"

"I'm one of them hard learners?" She jargoned. "Either that or I'm a sucker for punishment."

Darlene rolled her eyes. "No. It means you still believe there's someone out there for you; someone good. So now just say you don't care why he asked. You're going to go out with sexy-fine Rone Jennings and you're going to be fabulous."

"You're right, you know? I don't particularly care why he asked at this point. It's been years since I've been out on a date. And I've never had a serious relationship. I'm not going to question it. I'm going to try my best to keep it on track."

"In relationship you aren't in it alone. All your friends should help you two stay together. Though it's too early to say it's a relationship but you know what I mean."

Jennifer nodded. "Yeah, I get it. I just want to go out to prove to myself I can at least have a decent conversation with a guy without completely blowing it. I mean he's not some little boy like the others. He's a man—a *real* man."

"Girl, don't I know it. Think about it this way. Rone is a cowboy. He likes simple. He likes his women like he likes his beer."

"Cold?"

Darlene giggled. "No. He likes them tasty, full bodied and with a little burn."

Heat flushed Jennifer's face. "You wrong for that!"

"But you know I'm right." Darlene shrugged.

"I guess. Anyway, I need help."

"Okie-doke. So why am I here? What can I do?"

"You're here because I need help with everything. Even though I'm a grown-ass adult I can't seem to dress myself to save my life."

"Right! We need to go shopping!" Darlene fist pumped. "I'm seeing light blue. Something sexy and..."

"We don't have time for that and I don't have the money. The date is tonight."

"Tonight? That means we don't have time to go shopping. Bummer."

"It's just a date. Ugh! I really should stop calling it a date. It's dinner. I'm sure we can throw something together from what I have in the bedroom."

"Shopping would have been fun though." Darlene grinned. "What are we standing here for? Let's go see what you have in your closet! I love that pink dress you have."

"How'd you know I had a pink dress? I haven't worn it since before I moved here."

Darlene rolled her eyes and sighed dramatically. As they hurried down the hall to Jennifer's bedroom, her friend explained. "Remember when I had to go to that party in Bowsa? You lent it to me because I hadn't gotten paid yet and couldn't afford a dress!"

"I wore it with a large black belt?"

It finally dawned on her and she laughed nervously. "Sorry. Forgot."

They decided on the pink dress, a light, white shawl with a black clutch and matching heels. They weren't stilettos just high enough to make an impact and not cause her to look so short.

"Okay, so you have the clothes set. Do you have anything like earrings, necklaces?"

Jennifer shook her head. "I lost the few pieces I had in the move."

"Well, I have an idea. I have some jewelry at home. I'll run home and grab them."

"We don't have time for that." Jennifer frowned. "I have to get dressed and be ready for eight."

"Yes, and it's just after five now. You shower and do your hair, maybe grab a snack."

"I couldn't eat anything now. I'd just throw it up I'm so nervous."

"Then, maybe take a nap after your shower. I'll be back in a jiff."

Jennifer tried to calm down by counting backward and forward to ten. After agreeing to Darlene's suggestions, Jennifer hugged Darlene.

With her gone Jennifer suddenly had to contend with silence and the worry of what to do first. Her brain seemed to have reverted to the same state of confusion she was accustomed to feeling around her father.

He was a walking chaos pit.

She steadied herself by pressing her eyes closed and after opening them she hurried into the bathroom and stripped down for the shower.

She brushed her hand over her legs and frowned. It'd been almost three months since she shaved her legs. It wasn't like anyone was sleeping beside her and since she wore pants to work anyway, it didn't matter.

Jennifer climbed from the shower to rummage for a brand-new razor in her little kit by the sink and after finding shaving cream to go with it, she climbed back in.

Sitting on the side of the tub, she shaved her legs, being careful not to nick herself. That was the last thing she wanted, especially right before going out.

Once she was finished and she ensured all the hairs were caught, she shaved other places though those hadn't been neglected for three months. When Darlene returned, it was just past six thirty and Jennifer was even more agitated than before.

"Okay, this necklace goes best with it." Darlene lifted a beautiful one made of black stones.

"What is this made of?"

"I don't know. I saw it in Florida when I went a few years ago and loved the colour so I bought it. Don't worry. It's not real black pearls so you don't have to worry about losing it." Darlene laughed. "Here. Put these earrings in."

Jennifer took the studs and stuck them on. She glanced at her reflection in the mirror and had to say she looked pretty good.

What a difference a pair of earrings and a necklace made in her appearance and how she thought of herself.

She slid on some lip gloss, tuck away a strand of hair that had come loose from her ponytail and turned her head to see the side of her hair. The style didn't look as fetching to her as it did before.

Pulling it out, she brushed it all to one side then wrapped it under and pinned it down.

Much better.

Inhaling, she stuck her feet into her heels and did a small runway twirl in front of the mirror. "What do you think?"

Darlene grinned cheekily. "Beautiful."

"I hope he thinks so."

"If he doesn't, he's a moron and he doesn't deserve you. Is he picking you up?"

Jennifer nodded. "I told him he had to."

Darlene grinned then snapped her fingers three times. "You go girl. Look-at-choo! Takin' *chaaarge!*" Darlene punctuated her words by stopping a foot, while letting her neck glide to one side.

"I had to say something. Didn't want him thinking he was getting the milk for free."

Darlene laughed. "And with that image in my head, I should go. Call me when you get home."

"Nothing's going to happen between us, Dar. But I'll call you when I get home. It probably won't be late."

It was still an hour before Rone was to arrive. With nothing else to do, Jennifer removed the heels.

She gave Darlene a hug then sat on the bay window until she could watch Darlene's truck disappear down the road. She kept glancing at the clock, second guessing herself and the whole situation; slightly freaking out.

Each car to drive by the apartment sent her heart lurching. Then the car would zoomed by the house and her heart would break.

Finally, eight o'clock rolled around her phone buzzed.

Jennifer thought for sure it was Darlene checking on her, so she grabbed it without checking the display.

She made her way to the dresser and peered at herself. The room was so silent she could hear the tick of the clock to her left. It was the way the eerie sound made her feel that bothered her.

It curled her insides, sent her heart racing and every hair on her arms and the back of her neck stood on end.

"It's Rone."

"You're cancelling?" Jennifer asked, starting to remove one earring.

"Would you be upset if I was calling to cancel?"

"No. It would, however, be expected."

"Don't be such a cynic, Jennifer. I'm not calling to cancel on you. Is your window on the south side of the building?"

"Yeah."

"Come to your window—see me?"

Jennifer walked back to the window and looked down into the early night light. There, beneath her was Rone, waving an arm above his head. She couldn't help but smile. "All right. I'm coming down."

She hung up, took one final look at herself and replaced her earring. For a moment she stopped—just stopped.

Eventually, Jennifer slipped her feet into her shoes.

The beat of her heart was so loud she swore it was beating in her ear. Still, she slipped her shawl around her shoulders and checked the length of her dress.

It flared out around her ankles with style but didn't show her legs. After ensuring she had her card in her clutch she turned around to leave.

Jennifer caught her reflection in the mirror and swallowed hard.

You can do this. Just breathe. It's not that serious. Breathe.

Slowly, carefully, she descended the stairs toward her first real date.

Five

Rone leaned against his truck waiting for her. A few people exited the small building but none of them was Jennifer.

He had a million thoughts flashing through his mind from, she changed her mind to something happened to her on the way down. Shaking his head to clear it, he folded his arms across his chest.

When the door opened a third time and she stepped out, Rone was stunned. her light, pink dress hugged her beautiful breasts then flowed outward and down.

Matched with the shawl around her shoulders it blended perfectly with her rich, dark skin. He wanted to touch her, taste her, feel her smooth beneath his fingertips.

But it was too soon—he knew that.

The feelings pulsing through his body scared him. They couldn't be defined as lust. It was an appreciation for the perfect beauty of a real woman—a woman with meat on her bones and a class he'd longed for.

For a second, Rone couldn't remember how to unfold his arms. Sucking in some air, he fought for the use of his brain. He pushed off the truck and waved to her like a teenager going on his first date. His first date was nothing like Jennifer.

Not by a long shot—his first date was an air head who only wanted to date him because she thought Rone could sway his father into not throwing her brother in a jail cell whenever he did something stupid.

But Jennifer was a woman.

Feeling like a moron he opened the passenger door for her.

"You look lovely," he said.

"Thank you." She offered him a smile but Rone knew she was nervous.

The corners of her mouth trembled ever so slightly.

What would she say or do if he reached in and kissed the flesh that shook with her nerves? Would she slap him or turned her mouth into his?

She stopped in front of him and everything within Rone told him to trap her against the truck and take her lips. Instead, he hugged her lightly. Her scent swirled about him, wreaking havoc on his senses—hot strawberries.

Biting back a moan, Rone allowed her to climb into the truck, closed the door and walked around to the other side. His hands shook as he pulled open the door and Rone couldn't understand it. He was with a woman, a beautiful woman, still he couldn't quite put his finger on what was making him feel so giddy. After climbing into the truck, he turned to look at her.

"How are you with surprises?"

"Don't like them," she replied softly.

Starting the ignition, he shifted the truck into drive. When he'd pulled away from the small building, he turned from the centre of Barley toward Astrid County. If he was going to take her out for a good time it wouldn't be in Barley. "This one will be a good one. I promise."

"How comes you've never been to the diner before?" Jennifer questioned.

He glanced at her. "I have. Just mostly at nights. As the new Sheriff, you'd be surprised how much in office crap they want you to do during the day.

Something about regular business hours; then there are my rounds, calls and all that. After that I try to get some sleep before I have to head back in."

"So you don't eat?"

He chuckled. "Nah. I'm superman like that."

She laughed. It was a soothing sound that floated around him like a soft cloud. He glanced at her before returning his attention to the road. He wanted to see the way her face lit up and was rewarded if only for a moment.

"Your father is very proud of you, you know?"

"I know. He was over the moon when I was accepted to the US Marshals. Couldn't stop talking about it—he would tell everyone who would listen."

"When I just moved here he was the first person to even pay me ant attention. He has always been kind to me and I don't know if I told him how much I appreciated it lately."

"I'm sure he knows. Are you just going out with me because you like my father?"

"Are you just asking me out because of your father?"

Oh feisty.

"Touché." Rone laughed. "No. My dad may have some say in my work but when it comes to who I see I hardly ever listen to him. Of course, it is nice if he likes the woman I'm into."

"That is always a plus."

They made it into Astrid just a few minutes to nine. When he pulled up in front of his favorite restaurant and parked, he glanced over at her to see what she would say. Instead he watched her lean forward and peered up at the building, her jaws dropped and she looked at him.

"This is elegant," she said. "I feel slightly underdressed."

"You look beautiful, Jennifer."

She smiled. "Thank you."

"I brought you here because they serve the best seafood I've ever had."

"The best? Well, I hope you're right. I love me some seafood."

Rone chuckled and climbed from the truck. He was going to open her door for her but she did it herself and met him at the front. Pressing a hand at the small of her back he escorted her into the restaurant.

He tried not to react to the spark he felt from touching her and even managed to smile at the hostess when she approached them.

"Good evening. Welcome to Brochelli's. Do you have a reservation?"

"Yes, Jennings," Rone replied.

The hostess consulted the screen on her podium and grinned. "Ah, yes." She grabbed a couple of menus and walked them through a beautifully lit restaurant toward a private table.

"Here we are." She placed a menu to either side.

Rone helped Jennifer with her chair before taking his own.

"Would you like something to drink? Perhaps a glass of wine? We have a lovely Sauvignon Blanc chilling tonight."

Rone didn't care about the wine—truth was, he would rather have a beer, but he smiled and nodded. "I'll have a glass."

"And for the lady?"

"I'm not much of a drinker. I'll have a glass of root beer if you have it."

"Sure." The hostess nodded. "Your server will be Justine. I will see to your wine and your root beer immediately."

"Thank you," Rone told her.

After they were left alone, he focused on her again. It'd been years since he went on a date but the moment he saw her he was curious. Then, she hadn't gone out of her way to show herself to him. He had to chase her in a way, trying to find out her name. He found that unbelievably sexy. The way her eyes shimmered in the dim light enticed him.

Jennifer smiled and bowed her head.

"I guess I should tell you a little about me?" Rone asked.

"That would be nice."

"Well, I'm thirty six."

"Thirty six?"

He arched a brow. "Too old for you?"

She shrugged. "Not really. You'd only be too old for me if you were thirty seven."

Rone chuckled and eased back in his chair. "You really think I'm old?"

Jennifer shook her head as her shoulders rose and fell. "I didn't mean to infer. You were—and you're laughing at me."

"Don't worry about it." Rone nodded. "I'm not a vain man As I was saying, I have been in law enforcement since I was a kid."

She laughed. "That's dramatic, isn't it?"

"Yes. But with my father being the Sheriff, I didn't get away with anything in Barley. I had to be perfect most of the times."

"Most?"

"Yeah. When I was in Astrid or any of the other little towns around these parts, I got to be the real me. A pain in the butt."

"I'm sure you weren't that bad." She giggled.

"I sure like to think I was but as I got older it dawned on me. I wasn't a horrible kid because I got onto the police force. My father was happy I was making a name for myself in something positive. He wasn't keen on me following in his footsteps but when he saw there was nothing he could do to stop me, he gave up."

"If you can't beat them, join them, right?"

He smiled. "Right.

"Here you go. One glass of wine for the gentleman and a glass of root bear for the lady. Have you decided what you would like for dinner?"

"He was saying something about seafood?" Jennifer looked up at her.

"Oh!" The lady's face lit up. "We get everything fresh because we're right on the water. When I'm off duty and want to eat out I come back here. My favorite is the Lobster platter. It comes with lobster, scallops and shrimps, so good."

Jennifer laughed. "All right. I'll have that, please."

"And for you, sir?"

"The same, thank you." After she walked away, Rone brought the conversation back to her. "What about you?"

"Me?"

"Yeah. Tell me a little about you."

Her body slumped back into the chair and her eyes lowered. Rone arched a brow.

"There's nothing to tell, really." She began. "I'm twenty nine. I lived in Ohand with my father. My mom died when I was a baby. So, I lived with my father until he passed when I was eighteen."

"I'm sorry."

"Don't be. It was a long time ago."

Dinner went by in a flurry of conversation. From time to time, Rone noticed she became guarded and closed down.

He switched the topic.

For the most part she was intelligent conversation. Rone found himself so overwhelmingly amazed by her, he didn't want dinner to end. When it did come to an end, however, he invited for a walk by the water.

She accepted and pulled her shawl around her shoulders before tucking her small purse beneath her arm. Pressing his hands into his pockets, he walked beside her silently for a while before speaking.

"I didn't think you would go through with this." Rone admitted.

"Why?"

Rone looked out over the water and inhaled. His hair flapped gently against his head as the wind picked up the tresses in the dim light of the moon. "I don't know. You were so hesitant when I asked. But I'm glad you came."

He watched her shiver and slipped his coat around her shoulders. She smiled up at him and Rone had to hold his breath to keep any sound from leaving his body. Licking his lips, Rone returned his attention to the water. Staring at that wouldn't get him slapped.

"I'm glad I came too. This went better than I thought it would. Can I confess something to you, R.J?"

"Sure." He stepped in front of her and pulled his attention from the beauty of the water. Pushing his fingers into his front pocket, he stood there before her, waiting.

"I don't trust many men. I have my reasons. Due to that, I've tried not dating and was succeeding. Lately, I've been trying not to paint all men with the same brush. Guys stayed away from me and I return the favour. I guess what I'm trying to say is, thank you for tonight."

He smiled before hugging her tightly. For a moment he thought she wouldn't return it and when she did, Rone's body tightened with arousal.

Letting her go wasn't easy but he did and drove her back to her apartment. They talked for just a fraction of the ride but for the most part they were silent.

Close to her place, Jennifer reached over and covered his hand resting on the gear shift. For a quick second he looked down at where their hands connected and couldn't help the happiness he felt then.

Calmness flowed over him, and he slowed down slightly. The need to prolong the experience and connection with her as much as possible was deep within him. Slowing down didn't work well enough for soon they were parked in the front of the apartment building.

"I had a great time tonight," Rone spoke. Then suddenly felt like a moron.

"Surprisingly, so did I."

"A good enough time to do this again?"

She touched his shoulder and he stopped to face her. She said nothing but kept staring at him before a smile spread her lips. Her eyes sparkled and she nodded. "Good enough to do this again."

"Breakfast?" Rone asked.

Jennifer laughed and inhaled. "Breakfast."

He stood with his hands in his pockets facing her after escorting her to the front door. She bowed her head slightly. Swallowing the lump in his throat, he took a breath and inched in slightly while using one hand to lift her chin. He felt her tense and he sighed and merely brushed his lips against hers before stepping back. "Thank you for a lovely night."

"Thank you."

"I should let you go to sleep. I know you have to serve my dad breakfast in the morning."

She nodded. "Goodnight."

"Night."

He stood outside her building long after she was gone. Rone wasn't sure what he was waiting for but he just stood there, feeling his lips tingle in the most wonderful way.

It wasn't a full-fledged kiss but so help him he was aroused and ready to go. He looked toward the door again but turned the other way and climbed into the truck.

He glanced upward, not sure which window belonged to her but they were all dark. With the ignition humming, he took one final look up before pulling from the curb.

Rone even turned on the radio and tapped his finger against the steering wheel to the rhythm of Zac Brown Band.

Jennifer stood by the window and watched the truck disappear down the street into the night. It was well past midnight, but she just didn't feel like sleeping and Darlene was probably asleep already. She couldn't stop smiling.

Humming to herself, she walked into the bathroom and washed her shawl by hand. It was the only one she had that was of any use. The last two had holes in them. Those, she wore in the house during the winter.

Rinsing it in cold water, she placed it on a hanger and hung it over the door handle.

It took her longer than normal to shower, rub lotion on her body then dressed in a pair of booty shorts and a tank. After checking the door one final time for the night she crawled into her bed, ignoring the coldness of the sheets.

And though she was tired, Jennifer didn't fall asleep right away. She found herself lying there, smiling up at the ceiling. Never in a million years did Jennifer think it could be like that with a man. He was funny, intelligent and the way he gently touched the small of her back as he led her through the restaurant or while they walked along the waterfront left her tingling.

After dealing with her father's heavy hand, it'd shocked her at how gentle Rone had been.

How was that even possible?

Her father slowly crept in on her and Jennifer wanted to cry. She rolled over and stared at the alarm clock blinking two in the morning at her. She refused to let him tarnish the good night she'd had. She was happy and laughing. She sat across from a brilliant man and was herself and he didn't run screaming. He seemed to take pleasure in touching her arm, shoulders, the tip of her nose each chance he got.

Determination set in and she pressed her lips into a thin line.

She was going to enjoy the memory of Rone Jennings and think of the possibilities of seeing him again. Jennifer would cling to that and hope the image was stronger than the one of her father's beating her, telling her he would ruin her for every other man out there.

When morning came, she was still awake. But instead of being in bed, she was showered, and dressed. The sun found her sitting by the same window she saw Rone through the night before.

She waited, sipping on her favorite brew until her alarm clock blared.

Jennifer turned it off, walked her cup to the kitchen and grabbed her bag and keys.

She was going to be early for work, but it was Datsun's day to cook so she figured she'd go in and hassle him. The moment she arrived, she immediately wished she'd waited.

Beatrice and Raymond met her at the door.

"Ray, you guys know we're not open yet." Jennifer moaned.

"We know that," Beatrice replied. "We just wanted to know how your date went."

Jennifer stopped fidgeting with her keys and turned to face them. "Really? It's too early guys."

"Come on, Jenny." Raymond pleaded. "Give us something."

"Ask Rone." Jennifer returned to her keys. She turned it in the lock and let herself into the diner. She then quickly closed the door behind her before they could barge their way in. Taking a breath, she turned to see Datsun standing there, wiping his hands into a tablecloth.

"What was that all about? They've been sitting in their cars since about six thirty."

Jennifer smiled. "Morning. I went on a date with Rone last night and they wanted to know if I'm pregnant."

"Pregnant? It was only one date—right?"

"It's a long story." Jennifer made her way around him and hung her bag up in the back. She removed her apron from it and entered the kitchen while tying the straps in place. Her first order of business was to give the fryer a cleaning. It was their practise even though it was cleaned the night before to just give it a good rub down the next day.

"You went on a date with Rone? That must have been something." Datsun joined her and set his sights on the dishwasher.

She glanced at Datsun. "Yes. It was nice."

"Does he know about you and your past with your father?"

She shook her head. "I wanted to have fun last night. Telling your perspective date that your father used to beat you till you bleed and lose consciousness—well, I didn't think that was the best way to endear him to me."

"True."

"I think he suspects something though. He reached in for a kiss and I kind of just froze. He probably sensed it."

Datsun nodded. "Yeah, freezing would send up some red flags to someone like Rone. But don't worry about it. I'm sure he'll ask if he thinks it's a big deal. Then, you should tell him. Don't lie about it. Don't get angry or irritated. Talk to him."

"I'll think about it." Jennifer finished the fryer and headed out into the dining hall to set up the tables.

Six

Rone woke up with a smile on his face. It was the kind of smile that tugged the corners of his lips upward and left him feeling calm.

In Detroit, mornings were all the same. They usually led into a day of the mundane, unless a bust went south.

He loved his job but he couldn't tell the last time he'd gotten up with such happiness inside him. He'd loved Anne with all his heart but her sleeping over hadn't made him want to whistle.

When it came to dating, he couldn't remember a time he got up and the first thing he wanted to do was call a woman.

Still, he worked around the ranch, he listened to music for background noise. He hadn't been back long enough to settle in to hiring someone.

The station had kept him busy enough—the exchange of power from the last sheriff to him had been problematic. The old man wanted his son to take over, but the runt merely laughed and flew out to California to try being an actor.

His father hadn't been impressed, especially since he saw Rone as a traitor who'd left the town.

Justin and Chris helped out around the ranch when they could, but Rone couldn't keep depending on them.

Each morning he woke up he worked the ranch then clipped on his badge for the station.

Half the time he was exhausted by the time he climbed behind the wheel of the sheriff's SUV.

But that was life.

He twisted some rope around his hand and tossed it down a pole before pushing his hands into some gloves. He gripped a fallen piece of wire and pulled it stiffly.

Hooking it to the wood, he pushed a piece of metal into the post, bent it with the hammer before pounding it in to keep the wire in place.

"Yo! Rone!"

Rone stood and pushed his hat from his eyes. He smiled and pulled one hand from his glove to shake his friend's hand. "Justin, you're here early. What's going on?"

"Heard you went on a date last night. Wanted to see how it went."

"Really?" Rone laughed. "That's why you came here so early? It's barely six!"

"And I wanted to help you with this fence." Justin smirked. "It has been down for a while and I was afraid one of the horses would get out."

"Grab a pair of gloves." Rone put his glove back on and hunched down at the other part of the fence that was hanging loose. "As for my date. I enjoyed it. It's not the kind of date I expected though."

"It's with the waitress over at the diner, right?"

Rone nodded. "She was engaging and has this smile—I don't know man. I'm supposed to see her for breakfast"

"Well, we know how you are when you find something you're interested in."

Rone stopped working to look at his friend. "What's that supposed to mean?"

"Precisely what I said." Justin leaned forward to inspect what he'd been doing then looked up at Rone. "It means you're like a dog with a bone."

"Well, you're right about one thing."

"Oh yeah?" Justin hooked a screwdriver under the wire he'd been tacking to his section of the fence and pushed up to pry it from the fencing. "What's that?"

"I got a bone, alright."

"Damn it, Rone! That falls under T.M.I."

Rone shrugged and grabbed his hammer again. "You brought it up."

But no matter how hard he tried, Rone didn't make it in for breakfast.

He had a couple of kids to nab for spray painting graffiti on the side of the school and then the paperwork that went with it.

When he thought he was able to get out, he received a call from the county to the south requesting immediate help with a murder that fell into their laps.

They hadn't had one of those in almost twenty years. With his experience, they had no on else to help until an FBI agent could drop in.

By the time he was able to get free, it was well past lunch and he felt as if his world was sinking. The moment he dropped everything else off at the station and changed into an outfit he always kept in the bottom of his cabinet, he shoved his head into his Stetson and headed for the door with his secretary calling after him.

"Not now, Bea! I mean it."

Hurrying to the squad car he made his way over to the diner and let himself in the front door. The usual crowd filled the place and all shouted greetings at him.

He walked to the bar and climbed to one of the stools.

He didn't see Jennifer.

"Where's Jennifer?" he asked Datsun.

"In the back. Go on in."

Rone arched a brow but didn't say anything except to order a blueberry muffin and coffee.

In the back, he found Jennifer sitting down over a plate of scrambled eggs with toast.

"Hey."

She looked up at him.

"Sorry I wasn't here for breakfast. Something came up with work, but I wanted to see if you'd have lunch with me."

"Lunch has already been served." She replied with a small shrug. "And you don't owe me anything. Things happen."

Rone sat across from her. "I'm apologising because this was supposed to be our second date and I let work get in the way. I tend to fall down a black hole with blinders on when I work certain cases."

Her eyes fused to his face. She was reading him, he knew that. There was something within that stare.

"Do you want something to eat?" she asked.

Datsun walked in then with his muffin and coffee. When Datsun left, he pushed the food aside and focused on her. "This shouldn't be awkward. I'm sorry if I am making it that way."

"No. It's not you. I'm not used to this attention." Jennifer offered a smile. "I find myself wondering why. I'm not saying you're a bad person and I did have fun last night but I'm just being careful."

"Careful is good." Rone hung his head. He couldn't believe he allowed himself to get so buried into his work that he hadn't looked up once to think long enough to call her. "I get off work around six and then I'm on call but I can be all yours tonight or part of the night or for just a few hours. I'm putting myself at your disposal."

She shook her head. "Don't do that."

"Don't do what?"

"This... being nice to me. What's the catch?"

"The catch?" For a moment Rone didn't get it. When he did, he sighed. "The catch is, you have to spend some time with me. Get to know me outside of the makeshift cupids, including my father. That's all I ask. If this is about that kiss last night I shouldn't have done it. I mean...damn this is so hard. What I meant was. I should have asked first and I'm sorry I didn't. I can't say I'm sorry for kissing you though."

"You just said you were."

"I...Jennifer. I'm glad I kissed you. What I'm sorry about was the way I did it. Better?"

She gave him a small smile. "You're at my disposal huh?"

His cheeks heated but he reached across the table and squeezed her hand. "Can you meet me after work?"

"Where?"

"My place..."

Something changed in her eyes and she eased her hand from under his.

"We won't be alone, I promise. My father will be there. It's our weekly dinner. But if you want us to be alone, I can work with that too."

She smacked him playfully. "Leave me your address and I'll be there. But I have to go home after my shift. I'll need to a shower."

"You know, I have a shower at my place."

"Rone Jennings!" She gasped but laughed.

He smiled and quickly pulled his notebook from his back pocket. He scribbled down his address on a page, ripped it out and slid it across the table. "I'll see you tonight. Whenever you can get there, okay?"

"I'll be there."

"Do you have a phone number? I couldn't find one for you."

"Yeah," she replied.

Jennifer ripped off a piece of the paper he'd given her with his address, jotted down her number and handed it over.

He walked out in time to see his father sitting down. Smiling, he hurried over and fell into the chair across from Raymond.

"The two of you are something else," Raymond said. "She wouldn't tell me anything. You're not telling me anything. Give an old man a break."

"We had a great time. There's nothing to tell."

"Did you kiss her?"

"Dad."

"It's a logical question." Raymond pushed. "Did you kiss our Jenny?"

"Kind of—stop calling her *our Jenny*." Rone cringed. "It's kinda creepy."

"Come now, RJ. You're almost forty. You've kissed women before. So, it's either you kissed her or you didn't."

"I kissed her but it's not like you think." Rone glanced over his shoulders to ensure they were still alone. When he turned to his father again, it was to rest his elbows on the table and leaned in. "I reached in for a kiss and she went stiff."

"Stiff?"

"Yeah." He answered. "Almost like she thought I was going to hit her. Look, we'll talk more tonight. I have to head back to work. And by the way, I invited her for tonight."

"And?"

"She says she'll be there after she goes home and shower."

"Did you tell her you have a shower at your place?"

Rone laughed.

"You did!" Raymond cheered. "This is good."

Rone laughed again and patted his father on the shoulder. "See you later, old man."

"These kids—no respect for their elders." He chuckled. Rone kissed his father on the cheek and slipped his hat onto his head.

Seven

Jennifer sat beside Darlene trying to decide on what to wear for her night with Raymond and Rone. She wasn't any kind of fashionista. All her clothing were bought at thrift stores around the county. The only person who knew was Darlene because they were both in the same boat—very little money but wanted to look cute from time to time.

The upside was, if she didn't tell people, they wouldn't know.

On top of not being sure of what to wear, Jennifer knew she couldn't show up at Rone's place empty handed. Wine came to mind, but she knew the only thing Jennifer knew about wine was that she couldn't afford the good kind.

Darlene suggested beer and she readily picked some up.

"Okay, so you've done the pink dress." Darlene pointed to the coat bag that was now hanging over the bedroom door. She rose from the bed and grabbed it. "I brought you something you might like. It's a pants suit I got a few years ago. It's a tad big for me."

"Even so, your clothes would be too small for me."

"I made some changes to it when you told me about tonight." Darlene told her. "Just try the stuff on, would you?"

Jennifer accepted the bag. She opened it to find a beautiful pair of black pants along with a top with beautiful, flowing sleeves.

Jennifer tried the pants first. They were tight around her thighs and flared from the knees down. It zipped up without trouble and she walked around in it, testing it.

"Try dropping it like it's hot." Darlene teased.

"Ha!" Jennifer chortled. "If I dropped it, I'm not picking it back up."

Darlene laughed out loud.

The top was beautiful on her. The neck rested at the tips of her shoulders and that was the part she didn't like. It was showing too much cleavage.

"Darlene, I love the pants, but the top is a little too...showie."

"You're a woman, Jenny. Celebrate that." Darlene was busy looking through Jennifer's limited things on her dresser. "As a woman, it's your right to look sexy enough to cause traffic accidents."

"You go too far madam."

Darlene giggled. "But wouldn't that be something? Men can't take their eyes off you and drive into a tree."

Jennifer shook her head.

"Anyway." Darlene turned, holding up a pair of earrings. "All I'm saying is that you look lovely. Now, the same earrings from last night will work and you don't need a necklace with that top. You're good to go. I'm so proud of you, you know?"

"For what?"

"That you're putting yourself out there." Darlene pointed out. "You could have crawled into your own head, remembering all the horrid things that man did to you and be paralyzed with fear. I mean, it would be easy to let him win. I'm happy for you."

"It's hard." Jennifer admitted. "It's so hard."

"I know." Darlene sat beside her while handing her the earrings. "I know it's really hard because no one can just get over something like that. But I have your back. Take it slow."

"What if when he finds out what happens if he wants to run? What happens when he sees all the scars? Then what do I do? How do I explain it to him without him finding out how weak I've been?"

"Weak?" Darlene shook her head. "What you've been through would have brought down many a man. There's no weakness in what you've survived."

"But—"

"You deal with it. No more shutting out a man because of what that douche did to you."

Jennifer nodded.

She wanted to be this strong person Darlene was talking about. That woman sounded as if she could get through anything with her head held high.

But deep down, Jennifer knew she was nowhere near that.

A few times since she'd spoken with Rone at the diner that day, she'd locked herself in the bathroom and allowed that scared little girl that was buried inside her to sob until she was weak.

Then, she'd wiped her eyes and returned to the chaos of life.

But as she made her way home after her shift, Jennifer was determined to do better, to grow into this superwoman Darlene saw in her.

With Rone, she was going to put her best foot forward. The fear of being rejected because she was so physically and emotionally scarred would just have to stay in the back of her mind—she would force it to remain there.

Her body wasn't as smooth as other women. But the truth of it was, she couldn't sit around and be negative. It was time to step up and get on with it.

"I'm going to try this." Jennifer turned to look in the mirror again. Before Darlene arrived, she'd showered and washed her hair. Taking great care to ensure it didn't smell like the diner. She brushed the hair down to cradle her face and curled the ends leaving it soft enough to run her fingers through. She slipped the earrings in, slid on some lip gloss and smiled at Darlene.

"I'm glad you're here to hold my hand." She admitted to Darlene. "I tried calling Gale but she's probably away on another business trip. Honestly, it's been getting harder and harder to get a hold of her."

"Don't these big city types have cellphones?" Darlene asked. "I mean, we can barely afford it, but we have one. And it's always on us. What's her excuse?"

Jennifer sighed and shrugged. "Just—thanks for being here for me."

"I wouldn't be anywhere else, mama. You're going to be late if you don't leave now. Don't forget the beer and I brought over some flowers from the garden you can take too."

Jennifer hugged Darlene tightly. "I'm going to make sure I'm here for our girl's night tomorrow."

"Hey, if that sexy cop wants you for tomorrow night, you'd better cancel with me." Darlene giggled. "At least one of us should be getting laid."

"Laid?" Jennifer almost choked. "Um—no one's getting laid."

"Sure baby girl. If I was Rone and you walked in looking that delicious—is all I'm saying."

"Oh, sweet baby Jesus."

Darlene laughed.

"I'm not going to cancel." Jennifer fanned her face with her fingers. "Just be here like we planned."

Darlene patted her back. "Go. I'll wash the dishes in the sink then lock up."

"Thank you." Jennifer picked up her shawl and with a quick kiss to the cheek, she left the house. She found Rone's place easy enough and looking at it sent her heart racing.

It was a sprawling ranch—the kind you would see in those cowboy movies. Still, she climbed from the car, grabbed the flowers and the box of beer. When she knocked it took a while for someone to come to the door.

While Jennifer waited, she turned and looked around.

There was a black horse frolicking to her left in a closed off area. It was so beautiful.

"Jennifer!"

She spun around to see Raymond standing there. When she offered the beer, Raymond shook his head. "Hold on a second. R.J!"

"Yeah, Dad?"

"Someone's at the door for you."

For a moment, they waited until Rone looked around his father and smiled. "Jennifer!"

Raymond walked away and Rone hugged her tightly. The box squeezed between them and she groaned.

"Oh, sorry." Rone stepped back and accepted what she offered. "You brought me a present. You shouldn't have."

"I know. But I didn't want to come empty handed. Since I know nothing about wine, beer was the next logical step. Oh, and I brought you some flowers."

He grinned. "Why Jennifer. Are you propositioning me?"

"With flowers?" She arched a brow. "No. If I was propositioning you, I would be naked."

"Don't tease me woman."

She blushed.

"Come on in. Dinner is almost ready."

Walking by him she stopped and waited for him to close the door. He then led her down a beautiful corridor to the kitchen. He placed the box on the counter then put the flowers in water.

Raymond had suspiciously disappeared and the silence around them was only interrupted by a bubbling pot.

Rone moved around the kitchen as if he was meant to be there. Jennifer couldn't help staring in awe as she climbed onto a stool and he poured them some wine.

"I'm glad you came tonight," Rone said, softly. "I didn't think you would."

"Why?"

"Well, you were a little timid today and during our date. I didn't want to seem as if I was pushing you."

"It's not you, trust me." She sipped from her wine then arched a brow.

Wine had never been her thing and red wine always tasted a little—it was an acquired taste.

"One day I'm hoping to be strong enough to tell you about it." She nodded. "As for now I just want to get to know you—if that's okay."

"I'd like..." Rone was interrupted by the slamming of a door. He looked at Jennifer then rushed forward with her close on his heels. When they opened the door, it was in time to see Raymond's car speeding off down the dirt road leading from the ranch.

Jennifer looked at Rone then doubled over in laughing. She laughed so hard she snorted.

"It's not funny," Rone said but he was smiling.

"I'm sorry." She gasped through her mirth. "I'm sorry, but it's funny. Your father is still playing cupid."

"I should have known he would pull something like that."

"Me too. Shall we have dinner then?"

Rone nodded and closed the door.

They sat around the table and Jennifer even managed to reach over from time to time to squeeze his hand. Rone had her laughing and participating in their conversation.

Things were easy with Rone. He didn't speak to her—Rone spoke *with* her. Their conversation always taught her something and left her feeling better than when she walked in. There was no guessing he genuinely wanted to hear her thoughts and accepted them with a mind opened to learning.

Being around him wasn't at all like being around a sexy man. It was like speaking with a friend.

"I noticed you have a horse outside." She pointed out.

"Yeah." He sipped from his wine. "I have three now. We aren't breeders or anything but dad loves them being around."

"The black one?"

"Kicker. He was a beast when we got him. Now he's the perfect horse."

"You named a troubled horse Kicker? I think he was pissed off at the name than anything else."

"We used to have someone working here who quit after Kicker knocked him flat." Rone sighed. "We were lucky no damage was done."

Jennifer chuckled. "Well, I'm sorry to hear that but he is a beautiful horse."

"Do you ride?"

"No." She guffawed. "I've never been anywhere near a horse. I respected them enough not to do that. The last thing a horse needs is my butt on his back."

"You have a very nice butt."

She blinked at him then grinned. "Thanks. I'm glad you like it."

With dinner over, they carried their drinks and sat on the balcony The night had fallen over the small town and the moon was big, round and yellow in the sky.

She sighed and relaxed in the swing and pushed herself gently on it. Rone stood with his back against the banister watching her for a moment.

When he finally sat beside her, Jennifer had trouble breathing. Heat swarmed her face. Taking a breath to steady her beating heart, she moved closer to him and snuggled into his side.

When his arm went around her and pulled her in, Jennifer felt as though she had conquered Everest.

He caressed her shoulder sending shock through her body and boiling her blood. Licking her lips, she dared to look up and yearned for his kiss.

Their eyes met and when she broke the contact to stare at his lips, she watched with baited breath as he drifted closer.

This time she didn't freeze or pull back.

Though her mind screamed at her to run, she held still, gripped the front of his shirt as though it would make him stay and closed her eyes. She waited for his lips to meet hers. Finally, she had what she wanted, their mouths, caressing each other's.

She spread her lips, loving the tickle of his tongue.

To her great pleasure, his tongue slid within her depths.

Unable to control herself she pushed her tongue up and the moment they connected she moaned and whimpered easing closer to him.

An electric charge went off between her legs then sent spark through every vein.

Rone deepened the kiss, holding her chin tenderly, and giving to her a kind of passion Jennifer knew existed.

He cradled the side of her face with a large hand, his calloused fingers caressing her skin. With each stroke of his fingers, she felt it deep within her core and between her legs.

It was a hot charge, like being jolted sweetly by electricity. She shifted beneath him, craving that heat and pressing her legs together hoping to keep the sensation there.

He pulled away when she whimpered and Jennifer tried desperately to hide her disappointment.

"That was so worth the wait." He admitted. His voice was husky.

"Your voice changed."

"That's because you turn me on, Jennifer."

She buried her face into his chest.

"Hey. I'm sorry. I didn't mean to come on so strong."

She lifted her head and bravely dropped a chaste kiss against his lips. Jennifer shivered and caressed his chest. "It's all right. It wasn't like I didn't want you to kiss me." She ran out of breath and had to pause to fill her lungs. "I'm just—I hate being so shy all the time."

"Shy isn't a bad thing."

"Yes it is," Jennifer replied. "A man doesn't want a woman who's afraid of her own damn shadow and I'm more than afraid of my shadow. A man wants a real woman—you deserve a real woman."

"No. What I deserve is a woman who makes me feel something. Look, don't put too much thought into it. Just go with the flow."

"It's not that simple."'

"No?" Rone wanted to know. "I find it is less stress that way. We never want to live with regrets."

"Maybe."

She said nothing else. Leaning off him she grabbed her drink and took a sip. She put the glass down and rested her body into his arms again.

He pushed them in the swing as they sat there in the early night.

"I should go home soon." She whispered.

"Do you want to go?"

"No. But I work in the morning. All my stuff is at home and I couldn't just stay over a boy's house all night. It wouldn't be right."

He kissed her head sending a shiver though her. "You just called me a boy."

"You know what I mean." She touched his thigh gently before meeting his eyes. "But I wouldn't be mad at you kissing me again."

"It would be my pleasure," Rone said, softly, taking her lips again.

She felt as though she was being taken. He had a force about him that made her head spin. It dominated her and caused her heart to race with just the mere thought of those beautiful lips on hers. His kiss tasted like fire and unlike any other kiss she'd ever had. Inhaling his scent, she lifted a hand to caress his neck as she tilted her body back forcing him to hover over her. His weight pushed into her, sweetly crushing her.

She'd never felt a man against her like that before and she loved it.

Jennifer moaned, wrapped her arm around his back and slipped her lips from his. She needed to breathe. But he nuzzled her neck, kissing and sucking at the flesh. His face was rough with beard that sprang up during the day, but it felt amazing against her skin.

"Rone..."

He eased back and met her eyes. "We should stop."

"Why?"

"Because we both agreed we wouldn't rush this. If I don't stop, I will lose control and I never want to hurt you. Do you understand?"

"I think so." Jennifer smiled and nodded. "Sorry. I shouldn't have put you in that position."

"It's all right. I enjoy feeling you against me."

"So, what's next?"

Rone sat back as though he was thinking about it. "Do you have plans tomorrow?"

"I work in the morning and then I have a girl's night with Darlene."

"Sunday I get my first day off. I would like to surprise you with something."

"You know how I feel about surprises."

"I do." He kissed her ear. "I know you dislike them. But this one will be amazing. It'll be a day of lying around and just being with each other. Alone—without my father's meddling."

"I can go for that." Jennifer took a breath, steadying the rising fear within her. When he looked at her again, she smiled and touched his arm gently. "I really should go."

"Did you drive here?"

Jennifer nodded and allowed him to take her hand and led her from the balcony. At the front door, she stopped to grab her shawl from where he'd hung it. She tangled her arms around his neck, pushed to her toes and kissed him.

Just the thought of knowing he would accept her kiss made her want to do it over and over. Add to that the fact he kissed her so well—so perfectly—she couldn't resist it. His hands touched her hips, then snaked around her back, caressing as they went until he was holding her closely.

"If you don't go now I'll never let you leave." Rone whispered against her lips. "I'll see you on Sunday? Hell, I may not even wait till Sunday. I may stop by the diner."

Jennifer laughed. "So, I think I should say, I'll see you when I see you?"

Rone nodded and bent his head for her lips again.

Eight

Rone spent half the morning talking with his father. He sat across from Raymond in the kitchen and sipped from a mug of coffee.

"What do you know about her?"

"I know she's been hurt in the past." Raymond replied. "She doesn't like talking about it but I suspect it's been eating away at her. About a week after I met her, I found her outside the diner just sobbing. She said some women were lucky to have people in their lives who generally cared for them. She was crying, apparently, because she thinks these women take their families for granted."

"Seriously?" Rone tilted his head. "That doesn't sound like something good...her crying about that I mean."

"Nah. But she's a lovely girl. A little opinionated at times but a good girl. Why all the questions?"

"I don't know." Rone took another drink from his mug. "It's probably nothing."

"Come on. It's me you're talking to."

"I see sadness in her eyes. And when she looks at me, sometimes there's this mistrust there. Like I said—it's probably nothing."

"You're a good cop, Rone. If your gut is telling you something is wrong—"

"She's not one of my suspects, dad." Rone said entirely too harshly. He closed his eyes and exhaled loudly. "I'm sorry. I know there's something there. And I want to help—and I get it. She doesn't trust me like that yet. But this feeling—" He tapped his chest.

"I get it." Raymond smiled.

Deep breath.

"I was the same way with your mother, and she was stubborn as hell." He carried on. "She was a strong woman and sometimes all I want to do barge in with brute force and solve all her problems."

"But you couldn't."

Raymond shook his head. "And you can't either. Listen, we both know she comes with some demons. And yes, we want to help her—we want to rush in like knights on our white horses. But you have to understand, she's been fighting alone for a while.'"

"I get that too."

"Then give her time." Raymond patted his son's shoulder. "Show her you're the man she can trust to lay these burdens at your feet. And when she's ready, she'll come to you."

What his father said made sense. But Rone wasn't used to sitting around and doing nothing when someone he cared about was going through something.

Long after his father was gone, Rone pulled himself together enough to get some work done.

He walked his property while his friend Justin messed around with fixing the roof of the guest house.

There wasn't much damage, but he did have to pick up some garbage down by the swimming home. He allowed the locals to use it on Fridays, but he was seriously debating stopping that. No one seemed to take him seriously when he told them to clean up after himself.

Once he returned to the ranch, he brought the horses into an enclosed area for them to run while he mucked out the stalls.. Once he was sure they had enough sun, he marched them right back in and set out getting them some hay.

"Yo, Rone!" Justin called from the front of the yard.

"What?" Rone pulled a fork from the hook and jabbed it into a bay of hay. Dragging, he stepped back and watched it fall to the ground. He then used the fork to lift it into the stall and broke it apart.

"You have a visitor." Justin announced before dropping his voice into a sexy octave. "A very pretty visitor."

Rone's back instantly went up.

If Justin was speaking about Jennifer, he would strangle the twerp. Shaking his head to push away the rising anger He reminded himself that Justin was his friend, and he knew how Rone felt about Jennifer..

But he was a man who had a pretty girl, and he didn't like any other man even breathing in her direction.

"Well, send her back here." Rone called.

Pushing his hat out of his face, he turned as footsteps came around the corner. When he saw her, he felt his face light up. She was dressed in a beautiful, pink and white sundress that hung just below her knees. It hugged her breasts on top, showing off the fullest cleavage he'd ever seen on a woman. Her hair was tied up and away from her face showing no make-up but a thin sliver of sparkle on her lips.

"Jennifer." He sighed. "You're early."

"I know. I was really excited to see you. I could go away and come back later."

"No—I wish I could kiss you right now because you look so good." He chewed on his bottom lip. "I'm all sweaty."

She smiled and reached in, bum out and kissed his lips gently. "That'll have to do until you can get showered."

"Aww baby." Rone reached out and grabbed her around the waist. He pulled her into his chest and kissed her soundly. "You're so beautiful right now."

She giggled and wrapped her arms around his neck. Rone went speechless at the deepness of her eyes. There was no fear in them at that moment.

She was stronger, he could tell.

"You really like the dress?"

He nodded. "Is it new?"

"Nah. I've had it a while now but didn't really have a reason to wear it."

"I'm glad I gave you a reason to wear it. Come into the house."

Justin came around the corner then and she jerked away from him. With her body away from him, Rone groaned softly as the world kind of swam in on him again. Jennifer had been warm, and sexy on him and Justin just stole that.

Somehow, Rone managed a smile and faced his friend.

"I'm leaving for the day," Justin said. "It was nice seeing you, Jennifer. I'll see you guys later."

"Nice seeing you too Justin." Jennifer replied.

"I'll call you," Rone told him.

When they were alone, Rone finished the stall then took Jennifer's hand, leading her inside. He peeled his sweat soaked shirt over his head and carried it in his hand to the kitchen.

"Okay, I have to shower so make yourself—what"

She was staring at his right shoulder, then down his arm. He'd forgotten about his tattoo. It was tribal, large sprawling from his shoulder down to his elbows then across to the centre of his chest.

"You don't like it," he said.

"I don't know. I—It's huge."

"Yeah, I know." He lifted his shirt to put it back on, but she stopped him by taking it away.

Slowly, she climbed from the stool and caressed the ink from where it began, down his arm and up again. Her touch was soft with a tremble in it.

"Did it hurt?" Jennifer wanted to know.

"Yes. But it was worth it."

"It means something to you, doesn't it?"

"Yes. I lost a partner." He confided in her. "We called him Savage. It did something to me and for a long time I didn't know what to do to feel worthy of having him as a friend."

"I bet once you figured it out it was better."

He kissed her head. "I should shower."

"Could I talk to you?" Jennifer asked. "It won't take long. I thought about it all night and I really would like to talk to you about it now before I chicken out."

He arched a brow. "Okay, can you give me a second? Lemme just wash up a little."

Jennifer nodded. He hurried from the room and when he returned, he was dressed in a pair of track pants and a t-shirt.

Rone motioned to a stool after getting a bottle of water from the fridge. He placed a bottle of juice in front of her then sat with her. "What's on your mind?"

"I know we haven't known each other for a very long time." Jennifer began. "But when we kiss I feel—ah—I feel something and it got me thinking. That if you..." She stopped and rubbed a hand over her face.

Rone reached up and covered her hands with his. "Sweetie— just say it."

Her shoulders rose and fell. "Well, I was thinking we could em...you know?"

For a moment, Rone sat there, blinking at her wondering what in the world she was talking about. But the way she stuttered and fell over her words was so damn cute he just couldn't bring himself to concentrate.

Then she muttered a profanity and hung her head and it dawned on him.

Rone smiled and walked around the counter. "We won't do that unless you're ready and it's what you want."

"But it's what I want. Would you make love to me if I asked?"

"Honey, I'd happily do whatever you want to this body if you asked."

She pressed her face into his bare chest and Rone chuckled. "Look, Jenny. I know what it's like to rush things and have it exploded in my face. I'm quite content getting to know you and not rushing. So, when it happens it happens."

"But men aren't good with waiting. They tend to stray and then..."

"No. I won't stray, Jennifer. I promise you that." Rone dragged a hand up her arm. "I'm not going to lie and say I wouldn't want to have you right now. That's not what I'm saying. What I'm saying is, despite wanting you like I do, I'm perfectly happy with waiting."

"But you're so much more experienced than I am."

"That doesn't mean I want to push you into anything." Rone assured here. "Trust me, these things take time and I'm willing to be very patient. I love spending time with you, Jennifer and the last thing I want is to do something that will ruin everything." He kissed her head just as the sound of rain interrupted their moment.

He released her and hurried to close the window before the kitchen flooded.

"Well, I guess we won't be going out today. Your surprise was a picnic down by the river." The rain poured harder bashing against the window perhaps to show him what a moron he'd been to assume the weather would be perfect.

The sound of thunder scraped across the sky and he sighed.

"I guess I should have checked the weather this morning." She muttered.

"It's all right. We can have it here. We can clear a space on the living room floor, make a blanket fort and sit around—" She stopped and looked up as something fizzled and all the lights went out.

Rone did not like the sound of it.

The room was plunged into a mid-day kind of dimness and went silent except for the rain.

The humming of the fridge was gone.

The light on the voicemail stopped flashing and went out. She looked around then back at Rone.

"Light some candles and just hang here." Jennifer continued.

"Come on." He took her hand and hurried into the living room. He pulled the sofa away from the centre of the room as well as the center table. Rone spread the blanket from over the back of the sofa on the cleared space.

Jennifer added the cushions.

"Great idea. If you want more, you can go upstairs and grab some pillows from the bedrooms."

"Okay." She left the room, walking by him and leaving a faint smell of lavender behind her. He moaned, licked his lips but hurried into the kitchen to gather food and drinks.

Jennifer entered the large master bedroom and couldn't believe how beautiful it all was. The sheets and pillows as well as the cushions on the bed were black and red. She rubbed a hand over the smooth covering on the large bed.

It was soft.

Though the room only had a few pieces of furniture it was still breath-taking.

The bed sat in the center of the room, perfectly made with a lovely quilt on. A love seat beneath the window seemed perfect for a cuddle during a cold day with a good book and hot chocolate.

A guitar sat beside the love seat in the corner, and she wondered if Rone played.

The dresser had a few things on it along with picture frames. She took a moment to look through the pictures recognizing Rone, Raymond and Justin. There was another man along with an older woman. She was the splitting image of Rone—it had to be his mother.

Raymond spoke of her frequently and Jennifer knew without a doubt, that man loved his wife more than life itself.

She stopped at a particular picture of Rone in his US Marshals gear and almost climaxed.

He was dressed in dark blue, with a patch across his right breast that said *US MARSHALS* and one across his left breast that said *Jennings.*

He carried a massive gun pointing downward, a holster strapped to his left thigh and his pants tucked into his boots.

Dragging her finger over his face she had to tear herself away from how sexy he looked in the picture and grabbed an armful of pillows and cushions from the bed.

The last thing she wanted was for him to think she was snooping. Hurrying back down the stairs, she dropped the pillows on the floor.

"Rone."

"Yes?"

"This is...wow."

He took her hand and helped her to the floor, before sitting behind her and pulling her into his chest. Jennifer sighed, allowing the world to melt away from her as he lifted a grape to her lips.

"I love these." She told him before accepting the fruit. "I could eat grapes all day."

He chuckled. "Well, I'm glad this makes you happy. It's not much and I'm sorry it couldn't be outside but..."

Jennifer turned in his arms to slip both her legs over his. She pushed her dress down so she wasn't flashing him and leant in to nuzzle his neck with her lips. "This is perfect. I promise you."

"Perfect? This is amazing because I was going for beautiful."

She laughed softly, easing into his body and kissing him more passionately than she'd ever kissed anyone else.

He moaned and for some reason that gave her enough courage to reach behind her, grab a grape from the bowl and faced him once more. Pressing it between her lips, she fed it to him with her mouth.

Instead of taking the fruit, however, Rone kissed her, sucking on her lips then pulling the grape into his. He kissed her around it, dragged his mouth down her neck and kissed across her bare shoulder while his large hand pressed into her back.

The heat of his body emanated through his clothing into her, warming her body. When his arousal rested intimately against her, she moaned and rolled her hips out of the sheer need to see what it would do to him.

Rone growled and shivered in her arms.

"I want more." Jennifer whimpered. "I want you."

"Damn, Jennifer you make it so hard to say no."

"Then don't say no."

Rone groaned and pulled her into him even more. This time both his arms were around her, holding her so securely.

She melted into him sighing pushing every fear from her mind. She knew she would regret not doing this.

When it came to Rone, the absolute last thing she needed was regrets. Trialing a hand over his shoulders, she felt the raised flesh of the tattoo down to his hands. He was feasting against her neck, her chin and then her cleavage.

He sucked at the swells of her breasts while lifting her bum off the ground and pushing things out the way with his free hand.

He laid her on the floor, and for a moment just looked into her eyes.

Jennifer nodded with a smile and reached up to tweak one of his nipples with a nail.

"Jennifer..." He pushed her dress up and froze.

The passion she saw in his eyes before was gone and she knew why.

Embarrassed, she tried scurrying away. He grabbed her and held her in place.

"Jennifer, what happened? Who did this?"

Turning her face away, she felt the tears coming and felt completely furious with herself. She couldn't cry but what else was she going to do.

"Darling, tell me, please."

"I know you wouldn't like it. I'm not perfect."

"And I don't need you to be perfect that is not what I'm doing." Rone sighed. "Who did this to you?"

She turned to meet his eyes. "My father."

"Sweetheart..."

He trailed a tender finger up the scars against her thighs. When she saw his stare, her heart broke. There was a fire there, an angry fire she couldn't understand.

The softness of his touch over her scars sent tears tumbling down her face and as she tried to watch him, he went fuzzy in her gaze.

"Don't cry." He whispered, cradling her into his body. "Please don't cry."

"I'm not sad." She promised. "It's just—no one has ever been this tender and understanding about those before. I spent so many years trying to hide them."

"Those scars don't define you."

"I know..."

"Do you really, Jennifer?"

"I know. I really do—deep down, I do."

He said nothing else to her. He stripped her slowly then dragged his hands over her body. He touched her, caressed her, tasted from her flesh until she trembled and arched upward for his lips. The feelings charging through her were new, but she wanted them to last. Chances were, she would die if they stopped. She clung to him and pulled at his hair.

"Rone." She whimpered. "Rone!"

He eased down her body, spread her out like a meal and licked. Jennifer pushed at his shoulders, completely shocked at the vulgarity of his actions.

But he gripped her thighs, held them apart and plunged his tongue deeper.

Jennifer cried out, digging her nails into his skin and shoving her hips upward greedily. She loved the silken roughness of his tongue gliding over her tender bud turning her into one big blaze.

She trembled with each pass of his tongue and held on tighter with each suck from his mouth. It was exquisite, the completely madness of the feelings swarming her.

Every swipe of his tongue, every grip of his hands against her thighs and every sound to escape his body left her shaking.

"Rone..." His name tumbled from her lips. She couldn't control that anymore.

His reply was to move up her body. Somewhere in her daze she heard his zipper and spread her legs wider. It wasn't something she could control. It just happened. His weight pressed into her and his lips found her forehead.

Reaching down, she bravely wrapped her fingers around his arousal because she wanted to know what it felt like but most importantly, she wanted to give him the same pleasure he was sending through her.

He throbbed in her hand, hot and hard. When Jennifer stroke her hand brushed the head and hot, sticky liquid traced her palm.

His body shook and his head fell back.

Rone moaned and she hoped she was doing it right.

"Tighter." He whispered. "Squeeze."

Taking his instructions, she tightened her fist.

"Yes, that's it." Rone encouraged.

He took her hand away and inched forward. Rone kissed her as the head of his member found her entrance.

Jennifer wrapped her arms around his hips and pushed down against his bum. She didn't know what it would be like but the heat raging through her didn't leave much space or capacity for thinking.

He filled her slowly and it was amazing until he crashed through something like breaking the flesh. She screamed in pain and Rone went stiff atop her. She knew what happened and felt like a moron.

"Jenny, I'm so sorry!" He began pulling from her.

"Don't move." Jennifer told him. "Please don't leave me."

"I'm not leaving you—why didn't you tell me?"

"Please. Don't ask that now. Just, make love to me."

"But you're hurt."

She smiled up at him. "Rone. My friend told me my first time would hurt. I should have expected it. It's still a little sore but just give me a minute."

He didn't look sure but when she reached up and pinched one of his nipples, he held his hips still as though waiting for her to make the first move.

The pain subsided but not completely. For a while she simply reached up and kissed him, hoping to build his arousal again. She pressed her breasts into his chest, tangled her arms around his neck and buried her finger into his hair.

When he was hard and filling her again, she was ready for whatever he had to give her.

This time, it was even better. He slid within her as though he belonged there giving her something she was glad she was getting.

Though she couldn't put her finger on it, she knew what she was feeling was a good thing. Jennifer rolled her hips with his, meeting his every thrust.

"Rone! I'm going to—Rone!" She panted. Deep down she knew it was inevitable but she tried holding her breath to keep from breaking apart.

Her body mutinied, her teeth sank into his shoulders and a great river broke its borders within her.

She screamed with the storm, clung to her Rone and rode him from underneath. Her first orgasm, her first *real* orgasm left her panting.

Her sex throbbed beautifully around his large arousal.

"Open your eyes." He ordered.

She lifted her heavy eye-lids to look into his gaze. At that moment, he gritted his teeth and she felt a hot rush inside her body.

He had a majestic look about him as he gave himself over to the pleasure her body was giving him.

Her body, *Jennifer Cozel's body* was giving a man, a strong cowboy enjoyment.

She smiled and slumped to the floor. He gathered her into his arms and pulled her into his body. For the first time since she could remember, Jennifer felt cherished, and she didn't want it to end.

Nine

After Jennifer was asleep, Rone carried her up the stairs to the bedroom. He then spent a few minutes cleaning up the mess they'd made during their love making.

He really should have known she was a virgin but how was he supposed to believe at her age she'd never been with anyone else?

Feeling guilty, he chucked the soiled blankets into the washer but left their uneaten picnic where it was on the floor.

He climbed the stairs then slipped into bed with her, pulling her gently into his chest. Only now, her face was pressed into his neck as she breathed softly.

The next time he opened his eyes, Jennifer was still cuddled into him and he wasn't sure if he should wake her. He also didn't know what time she needed to be up for work. Groaning at his predicament, he leant over and kissed her. "Jenny, baby?"

"Mmm?"

"Sweetie, wake up."

"What's wrong?"

"Nothing. But what time did you want me to wake you tomorrow? I know you have work."

She sat up, pulling the sheets to cover her chest. Her hair was pressed into the side of her head. He smiled and reached across to fix it, but she blushed and looked away from him.

"What time did you want me to wake you up in the morning?" He repeated.

"Four thirty. I have to go home for clothes. I'm hungry."

"Stay right here." Rone hopped his naked body out of the bed.

"Wait!"

He stopped and turned to face her.

But she said nothing.

She merely stared at him and he found himself getting aroused under her gaze.

Licking his lips, he slid his hand over his body, slowly downward to his penis. He stroked it a few times with her watching before smirking and walking from the room.

"Tease!" She flung after him.

Laughing, he made his way into the kitchen. The ice-cream had long since melted and nothing seemed edible after their little detour. They'd snacked after their first session of love-making but other than that he was starving as well. He laughed again and wondered how this one woman seemed to make him feel as if he was flying.

The sound of the shower running upstairs caught his attention. Thankfully, that pulled his attention to back to what he was supposed to be doing.

In the fridge, he grabbed a giant, peeled pineapple and sliced it up. Next, he made some new ham sandwiches along with some chocolates. He emptied the picnic basket and stocked it with the new food, tossed in a few bottles of water and a couple of juices.

"Rone, I changed the sheets. Where's your washer?"

"You changed the sheets? Why?"

"Um—a woman's first time." She bowed her head for a moment. "I guess we carried some of it to the bed afterward."

He walked over to kiss her cheek. "I'll take them. Go back to bed, sweetie."

She kissed his neck and did Rone suggested. With her gone, he checked the sheets to noticed they were, in fact, soiled.

As he made his way back to the kitchen, he wondered how badly he'd hurt her. Sure, he understood her first time would be a little painful, but he didn't like the idea knowing he'd caused her to hurt.

When everything was stacked on the tray, he climbed the stairs again and sat in the centre of the bed with her.

"I know this wasn't what I promised."

"Rone." She touched his face. "I'm very happy right now, so no apologies. Okay?"

He nodded and placed the basket between them. Rone handed her a sandwich and watched as she broke off a piece. When she was chewing, he reached for his and took a bite. "Why didn't you tell me?"

"Tell you what?"

"Jennifer. You were...you've never been with another man. I don't feel right hurting you like that."

"I didn't think it was a big deal." Jennifer replied. "And then I thought if I told you, you'd never touch me. Men tend to run from virgins."

"That's not what I would have done. I would have been more careful." Rone put down his half eaten sandwich just so he could focus all his attention on her. He wondered what kind of men she'd dated over the years but he didn't ask. The situation didn't call for prying. It called for a form of tenderness he thought he'd lost a long time ago.

She nodded. "I'm sorry. I should have said something but let me tell you I'm new at this, okay? So just—you're going to have to help me out a little."

"I'm so gamed. Now, let's eat because I have a plan for this body of yours."

She giggled and covered her lips before averting her eyes. Rone laughed softly, leaning in to kiss her lips, then her nose then forehead. "I need to start behaving myself around you."

"Wouldn't that be working backward? What happened to the man who was brazen as all get-out to walk over and ask me out to dinner?"

"I'm not sure." Rone laughed. "But I'd like to have you for dinner a little later."

"See? Rone Jennings, you can't be good even if you tried." He smiled.

She spent a few hours simply lying against Rone's chest, caressing her fingers over his tattoo, feeling the skin in it—the life of it. It was a different kind of feeling and whereas she had been a little disturbed by the elaborate ink before, now she knew what it meant and found herself being turned on by it.

She wondered what would happen if she ever told her father she wanted to get one. He'd freak and beat her to a pulp was the ultimate decision.

Shivering, she felt loved when Rone pulled her closer to his body. A few years ago she never thought she would be with a man much less a man who held her closer just because she shivered.

"I noticed you had a guitar." She broke the silence.

"Mhmm."

"Do you play?"

"A little bit."

Shifting, she pushed to her elbow and looked down into his eyes. "Can you play me something?"

"Serious?"

She nodded and he eased from the bed. When he returned, Rone sat with his back against the headboard with his wonderfully muscular legs stretched out.

Jennifer wrapped the sheets around her and sat in the center of the bed facing him while he strummed the cords as though trying to find the right key. Then to her shock, Rone began singing, in a beautiful, masculine voice that sent shockwaves through her.

Though the stars are beautiful even when they fall.
Though the moon kisses the trees when the night calls.
Though the sunlight is amazing and I am enraptured,
They fail in comparison to the beauty of you.

Jennifer gasped softly.

He stopped and met her gaze. She covered her mouth, hand shaking, and eyes dazed with tears. "That's so beautiful."

Rone put the guitar to stand on the floor, leaning against the bedside table and pulled her into his arms. "Thank you. Then why do you look so sad?"

"I'm not." She sniffled. "I've never had a man sing to me before—well a man who can actually sing. Drunk guys over the years doesn't count."

Rone laughed.

"And that song...I've never heard it before but it's lovely."

Rone's breath brushed her ear and traveled downward until he kissed her shoulder.

"When I was younger, I thought I could be the next Johnny Cash. I used to write songs for a friend of mine. He used to sing them to girls and *voila!* This is one of the unfinished ones—for the life of me I just can't seem to finish it."

Jennifer pulled back to stare at him. "Wow. I learn something new and wonderful about you every day."

"You are such a bad influence on my ego," Rone replied. With her against him again, he shifted down into the bed.

"Do you ever think of going back into song writing?"

"Sometimes. Sometimes I wonder what would happen if I'd gone to Nashville. Matt and I were supposed to go together."

"Matt? Who's Matt?"

"The country singer."

"Matt Sheppard?"

Rone kissed her head then nodded. "Yes. Apparently, he's on a world tour at the moment. He probably doesn't think about me at all."

"Well, maybe you should call him."

"Maybe..."

Jennifer kissed his chest then lifted her head to look into his eyes. He smiled at her and warmed her soul. That was when she cuddled into his side, closed her eyes and allowed sleep to take her.

By the time she felt his lips against her neck and shoulders, Jennifer had a wonderful sleep. Moaning, she arched slightly against his lips and smiled.

"Good morning, darling." Rone whispered, kissing up her back to her cheek. "I know it's early but I have to go to the station. You should get up to head home for clothes."

"I don't wanna." Jennifer giggled sleepily.

He felt her bum and spanked it playfully. "Me either. I would much rather stay home and—sleep with you."

"Oh, boo Rone Jennings. You're so boring."

He growled at her before nipping at her shoulder. "Can I see you later?"

She rolled over in the enclosure of his arms and cradled his face. For a moment she stared into his eyes not sure what she was looking for. Eventually she eased up slightly and kissed him until he trembled against her.

"Of course, you can see me later." Her voice cracked. "What time do you get off work?"

"I'm not sure. If it's too late..."

"Doesn't matter what time, Rone. Just come."

Nodding, he kissed her, this time with a grope of one breast then the other before groaning and climbing off the bed.

"I made some breakfast downstairs when you're ready. And I found all your clothes and placed them right there." He pointed to a large chest where her dress was folded neatly.

"Thank you."

"I'll see you tonight?"

"I'll see you tonight." Jennifer nodded.

She watched him remove his gun from a wall safe and shoved it into his holster before grabbing his badge from the dresser. When he hauled on his jacket and reached for his hat, she trembled at just how sexy he was.

The dark hat matched his silver-blue eyes perfectly and left him looking like a wild man. He kissed her again before leaving.

At the window, she watched until he was long gone before sighing dramatically and falling back to the large bed. Her happiness was interrupted by her eyes catching the clock. Gasping, she flew from the bed but took enough time to make it. She placed the pillows back along with the cushions before hurrying into the shower.

The bathroom was beautiful. She'd been using the one downstairs but after they climbed into bed, she was too comfortable to get out again for something as trivial as the bathroom.

The claw foot tub sat, white and majestic, in almost the center of the room with a black and gold stool at the head. Across from it was a shelf piled high with fresh towels.

To the far right in a corner was a standing shower and beside that were the toilet and the sink. For a moment she stood there, wrapped in a towel just staring at the luxury around her.

When she finally unglued herself, it was to take a fast shower then quickly dress.

In the kitchen she ate just a bit of the breakfast he made, skipped the coffee and was out the door in a flash. She locked the door from the inside, then pulled the door shut behind her.

On her drive back to her place, she hummed, even whistled.

The morning was silent with barely any vehicles on the street. She drove by the diner and to see it only had Datsun's car in the parking lot out front.

Taking a breath, she prayed no one saw her flying in the opposite direction so early in the morning.

Giggling at the concept of being so bad and talked about, she made her way home.

Walking by the rental office she pulled out her cheque book and was writing up the rent for the next month when Bosley called her name.

"Morning."

"You're up early, Jenny," Bosley said with a smile. "I have a message for you."

"A message?" Jennifer placed her cheque down on the counter and accepted the crumpled piece of paper he handed over. "Who's this Michael person?"

Bosley shrugged and collected the cheque. "He's been hanging around here since yesterday evening. Says he'll be staying at Macey's B and B and left the number."

"I don't know a Michael." She crumpled the letter in a fist. "It's probably a mistake."

"Hey. I'm just the messenger." He waved the cheque at her. "Thanks for this. I just wished the others were like you."

Jennifer afforded him a smile but climbed the stairs to her place slower than usual. She kept wondering who this Michael person was and what he wanted.

She'd never met a Michael even when she worked with Gale in the city. Still, she'd better call Gale to make sure.

In her apartment she changed into a pair of black track pants and a tank top. She pulled a plain black tee-shirt over that and grabbed her work bag. She had a few minutes to spare so she called Gale.

"Morning!" Gale was cheerful.

"Whoa. I never could understand how you can be so cheerful so dang early." Jennifer chuckled. "How are you?"

"Pretty good. I'm coming to see my best friend in a few days!" Gale replied with a giggle. "I was on my way out to the gym. What's up?"

"I have a lot to tell you but that'll have to wait. Do you know a Michael?"

"Plenty of Michaels. What's going on, Jen?"

"I'm not sure. Have I met any of these Michael's you're friends with?"

"I don't think so. Not unless you went with me to Jamaica at some point that I can't remember. Jennifer talk to me."

"I spent the night out last night. Came back just now to a note from some guy name Michael. I'm just trying to make sure when I talk to him I don't do something stupid like make him see I don't remember who he is."

Gale laughed. "Now that would be awkward. Before you go though, anything you wanted me to bring when I'm coming?"

Jennifer thought about it then shrugged. "Nah. But we'll talk before then."

"Okay, darling. You have a good day, okay?"

Jennifer nodded needlessly. "You too, mama. Talk later."

That was a bust.

Soon she was in her car again, driving toward the diner. This time she wasn't as high as in the morning. This time she was rocking her brain trying to figure out who this Michael was.

As much as she wanted to just forget the crumpled piece of paper sitting beside her on the passenger seat of her car, she couldn't.

Ten

Rone walked into his office and pulled his hat from his head. Chucking it to his desk he hauled off his coat and dropped it in one of the chairs across from his desk. He was suddenly feeling disgruntled about being at work.

He'd so much rather have Jennifer wrapped around his body. He bit back a moan which was probably for the best since Megan Duffield, his deputy walked into the room and handed him a piece of paper.

Without even looking at it, Rone knew something was wrong. She looked annoyed at having to give him the note. When he glanced at it, his mood changed.

The location on the report caught his attention—Bethune Apartments. Something curled his insides as he flopped to the chair behind him.

Though Jennifer wasn't home at the time the report was made, it still bothered him that some stranger was just there, sitting in his car staring at the place.

"This came in yesterday?" he asked.

"Yeah. I checked it out. The guy was gone by the time I got there. Mrs. Charles on the first floor didn't like some strange, black man sitting in his car, *casing the joint,* as she put it. I tell you, some people are just paranoid."

"Yeah." Rone muttered. "I guess. But just because you're paranoid doesn't mean someone isn't out to get you."

"You too? That's what Bea said. So? I guess the rain ruined your picnic yesterday huh."

"You would think so." Rone laughed. "But not really. We had it inside."

"This woman must really be something."

"She is." Rone took a breath and looked up at Megan. "She's just—I don't know. There's this quiet elegance about her—such purity. Sometimes I find myself thinking how much I would ruin her by being with her."

"Don't be such a dork," Megan said. "She's not going to be with you if she thinks you will ruin her. You're a cop for crying out loud—you're one of the good guys."

"Thanks Megan."

"She suggested I try writing again."

Megan looked shocked and he knew why. Since Matt left, Rone stopped writing. The urge was gone.

"She's right, you know?" Megan nodded. "You were good at it."

"Has Justin and Chris been around here yet?"

"And he changes the subject." Megan sighed. "Justin headed to the city. Something about a rare putter he wants to get at a good price on. Haven't seen Chris." She slid into one of his chairs and leant in. "Can I ask you a question, Rone?"

"Sure."

"This is really awkward for me. But er...you have to promise not to tell him I asked you this."

"Megan."

"This is weird for me—I just...what kind of women is Justin into?"

Rone sat forward and arched a brow. Did his quiet, bright-eyed deputy love his best friend? He smiled. "Well. Let's see here. He likes a woman who can call him on his bull, but she can't be too out there, you know? He's a country boy. She must like getting her hands dirty. But most importantly, she has to be adventurous."

"In life?"

"And in his bed."

Megan's cheeks took on a plush, red colour.

"Advice from a friend?"

Megan nodded. "Yeah. Sure!"

"If you are serious about Justin don't beat around the bush. Don't act all shy and unsure of yourself. If you want him, go for it. Show him you can be up front but also a woman and you've got him for sure."

Megan laughed. "And how do I be brass but soft?"

Rone shrugged. "You got me there. Maybe what you need is a woman's point of view? I suck at things like this. Maybe I could get you and Jennifer talking?"

"That would be great. I don't have many women friends here."

"All right. Why don't you come with me at lunch time today to the diner?"

"Today? I-I don't know about that."

Rone sighed. "See? How can you chase down the Butler boys and tackle them, beat any man around here in skeet shooting but when it comes to a man you get all flustered?"

"You're right. You sure suck at these things. I'll try and talk to your girl about it today." Megan rose and walked from the office but Rone sat where he was grinning.

Just the mere mention of Jennifer being "*his girl* " made his heart soar. Bea pushing her head in the window and telling him there was a call-out for the Butler place pulled him from cloud nine and shoved him back into the world of law enforcement. He shoved his hat to his head, grabbed his coat and dashed out the door.

It didn't take long for him to pull up in front of Martin Butler's place and frowned. On the front porch, Martin was brandishing a shot gun while his daughter, Darlene was trying to leave with her suitcase.

Rone knew the man was drinking again from the way he wavered ever so often on his feet. Every time Martin over-indulged—which was every damn day—something always went wrong. Shutting off the engine, Rone unclipped the latch on his holster and shoved from the car.

"Martin," he called. "It is way too early for this shit."

"Sheriff. You have no business here."

"You don't think so? First of all, put down the shot gun," Rone ordered, hand on his own weapon. He wasn't sure if Martin would fire on him but he wasn't about to take that chance. A drunk was unpredictable.

Martin didn't budge or turn to look at him. He just kept staring at his petrified daughter with the gun trained on her.

"Martin. I'm not in a good mood right now. Do you seriously think I want to be here, with you right now dealing with this bullshit again? Put the gun down because if you make any sudden moves toward her or me, I will drop you like a sack of potatoes."

"You wouldn't." Martin turned to look at Rone then.

"Are you really willing to test me? One last time, Martin. Shotgun, on the ground, now."

The older man took a breath and bent forward lying the gun on the floor. Darlene took that moment to run toward Rone with her suitcase in one hand. He caught her against her chest and she sobbed softly. "You alright?" he asked her.

She nodded into his chest.

"Get in the car," Rone told her. Though he didn't take his eyes off Martin, he listened until Darlene slammed the car door before approaching Martin. The moment he was close enough he smelled the whiskey. It was as though Martin bathed in the stuff.

"How much did you have to drink?" Rone questioned. He picked up the shot gun, ejected the bullets and cleared the chamber them tossed the shotgun into the house through an open window.

"No more than usual."

"Turn around, Martin." He pulled out his cuffs.

"You're going to arrest me? For what? I didn't do anything wrong."

"How about illegal confinement to start?" He gripped Martin's hands and pulled them in behind the man's back. Once the cuffs were on, he took a breath. "How many times did my father beg you to go clean? You can't even stay sober for your baby girl. Do you see how much you hurt her?"

Martin made no reply.

"What'd I tell you about me coming back out here and you waving a shotgun? Huh? Jared and Paul left so you have to make Darlene's life hell? What's the matter with you?"

Martin said nothing.

"You know—I don't care. Let Judge Birmingham figure it out. Move."

Back at the squad car, he pulled out his radio and called the office.

"Yeah Sheriff?"

"Bea, can you call the diner and have Jennifer meet me at the Butler ranch? Tell Datsun it's an emergency."

"Right away, Sheriff."

With the radio back in the hook, he turned to Darlene. "Darlene, can you go sit under that tree? I need a place to store him until Jennifer gets here to pick you up."

She nodded and scrambled from the car. Once she was seated, clutching the case against her side, Rone moved her father to the back of the squad car.

He then started yelling at her then, calling her every vile name in the book. Rone saw just how visibly shaken she was so he slammed the door, barring any sound from coming out. But Darlene still looked terrified.

He pulled the door open and glared at the man. "Don't make me gag you."

Fear ripped through Martin's eyes so he clamped his mouth shut.

"Let me explain something to you." Rone snapped. "Do you know how many men out there who wished they had a daughter who cares half as much as yours do? That's your little girl! That is your princess. Why do you take such god-damn pleasure in seeing her cry?"

He paused.

Martin said nothing which only serve to piss Rone off even more.

"You should be the one fight to protect her from broken hearts." Rone pushed. "One of these days you're going to wake up and need her to hold your hand. She won't be there. One day she's going to give up on you. And trust me, Martin. That is the worse feeling—knowing someone gave up on you." Rone slammed the door again then walked over to sit beside Darlene.

"He wasn't like that when mom was alive." Darlene spoke. "I thought since Paul and Jared were gone, all he needed was someone to stay behind and take care of him. But he's turned into this angry, gun-wielding, hateful person I don't even recognize anymore."

"Everyone has their breaking point, Darlene." Rone replied. "I'm not making excuses for him because what he's been doing is more than inexcusable. What I'm trying to say is, I think he's reached his. A normal person would reach their breaking point and walk away to gather themselves. He's lost all the senses of a rational person and the alcohol doesn't help. There's nothing else I can do for him."

Rone shook his head, glanced over at Darlene then looked to where her father was sitting, leaning against the glass in the backseat.

"But you can't save him, Darlene." Rone continued. "My father was called over here eighteen times since your mother's death. We've had to arrest your brothers because he riled them so bad, they both snapped. You're going to have to let it go because the next time Megan or myself may not be able to get here fast enough."

She sobbed softly. "I know. I was just hoping..."

"I know. But you can only help your father if he wants to be helped."

"It's not that simple."

"Yes, it is." Rone frowned. "Think of it this way. Yesterday, you passed Martin and he's in a hole. You stop, extend a hand and helps him out. Today, you pass the same hole and he's in it. You did the same thing you did yesterday—help him out. Tomorrow, you pass the same hole and he's once again—you guess it."

"In the hole and I help him."

Rone nodded. "How long until he pulls you in?"

"What's going to happen to him?"

"I'm going to have to charge him," Rone replied. "This isn't the first time we've been called here for him acting like this. One day he could kill someone."

"You mean me.'"

The answer hurt Rone to his core. But he nodded. "He may get probation and a restraining order. I don't know."

"I don't think he'd survive prison."

"He didn't turn the gun at me. That may count for something." Rone shook his head and pressed his lips into a thin line for a moment. "The judge may give him a little jail time to show him they're tired of seeing him."

Darlene sighed. "I tried, you know. I really tried. When everyone said I should leave him for my own safety. How could I? He's my father."

"I understand."

She sighed. "I stuck around and stood by his side. I figured, we all lost mom and we all have to deal with it in our own way. But when is it less about the loss and more about him losing his mind? Now he pulls a gun on me. Me. His own daughter."

Rone didn't know what to say then. He merely bowed his head for a spell before watching Martin in the car with his head down.

"I'll do what I can for him—for your sake. Other than that, I honestly don't know if I care anymore."

"Thank you," Darlene whispered. "I keep telling myself it's the addiction and not the man. But—"

"But now you're thinking the addiction and the man have become the same thing."

She nodded. "Am I horrible?"

"No." Rone replied, rubbing her back. "You're not horrible."

Jennifer's car pulled up beside his cruise then and she bolted from the driver's side. "Darlene?" she cried running toward them. Falling to her knees she hugged Darlene tightly before reaching over to cradle Rone's face. He saw fear there and when he smiled at her, relieve filled her eyes.

"She's fine," Rone promised. "I just wanted someone to come get her. I'm taking her father to lock up and didn't want to have to drag her there too."

"I'll take her home," Jennifer said. "What happened?"

"I'll let you two talk." Rone rose and helped them to their feet.

He kissed Jennifer, slowly, drawing pleasure from her tongue swirling around his. Reluctantly, he pulled back and hugged Darlene.

"You remember what I said." He spoke. "I'll swing by later."

He entered his car and pulled from the front yard. When he glanced back at Martin, there was something about the way the old man looked ahead; something devoid of emotions and all life.

Eleven

After Darlene explained what happened, the ride over to Jennifer's place with Darlene was a quiet one. They climbed the stairs in silence and made lunch in silence. Jennifer didn't know what to say to Darlene.

Nothing she could think of made any sense or added anything to alleviate the gravity of the situation.

Her father had tried killing her.

How does a person explain that way?

Darlene was visibly shaken. She was clutching her small suitcase tightly to her chest and softly humming as though slowly losing her mind. It took some doing to get the suitcase away from Darlene and set it beside the bed. She then led Darlene to the bathroom to wash her hands then back into the small dining room to sit at the table.

Silently, she made Darlene something to eat—a ham sandwich and a glass of apple juice. Jennifer didn't eat with Darlene. Instead, she remained close to the sink.

Jennifer waited with her back against the counter, keeping and eye on Darlene. She folded her arms across her chest, debating how to bring up the subject about what they both would know to be the truth.

The only sound was periodical vehicles passing below them and once in a while someone calling to someone else across the fences.

Shaking her head, she turned and began washing the dishes in the sink. It would buy her some more time to gather her thoughts.

"I know what you're thinking." Darlene's voice cracked a few times.

"What am I thinking, Darlene?"

"You're thinking *I told you so*. You told me to leave. You knew what was coming." Darlene poked her half-eaten sandwich with a finger. "How did you know?"

Jennifer felt sick. "I know abuse."

"I should have listened to you."

"That's not what this is about, Darlene." Jennifer tossed her hands up. "We can't dwell on what you should have done or could have done. I've spent so much of my life wondering how much different life would have been if I'd been strong enough to leave—or just push him down the stairs one night when he was so drunk he couldn't even see straight."

"And what answer did you come up with?"

"There really is no way to tell." Jennifer replied. "That is why saying woulda, coulda, shoulda isn't helpful."

Darlene exhaled loudly. She stared down at her sandwich but didn't pick it up again.

"This is about what to do next." Jennifer continued, facing the sink. "I would tell you *I told you so* if I thought it would help. It won't."

"So many nights I would lie awake and wonder what would happen if I just walked away." Darlene swallowed. "But then I stop and think...where would I go? What would I do? I have *nothing* out there. I have nothing here."

"That's not exactly true." Jennifer's voice cracked. "You don't know what's out there. As for here, you have me and Rone—that may not mean much."

"It does." Darlene nodded. "More than you'll know."

For months, Jennifer saw the signs of abuse. Most people wouldn't notice them—but after living through her own hell, Jennifer was sure. Repeatedly, she brought it up to Darlene, but all her friend said was "*he needs me*" or "*he's old and he has no one else.*"

But bruises on Darlene were getting harder and harder to hide. Even so, there was nothing Jennifer could do and talking wasn't helping.

After a while, Jennifer stopped trying and prayed.

You can't help someone who doesn't want to help themselves.

With the dishes finished, she wrung the cloth out and hung it over the tap after turning it off. Drying her hand in a hand cloth, she folded it and placed it on the counter before facing Darlene at the table.

"Look. You can stay here as long as you want," Jennifer said. "We can share my bed. It's big enough."

"What happens when Rone comes over?"

"You let me worry about that." Jennifer told her.

"But…"

"No buts, Darlene." Jennifer told her.

'What if you two want to—well, you know?"

Jennifer blushed. "If Rone and I want to get—well, you know? We can use his place."

Darlene sighed. "I hate being such an inconvenience."

"You're not an inconvenience." Jennifer explained. "You're my friend. Gale is coming in a few days so I'm going to have to figure something out—maybe get a sofa bed or something."

"Jennifer. You don't have to. The house is there. Dad is in lock up. I can stay there."

"You can't go back. If they let him out, he'll be going home and if you're there he won't be happy to see you. No, I'm not having it." Jennifer flopped into the chair across from Darlene. "If I have to buy an air mattress and sleep on the floor so be it. You're not going back to that house."

"I'm sorry about the timing of this. I just thought..."

"I know what you thought. You could change him. He's only upset. It won't happen again. I used to think that for the first year my father began making my life hell. Then after a few more months of that I knew I was screwed. No one can change these men—I don't think anything can."

A strange, awkward silence swam through the room and Jennifer inhaled. The sound of the breath was sharp and almost hollow.

"Can we talk about something good? Talking about my father is making me depressed even more than I already am."

"Okay. What do you suggest?"

"How are you and Rone doing?"

Jennifer smiled, snagged a grape from her friend's plate and shoved it into her mouth. She thought about that question and shrugged. "We're good. He can't seem to keep his hands off me. We—we slept together."

"That *is* good news! Wait...Did you tell him you were a virgin?"

"No." She shook her head. "The truth is I thought I had more time before we take that step. Passion had always been a myth, you know? Like unicorns and the easter bunny."

"The easter bunny? Not real? Girl."

Jennifer laughed. "You know what I mean. But the fear I saw in his face when he realized I'd never been with anyone else. I thought he would have cried."

"Well, of course, it broke his heart!" Darlene reached over to smack Jennifer's arm. "He likes you. He didn't want to hurt you."

"That's what he said."

"So? How was it? How was he?"

"I have nothing to compare it to." Jennifer hung her head. "But after the hurting, it was wonderful. I didn't think such a large man could be tender or soft but when he touches me, stroke my arms, lay over me..."

"How do you feel when he's on you?"

Jennifer paused and quirked a brow. "What do you mean how did I feel?"

"Do you feel disgusted? Turned on?"

"Disgusted? No, far from it." Though her cheeks burned with her shyness, Jennifer felt no shame in sharing with Darlene. "He smells so good. His body is so—so perfect. Trust me; disgust is not what I felt. I'm trying to take things slow with Rone. But each time he looks at me I lose it. And today when he kissed me, it took everything to let him walk away. I'm seeing him tonight."

"Damn. I should go out, give you two some alone time."

"You don't have to do that, sweetie. Rone will understand. We can go out and you can come with us. It makes no sense leaving you cooped up in the house. It'll be a party."

"Oh girl, please. I'm a grown-ass woman." Darlene batted a wrist. "You and your man need some alone time together. If you want to stay in let me know." Darlene pushed the rest of the sandwich into her mouth and snatched her plate from the table.

Jennifer watched her wash it and took the time to get more grapes from the bunch.

"You know," Darlene began. "I've had my eyes on Rone's friend, Chris. But he doesn't even know I exist. He has money and I have nothing. What would he want with me?"

Jennifer chuckled. "You're preaching to the choir sister."

Darlene laughed.

"Look. I have nothing but this apartment, that beat up old car and my life to my name. So Rone doesn't want me for my money and perhaps not even for my looks. I wonder what he really wants from me but I'm trying not to let my father's ghost mess with what I'm trying to build with this man. The hardest part of this whole thing is not to get ahead of myself."

Darlene sat while drying her hands in the same cloth Jennifer had earlier. Jennifer leaned forward and pressed her elbows on the table.

"And just when I thought my life was finally moving forward? I have some douche bag coming into town looking for me."

"Friend of your father's?" Darlene wanted to know. "That's possible, right?"

"I don't know." Jennifer shrugged. "Not sure I want to know. I was going over to see who it was after work today before I met up with Rone. But it can wait. It's probably one of Gale's friends I met before and they want to talk to me about something or another."

"Gale's friends hunt you down often?"

She grinned. "No. I'm just saying—I don't meet a lot of people on my own."

She didn't tell Darlene what Gale had said earlier because she didn't want to add any more to Darlene's plate. "Let's watch a movie."

Rone got off work and drove down the street to the diner. When he walked in the door, a few people turned to wave at him, but he barely acknowledged them.

His father was seated in his regular spot by the window reading. He didn't see Jennifer and after a quick chat with Datsun he realized she hadn't gone back to work but stayed with Darlene. Checking his watch, he walked over to sit with his father for a minute.

"You look tired," Raymond hugged his son and sat back. "I heard you had to arrest Butler again."

"Yeah," Rone said simply, reaching for his father's glass and taking a sip. It was lemonade. "He was holding Darlene at gunpoint. Can you believe that? I need something a little stronger than lemonade."

Raymond hung his head a moment before inhaling deeply and looking at his son. "He used to be a good man. But after Phyllis died, he just lost it. He started drinking and at first, I understood. After your mother died, I got a few drinks in me."

"But you didn't let it take over your whole life."

"Of course not." Raymond sighed. "I had a son. No matter how much I was hurting, I couldn't keep knocking 'em back. I didn't want strangers raising my kid. Besides, your mother would haunt me."

Rone arched a brow.

"For years I begged him to get clean." Raymond told him. "Even after the last time when Jared and Paul finally had enough, I told him if he's going to live in the house with Darlene he needed to stop because if he didn't she'd leave him."

"You can't reason with a drunk, dad." Rone told him. "You taught me that."

"Okay, let's talk about you and Jennifer."

Rone arched a brow and eyed his father. The old man had an air of mischievousness in his eyes. "Why is it, every time we get together lately our conversations always go to me talking about Jennifer?"

Raymond laughed. "Because at the mere mention of her name you go all loopy-eyed."

"I don't go all loopy-eyed!" Rone protested. "What does that even mean?"

"I'm looking for Jennifer Cozel," A masculine voice said from behind him.

Rone's head snapped up and he turned in his seat to see who was asking for Jennifer. The man standing there was tall, dark skinned—he looked as though he'd walked out of one of those posh suit magazines. Instantly Rone didn't like him. Not because he was dressed so immaculately, but because he was asking for Jennifer.

"Well, she had an emergency today," Datsun was saying. "But you can ask the Sheriff over there. He should know."

The man nodded and walked over to where Rone was sitting with his father. "Good evening," he greeted extending a hand to Rone. "I'm Michael Kitchens. Which of you gentlemen is the sheriff?"

"I am." Rone all but growled and ignored the hand. "What can I do for you?"

"I'm looking for Jennifer. I was told you could tell me where I can find her."

"You're the man who's been sitting outside her place," Rone said, coolly. "What do you want?"

Michael retracted his hand slowly, rubbed his palms against his thighs before his shoulders rose and fell heavily. "No disrespect, but this is between me and Jennifer. So, if you can't help me I'll sit around her place until she shows up."

Rone started rising but his father gripped his shoulder to steady him.

"Look, Mr. Kitchens." Raymond began. "Jennifer is loved around here. And we're not going to point some strange man in her direction. We may be a small town but we're not stupid."

"This is nuts!" Michael cried. "She's a grown woman! She can see whoever she wishes. Do you treat all her boyfriends like this?

Rone did rise then and eyed the man. "Boyfriend?"

"Down boy." Raymond stood and moved between Rone and Michael.

Michael probably got the picture for he hurried out the door. Rone watched him drive away in a luxury car before the power gave out of his legs and he flopped to the chair again.

"She has a boyfriend." Rone finally managed to spit the words out long after the world went silent around him.

"Now son, he didn't exactly say that." Raymond patted Rone's shoulder affectionately. "He was merely asking a question."

"I'm sorry dad, but I have to go."

"You're angry. Don't go see her now."

Rone took a breath. "I have to. I want to check on Darlene."

"Rone?"

"I know what I'm doing, dad."

Stuffing his head back into his hat, Rone exited the diner with his father calling after him to go for a walk first.

Still, he climbed behind the wheel and glanced in the mirror before pulling from the parking lot.

Long after making it to her place, he merely sat in the vehicle, staring up at the window. From time to time the light in the room was blocked, telling him someone was moving around.

He wondered if it was Michael and how comes they hadn't slept together yet. It felt strange to him the jealousy surging through him. Even imagining another man touching Jennifer made him want to slam his first into something, someone—anything.

His father was right. The anger cursing through him was not conducive to a police conversation. But he was an adult. He could get through this without losing his temper any more than he already had.

Easing from the front seat, he made his way into the building. The elevator was out of service, so he took the stairs. At the top, he tried remembering what number her door was but couldn't.

When he heard Darlene's voice and Jennifer's laughter he followed it to a door and knocked. It took a moment before anyone answered but then Jennifer did.

"Rone!" Jennifer said happily.

He brushed by her into the apartment.

"Rone? What's wrong?"

"I would really like to talk to you right now, Jennifer," Rone said. But he didn't have time to discuss it for Darlene stuck her head out a door. "Darlene...how are you feeling?"

"Good. Am getting ready to go out for a walk then heading over to Michelle's for the night. If you've come to check on me, I've been good."

"I know. Michelle? Datsun's girl? She's back in town?"

Darlene nodded. "Just for about a week then she's off again. I just haven't had the time to go over there. Since I don't work tomorrow, I might as well."

"Good." Rone took a breath. "I wanted to update you on your father."

He spent a few minutes explaining things to her and after she left, he turned to look at Jennifer who was eyeing him with rabid anger.

"What is your problem?" She demanded.

"My problem? Jennifer, my problem is I opened up a part of me to you that hasn't been touched in years and you stomped on it."

"What?" Jennifer snapped. When he tried warling away she grabbed his shoulders and shoved him hard against the wall. "Don't you dare start this shit and then walk away. I will *not* have it. Now, talk."

Rone grunted when his back hit the wall and when he met her eyes, he couldn't remember seeing that much anger anywhere. But he didn't really care.

"I met your boyfriend," Rone said simply.

She laughed bitterly and shook her head. "Of course you've met my boyfriend! It's you, you dumb, clueless jerk!" She released him and walked away.

"I meant your *other* boyfriend," Rone replied.

"My other what now?"

"Michael."

She sighed and when he looked at her she was pressed into the wall, gently tapping her forehead against it. "I'm going to kill him."

"You can't threaten someone in front of a cop."

"Look, I don't know who that is. I swear. I came home to a note saying he was here looking for me."

"And how am I supposed to believe that?"

"Damn it to hell! Rone, I don't have another boyfriend." Jennifer snapped. "Please believe me. I don't know who this Michael person is. Before I moved here, I had one boyfriend and I wouldn't even call him that—hell, we never even kissed. Since I've been here I've dated two or three times but they were all long distance and none of their names were Michael."

She closed the distance between them and stood in front of him, gripped his shoulders and captured his gaze. Rone felt weak with the power of what he felt for her and closed his eyes. Bowing his head, he pressed his forehead to hers.

"I'll kill him." Rone whispered.

"Rone." Jennifer chuckled. "Don't be so dramatic. While I appreciate you trying to protect me and even though I think it's very sexy, I'll handle it. All I have to do is find out who he is and what he wants. Then he can go away, and you can stop being so angry and kiss me."

He pushed some air out his mouth, feeling like a complete an idiot. Wrapping his arms around her hips, he pulled her full breasts into his chest and took her lips.

Rone moaned when she tangled her arms about his neck and allowed him access to her warm, delicious mouth. He sucked her tongue in greedily then plunged his into her mouth.

He was weak and shivering from her kiss.

Twelve

What was wrong with her?

All Rone had to do was look at her and she was putty in his very large, very skillful hands. She shouldn't be questioning it. Rone came back for more. He had her and he seemed to be just as eager and wanting as before. He was looking at her again, in that same way he did the first time he'd peeled her clothes from her body and touched her softly.

He stalked her toward the room, moving slowly like a beast, out to maul her. Each time she smiled at him his eyes flashed a hot, dangerous flicker that pulled moans from her throat.

Her heart fluttered even as she backed down the hall, dragging her hands against the wall to feel her way for the bedroom door. She didn't care about anything at that moment. She knew her bedroom like the back of her hand and moved easily across the room.

Jennifer climbed onto the bed backward with Rone stalking her across the small space. He grabbed her ankle and pulled gently forward. She slid easily across the sheet and slammed into his body quite intimately.

Her wetness hit his abs and he groaned while he spread her wider and gripped the seat of her panties with his free hand.

In no time at all, he tossed the damp material behind him and leaned forward to kiss her again before slipping his mouth over one shoulder and down her arm.

His lips felt wonderful against her skin, tickling her spots and leaving her panting helplessly.

From time to time, he would lick at her just enough to make her crazy only to back away drawing his name from her lips. Words her mind couldn't wrap itself around spilled from her mouth and for a moment Jennifer was scared she'd said something she shouldn't.

But he didn't stop.

Wrapping her arms around his shoulders, she arched into him and whispered his name until she couldn't think anymore. He'd slid down her body, licking, sucking and nipping until he was kneeling between her legs.

Jennifer pushed to her elbows.

This time she knew what he was about to do and she yearned for it.

Their gaze locked and she nodded. Rone licked his lips before falling forward, pressing his tongue against her bud and twisting from side to side.

A heated pulse began deep within Jennifer's very core only to spread her body with each pass of his tongue. When he sucked against it hard, her elbows gave out, slamming her into the bed even as her legs fell wider. He was eating her alive and she wanted and encouraged every bit of it.

With her breathing quickened, and body feeling as if she was flying, Jennifer allowed the sweet fire to engulf her completely.

The powerful orgasms she had grown so accustomed to with Rone swept through her body, picking her up and shaking gasps and shouts of pure bliss from her lips.

Rone pressed a large palm against her abdomen and pressed slightly, heightening her pleasure, sending another orgasm rushing through her core.

When she flopped to the bed, panting for precious air, a smile spread her lips.

Giving Jennifer pleasure was unlike being with anyone else.

She was a grateful lover, an expressive lover, a lover who wasn't afraid to lose complete control of her body. Tasting her was another thing all together.

It took him to another place—a place he never wanted to forget.

When she gushed against his tongue, he moaned, gripped her hips and continued his ministrations until finally, she trembled against his mouth.

Rone crawled up her body, licking her juices from his lips and loving her taste.

He smiled into her face, pressing his body into hers. To his surprise she wrapped her legs around his hips, pushing down against his ass.

"What happened to my shy Jennifer?"

"Her body is burning right now and until you put out the fire you're not going anywhere."

He chuckled. "Is that a promise?"

Jennifer laughed and reached up for his lips. At that moment he slipped into her, watching her mouth open into a silent scream. Her face contorted beautifully into a passion frozen gaze that sent a kind of flame surging through every fibre of his being. She arched back, pushing her beautiful breasts upward. He couldn't fight temptation. Rone bowed his head, taking one nipple into his mouth and lashing it with his tongue before sucking.

"Rone!" Jennifer cried.

Rolling his hips, he pushed into her, feeling his arousal slip deeper.

She tightened beautifully around him pushing his climax closer and closer to the edge. Her aroused scent wrapped itself around him tugging at every part of him.

His heart hammered inside his chest as sweat dripped down his back and forehead.

Lifting his head, he rode her faster, harder. The bed creaked mercilessly beneath their combined weight but he couldn't stop.

He felt her break around him over and over, leaving him breathless and mad with desire. Finally, his body couldn't hold anymore. Every bit of control he had within him disappeared and he sank deep into her until their bodies seemed to be one, fireball.

A loud, primal sound was torn from his body as he let it all go. She closed around him, sweetly milking his body, leaving him pulsating atop her.

He rolled to the side and pulled her into his body.

The last thing he wanted to do was fall asleep on her. Kissing her head, he couldn't help but smile. "I want all our disagreements to end like that."

Jennifer giggled and nipped his side with her teeth. He grunted. "Don't tease the bear."

"What if I love being mauled by you?" Jennifer questioned.

"By all means—tease away."

He enjoyed their soft banter after lovemaking. There was a playfulness about Jennifer that he never found in any of the other women he'd been with. He welcomed that softness and that lightness. She dragged her fingers softly against his side. The soft caress pulled a sigh from his lips leaving him weak in her embrace.

"I'm glad you're not with someone else." Rone whispered.

"I never had the courage to be with anyone else."

"So, why me?"

"Why you?" Jennifer shifted against him. "I don't understand the question."

"Why do you feel courage to let go with me?

"I don't know." She sighed. "You look at me with something in your eyes that pulls at me. I didn't have a choice, you know?"

He laughed softly. "We always have a choice, Jennifer."

"Not with this," she said, defiantly. "With other men I've been self conscious and nervous and depressed. With you, I get nervous and all I have to do is have you look at me...damn. Listen to me go on and on like some love-sick teenager."

Rone smiled and kissed the top of her head. "Hearing you can't resist me does something—wonderful to me. Anyway, it doesn't matter anymore, my sweet. We have all the time in the world."

"You really think so?"

Rone nodded.

"I never had any experience with a man that's been good. Well, before I moved here that is. My father was a schnook, and he was it for role model in my life. I don't mean to burden you with my past."

"You never burden me. If talking about it will make you happy, then I'm all ears."

"Why are you so different?"

"I'm not sure how to answer that." Rone shook his head. "I guess I could answer it by saying my father is who he is. I learn everything from him."

"And he's a good man, Rone. A very good man."

"He is. You should get some sleep, baby. We both have work tomorrow."

She moaned sweetly against him, a sound Rone was beginning to love. He waited until she fell asleep before he pulled his body from the bed and walked over to his pants.

He rummaged through for his cell phone and exited the room to make a phone call in the hall.

"Barley Sherriff's department."

"Megan. Can you do me a personal favor?" he asked.

"There's this guy, Michael, over at the bed and breakfast. I want you to find out all you can about him for me."

"Michael? Got me a last name?"

"Sorry hon. That's all I got."

"You're asking for a miracle." Megan sighed dramatically.

"I thought you said you're the miracle maker?" Rone teased.

"All right. I'll see what I can do."

"Thanks. Don't let Jennifer know you're looking."

Megan chuckled softly. "She told you to stay out of it, huh?"

"Yeah."

"Typical man."

Rone hung up and went back into the room. He placed the phone on the dresser and sat on the edge of the bed watching her sleep. He knew she said she would take care of it, but he was worried this man wanted to take advantage of her.

Even if he was her brother, Rone wasn't about to take any chances. He just wanted to make sure everything was on the up and up.

Though he wanted to think about it all more, he just couldn't seem to keep himself out of her bed. He needed to feel her body against him. He was falling in love with Jennifer but he didn't dare say anything to her. The last thing he wanted to do was scare her away.

He had to be careful.

Rone tried remembering the last time he was truly scared of something. Even though he couldn't remember, the thought of Jennifer walking away terrified him.

Sighing helplessly, he gave in to the weakness and climbed back beneath the sheets.

"Rone?"

"Mm?"

She shifted and sat up. "Are you all right?"

"I'm fine." He pulled her down so that half her body rested on top of him and the other half stayed on the bed. He wrapped his arms around her, caressing her soft flesh while brushing his lips on her forehead. "Never been better."

She moved, tucking her head under his chin. His body reacted to her sliding over him by trembling.

Thirteen

She woke up in Rone's arms.

Nothing came closer to paradise than that. For a moment, Jennifer simply eased away from him and watched his face, peaceful in sleep. She made no other movements for she was afraid to wake him.

His handsome face made her sign as peace ran through her. For the first time since meeting Rone, she felt like she was doing something right with no regrets or second guessing.

Being in his arms was bliss—there were no other words to describe it. Sighing, Jennifer moved closer to Rone's hard body and kissed his chest. She watched him shiver, heard him moan and did it again.

"You're a tease," Rone said, his voice husky.

When she looked into his face, his eyes were closed but he was smiling. Caressing a hand against his forehead to push some hair away, Jennifer kissed his lips. She meant for it only to be a chaste one but he wrapped his arms around her, pressing his palm to the back of her head and deepened it.

"It's early." Jennifer whispered, panting from his kiss. "But I have work."

Rone opened his beautiful eyes then and turned to glance at the clock. "You're right. All right, you shower and dress I will make you breakfast."

"He cooks." She joked.

"Baby, I do so much more," Rone replied and kissed her deeply.

She knew she couldn't stay that way all day.

They both had to get to work.

Groaning, she hurried into the shower, closing the door behind her. She tried not to think how badly she would rather stay in bed that day. Still the bills needed to be paid and life had to go on.

Her shower didn't take long and soon she was wearing a black pair of jeans and a black top with the *G.I Joe* Cobra on the front. Taking time to tie her hair up, she grabbed a notepad and pen.

Shoving them into her little bag, she turned for the door but the phone began ringing. Jennifer groaned, rushed back across the room to the bed and grabbed the phone.

"Hello?"

"Hey sweetie. I thought I should call you before you were out the door."

"Hey Gale! I have so much to tell you. When are you getting here?"

"Day after tomorrow." Gale replied. "I have to run to New York right quick then I'll be all yours for three days."

"Sounds like a plan." Jennifer gigged. "Can you email the info to Darlene and I'll grab it from her today? You still have her email from last time, right?"

"Yeah. I do. I'll do that."

"Okay, hon. I'd love to chat but I have one of the things I have to tell you about in the kitchen. I will see you soon."

"Love you."

Jennifer grinned. "Love you too, Mamacita."

The day was starting to look much, *much* better as she hurried from her room to find Rone shirtless and moving around her kitchen like he owned the joint.

His hair was a mess; finger raked backward, his body, muscular from years of training in law enforcement and a very delectable butt that made her tremble.

She walked in, placed her bag on the counter and kissed his shoulder.

"I boiled the kettle. You don't have coffee," Rone said, handing her a warm mug.

Leaning in, she accepted it and took a sip. "Mmm mint."

"Thought you might like it." Rone grinned at her. "Dad always said mint made everything better. Anyway, I'm making some scrambled eggs. I see you have bread so we can do toast."

"I love scrambled eggs." She leant her back against the counter. "Can you add some ketchup on the side of the plate for me?"

Rone nodded and walked to the fridge. When he stood beside her again, it was to squirt some ketchup onto her plate then hand it to her. "I like this."

"Making me breakfast?" She asked.

"Mmhm. I could get used to it."

Jennifer laughed softly, thanked him with a kiss then sat at the table to eat. It'd been a long time since she sat down and ate breakfast at the table and she'd never really had breakfast with another person. She chewed and watched Rone for a while.

"Your tattoo is starting to be so damn sexy to me," Jennifer said, then flushed heatedly.

"I think you're starting to show your real self and I like it." Rone laughed.

"I didn't even realised I said that out loud until the last word came out."

Rone smirked at her before pushing a piece of toast into his mouth.

For a while later they sat there, eating, talking and stealing kisses. Jennifer couldn't remember a time in her life she was so happy. When it was time to go, she stood by the door enjoying one final kiss, one final touch.

Rone was dressed and ready also and escorted her to her car. She kissed him through the window.

"Before I forget. My friend Gale is coming to visit day after tomorrow."

"Does that mean I won't see you for a while?"

Jennifer frowned. "Of course not. I want you to meet her."

"Of course. I'll see you later tonight?" he asked.

She grinned and nodded.

He stepped away from the car, blew her another kiss and she was off.

Jennifer walked up to the door, folded a fist and smashed it into the door over and over.

This idiot had almost cost her Rone. They already head a tenuous hold on the relationship between them she wasn't about to let some ass-tard from the insane side of the track ruin that. When no one responded to her knock she kicked at the door.

Finally, it swung open and she eyed the man standing before her, sleepy-eyed and confused.

He had low cut hair, with a body that made her think he's spent too much time in a gym. He had dark skin with matching brown eyes and thick, full lips.

"Listen." She snapped. "I don't know who you are or what you think you're doing but stay away from me! And if you go near Rone again you will regret it. Got that?"

He stared at her in that same way her father would look at her when he just woke up right before the evil set in. She set her shoulders, braced her feet, curled her fists and lifted her chin.

"Do you understand me?" Jennifer demanded.

He nodded. "I understand you. But I came all this way to find you. Don't you at least want to know why? Damn, we can't have this conversation in the halls. You want to come in?"

She eyed him.

Is this fool kidding?

"I guess not," he said. "Can you give me a second to haul on a shirt? Please. I need to speak with you."

Inhaling deeply, Jennifer glared at him but crossed her arms and shook her head knowing she was going to kick herself later for what she was about to do. "Fine. Five minutes."

"That's all I need—more or less."

He disappeared into the room. There was a shuffle for a moment then returned dressed in a pair of black pants with a red graphic shirt. He walked out of the room and the two entered the living area of the house.

It was cluttered with things the owners probably thought were antiques. Still she sat in a sofa that could hold only her forcing this man to sit across from her.

"My name is Michael Kitchens." He began. "I'm your brother."

Jennifer's head snapped up to lock eyes with him. It was as though someone was standing beside her with their fingers stuck in her ear. Her heart was racing so loud her body became numb. She swallowed. "I don't have a brother."

He tossed his arms up dramatically. "I beg to differ."

"I don't have any money," Jennifer pointed out. "If you were hoping to rip me off or something in some kind of scam, you're barking up the *absolute* wrong tree."

"You think I'm here to rip you off? How jaded are you?"

"How are you my brother?"

"I didn't know about you until about four months ago. My mother was dying and made one of those dramatic deathbed confessions."

"My father never told me I had a brother."

"He didn't know."

Jennifer arched a brow.

"Mom, my adopted mother, said my real father was abusive." Michael explained. "When I was born, our mother had the nurse take me away then told my father I died during childbirth. Apparently, he didn't even check for a body. The nurses realized why she did it and helped her hide me."

"And she stayed with him long enough to have me," Jennifer said bitterly. "Then died leaving me with him. Great. Not only did my father hate me, now I get to know my mother loved you more than me."

"Did he..." Michael reached for her hand, but she drew away from him and rose. "Jennifer..."

"What do you think?" Jennifer snapped. She walked to the window and stared out for a bit trying to go over everything in her head. She should have known. Michael had her father's eyes--the same hard brown eyes. There was a kind of hitch in his voice that reminded her of him, but Michael seemed softer and kinder.

"I can't deal with this right now. I should go."

"You will speak with Rone."

She shifted to face him. "How do you know that?"

"The way his back went up when I spoke with him yesterday? There's no doubt he thought we were lovers and he was jealous."

Jennifer shook her head and returned her focus outside. The street was dead aside from a lone car puffing down the road.

"Stay away from Rone." She told him. "He doesn't like you at the moment and I'm not sure I'll be able to convince him not to pound you into the ground—if I was to believe you're my brother, that is."

"You know I'm your brother, Jennifer."

"Oh yeah? And how exactly do I know that?"

"From the pictures I've seen, I look just like our father!"

"Yeah, and I look like Queen Latifah, doesn't mean we're sisters!"

"Jennifer..." He reached for her again.

This time Jennifer folded her fists and lifted her chin. "Don't you touch me!"

"I know this is a lot. I was warned you wouldn't jump for joy. I'll be here as long as necessary."

She took a breath and walked by him out the door. She didn't head back toward the diner since her shift was over. Jennifer turned right and walked down Main Street. It didn't take her long to enter the sheriff's building. There wasn't anyone at the front desk and frustration kicked in.

"Rone? Rone, you here?"

An office door opened and a woman poked her head out. "Megan. Have you seen Rone?"

"Yeah, he should be in his office. Down the hall, the door on the left. Is there anything I can help with? Are you okay?"

Jennifer shook her head. "Thanks though. I need Rone right now."

Megan nodded and she hurried down the hall to the sole door on the left.

She knocked.

"It's open."

Barging through the door, she dove into his chest, wrapping her arms tightly around him. She buried her head beneath his chin and snuggled into his warm strength seeking comfort.

"Baby?" Rone rubbed her back. "What's wrong? Talk to me."

But Jennifer had no words. She simply allowed him to hold her as her body shook and tears soaked his shirt.

"Sweetie, you're crying. Please tell me what's wrong. What can I do?"

"I have a brother." She sniffled. "My mother told my father he died during childbirth just so he wouldn't get his hands on him. How pathetic is that? And with me, she died without making any plans to save me. Do you know how much it sucks knowing she went through all that before he was born and just left me?"

"Wait...a brother? Here?"

"Michael—the man you thought was my boyfriend."

"He's your brother?" Rone pulled her away from him and stared down into her face. "I take it you're not happy about that fact?"

"I don't know. All my life I prayed for a brother to protect me from him. But a brother never came. Now, I find out I actually have one I don't know if..."

"You need one."

Jennifer nodded. "Am I a horrible person?"

Rone smiled and kissed her head. "No. You're not a horrible person. I tell you what—why don't I take you home tonight and we can cuddle."

Jennifer couldn't help laughing.

"See? There's that beautiful laugh I've come to adore so much...but I was serious. If that's all you need from me tonight I'm more than willing to give it."

"Thank you. But can you come to my place? I could make us some...wait no we can't. Darlene is there and we wouldn't have space or privacy. You understand right?"

He nodded. "Can I take you to the beach for a little bit of time together? I've missed you."

She snuggled into him again. "Sure. I've never been to the beach at night with a man before." She lifted her head to wiggle her brows at him. "Seems I'm doing a lot of firsts with you, Rone Jennings."

"And trust me, sweetheart. I'm not complaining." He lowered his head to take her lips.

Fourteen

"Darlene, I'll be back."

"Jenny? Where you going?"

Jennifer removed her apron and placed it on the back of a chair. "It's been a few days since I got the mail. Since I remember now I'm gonna go get it."

She hurried from the apartment and down the stairs. After stopping to say hello to Mosely, she grabbed her mail from the box and climbed the stairs slowly.

She skimmed through them and stopped on one letter with a lawyer's name and address on it.

Arching a brow, she shoved the rest into her back pocket. Sitting on the final step at the top, she ripped into the envelope, pulled the letter out and unfolded.

Dear Ms. Jennifer Cozel,

Your father Marshal Cozel is our client until the business of his will is completed. As per Mr. Cozel's request you were not to be contacted or informed of his will until eleven years after his death. It has been eleven years since Marshal Cozel has been dead and in keeping with his request we require a meeting with you to settle his estate. Should you have any questions, please call Barry Lowe, Solicitor of Lowe, Raymond & Tosh Barristers and Solicitors at your earliest convenience or visit our office at 45 Bremlaw Crescent, Ohand County.

Jennifer stopped reading. For a moment all she could do was sit on the step and shake. Her father had a will?

He waited eleven years to have her be informed of it and she knew why. The jerk had to control everything.

"You couldn't control death could you!" Jennifer snapped.

Glancing at the letter again, there wasn't much else in it. She wasn't sure what she was going to do. Sure, she was curious as to what her father owned to be placed in a will.

. Knowing her father, he probably wanted her to go and hear the lawyer read that he'd left everything to everyone else but her.

Not that he had anything in the first place, but she was still curious.

Taking a breath, she shoved the letter back into the envelope, folded it and shoved it into her bra. They were finally having a good time and she wasn't about to bring it up and ruin Darlene's evening.

After having dinner, Jennifer washed the dishes while Darlene rinsed. They chit-chatted about everything from the first time they met until they found out they were working together.

Jennifer felt something for Darlene—a special friendship she thought she had with Gale. Only with Gale it was different. Jennifer didn't have to try to be something else around Darlene and her friends. When they all hung out, Jennifer was nothing but herself.

With Gale, she was always worried she'd say the wrong things.

"I'm glad I found you Darlene—or rather, you found me."

"Me too." Darlene hugged her. "I tell you sometimes I feel like my brain is about to explode and you somehow stop that. Do you ever think you can do more than what you're doing now in life?"

"Every day. But I can't do better yet so now I do what I can."

"What about school? You always wanted to go back and finish your teaching degree."

Jennifer nodded. "Yeah. That was the plan." She stopped to dry her hands on a table cloth and took a breath. "Somewhere along the way, I just couldn't do it. Aside from the money thing I couldn't bring myself to go back."

"The fear of failing?"

Jennifer nodded again. "Grab us some drinks, would you? Let's sit in the living room."

They gathered a few sweet snacks and drinks and retired to the living room. They sat beside each other, legs lifted to the centre table, backs pressed into the tattered sofa.

"You know something, Dee?" Jennifer questioned.

"What's that?"

"I'm happy. I never thought I could ever say that about myself but I'm so happy. I mean the only dream I had was to live to see my twentieth birthday. Other than that, I had no dreams. Now, I feel alive."

"That's no way for a child to live." Darlene spat. "He took everything away from you."

"In a way, yes. But if he hadn't I probably wouldn't be here with you and Rone. I have to use that to outweigh the things he's done."

Sitting with Darlene, Jennifer took a breath and lifted her cooler to her lips. She took a long drink and placed it back on the table. The two had been sitting in silence since Jennifer told her about Michael.

No matter how many times she said it, Jennifer was still at a loss for words or thoughts about whether to believe he was her brother. Just one look in his eyes and she knew but damn it where was he when she was lying on a cold floor, beaten within an inch of her life and bleeding?

"You can't blame him, you know?"

Jennifer inhaled a sharp breath, held it then exhaled.

She wanted to.

"I know. Shit. I know." She stopped, shook her head then tried again. "He didn't know. No one told him until the woman he thought was his mother all his life was dying and told him what happened."

"I know, baby girl," Darlene began. "It's hard after the hell you've been through to see anyone else in this as a victim. But he was. Maybe you shouldn't talk to him for a little while. Get your head straight then go back—what do you think?"

Once more Jennifer inhaled. She rubbed her suddenly sweaty palms against her thighs and stretched her back. "Maybe. I just don't want him to think I'm a horrible person because I can't deal with this. I mean, you'd think I'd be stronger."

"You are. Just because one thing shakes you don't mean you're weak."

"Can we talk about something else? I don't feel like we're getting anywhere with this line of conversation."

"Sure...how are things with you and Rone?"

Jennifer felt giddy. "He's amazing. I woke up beside him and my heart does this...this...thing."

Darlene laughed. "Well, that's a good thing. You love him."

"Love? Er..."

"Yeah. You know? Love? L-O-V-E?"

Jennifer coughed. Suddenly it was like she couldn't breathe. She smiled at Darlene for a moment before panting for air. She knew it was the beginnings of a panic attack.

Thankfully, Jennifer knew what to do—she leant forward with her face between her knees.

Darlene rubbed her back muttering for her to breathe slowly but she just couldn't catch her breath. She couldn't fall in love with Rone! That was the last thing she should do!

"Breathe, sweetie. You have to breathe."

"I'm—so—sorry!" She panted.

For a while she sat like that until the feeling subsided. Sitting up, she looked over at her friend and licked her lips. "I can't be falling in love with Rone, Dee...I really can't."

"Why not?"

"What if he doesn't feel the same way?"

"What if? You can't let yourself think that. You've slept with him. When you found out about Michael, where did you go?"

"To Rone."

"And what did he do?"

"He held me..."

"And when he thought Michael was your man." Darlene continued. "He got jealous?"

Jennifer nodded.

"I'd say he feels something for you. Don't overthink this. Just see where it goes. If its not going where you want it to then let it go."

Jennifer reached over and squeezed her hand.

"I was thinking," Jennifer said softly. "Your dad really loved your mom. Do you see what her death did to him?"

"Some of us can only pray to find a man to love us so much." Darlene admitted. "Some of us get lucky."

Jennifer smiled sadly.

Silence.

"I see you brought home an air mattress." Darlene broke the silence around them.

"Yeah," Jennifer replied. "I went in to look at the futon and I couldn't justify spending all that money on it. I didn't have a choice—I had to get something since Gale comes tomorrow and I wanted to give her the bed. You and I will be banished to the living room on it."

Darlene giggled. "It'll be like old times. Remember when we used to sleep outside in the backyard over at pop's in a tent on one of those plastic beds? Some of the best times of my life."

Jennifer thought back to the first few months she met Darlene. They would stay awake all night, giggling and eating everything that wasn't good for them. Darlene's brothers would make sure her father didn't come out. "Remember the night Paul and Jared caught us skinny dipping down by the river?"

Darlene laughed out loud. "Oh yeah! I thought you were going to die from embarrassment!"

"And the fact that Paul had to say *damn girl! Where have you been hiding them tits?* Didn't make it any less traumatizing." Jennifer covered her face with her hands for a moment.

Darlene doubled over.

Jennifer chuckled. "There's no filter on that one."

A knock sounded at the door and Jennifer rose, still laughing softly to answer it. When she pulled the door opened, Rone stood there in his black hat looking extremely sexy but tired and weary. She opened her arms to him and after pulling his hat from his head, walked into her.

When she hugged him he sighed loudly.

For as long as he needed her to, she stood there, pressed into the wall with him against her chest. When he finally lifted his head and kissed her, she smiled.

"Long day?" Jennifer questioned.

"You have no idea." He kissed her again before walking away to kick off his shoes. He hung his hat on the hook by the door and the two walked into the living room where Darlene was still sitting.

"Hey Darlene." Rone greeted her. "I heard you went to see your dad."

"Yeah. I may want to strangle him right now but he's still my dad," the waitress replied.

"You want something to eat, sweetie?" Jennifer asked. "I made dinner."

Rone nodded. "I can get it."

"No." Jennifer pointed to a chair. "You sit, I'll feed you."

When Rone smirked at her, Jennifer knew precisely what he was thinking. She remembered the way he spread her wide and feasted from her body. Shivering, she hurried from the room hoping Darlene didn't notice.

In the kitchen she grabbed a plate and dished out some food. After she had that in the microwave, she poured a glass of juice, added some ice-cubes and dropped a shot-glass filled with lemon juice on top.

She set everything on a serving tray and went back to find Darlene and Rone in a deep conversation.

"You, mister, eat." She ordered playfully.

"Yes ma'am." Rone drawled. "This looks good."

"He was telling me what was happening with dad." Darlene pointed out as she sat beside Rone and rested a hand on his thigh.

"Is there anything we can do?" Jennifer wanted to know. "Did anyone call Paul and Jared?"

"Well, I did," Darlene said. "Jared said as long as I was safe, he didn't have a reason to come back here. Paul said he'll think about it and let me know. But I don't think he will."

"The judge said she'd release him into therapy and rehab. He will have to do it for a year then they will evaluate him again. If he fails...well, I guess I don't have to tell you it will end badly for him."

"We both know he won't make it a year." Darlene snapped.

"They are giving him a chance to save himself," Rone said. "Since no one else seem to be able to. I want to be hopeful, but this is the best alternative to prison."

Darlene sighed. "Why didn't he just listen to Raymond?"

"Because—Darlene, your father is an alcoholic." Rone explained. "There's no reasoning with him when he's drunk and when he's sober he can't concentrate on anything but his next drink. None of this is your fault. Jennifer tell her."

"He's right," Jennifer said. "Don't feel horrible about it. Keep your head up."

Darlene nodded and picked up her glass. "If you'll excuse me...I'm going to call Paul."

Jennifer watched her leave before snuggling into Rone's side. He stopped eating to wrap his arms around her and rubbed her shoulder affectionately.

"She loves him, Jennifer." Rone spoke softly. "You can't fault her for that. With friends you can just cut them off but with family—well you're kind of stuck."

"I know. I get it." She licked her lips. "I just wish there was more I could do."

Rone went silent.

Jennifer eased from him to allow him to eat. But instead, he stood and walked to where she was to pull her backward into his chest. Feeling his strength behind her caused her to shiver and nuzzled his chin with her head.

"Would you think any less of me if I tried getting to know Michael?" Jennifer questioned.

"I know you told me to let it go."

"Rone?"

"I wanted to make sure you were safe," Rone said. "Promise, you'll forgive me."

"You looked into him, didn't you?"

"Yes."

Inhaling she turned to look up into his eyes. "I know you want me to be safe, Rone. There's nothing for you to apologise for. He is my brother. He is my father's twin. I need your blessings for this though."

He stared into her eyes for a moment then a smile curled his lips. "Will it make you happy? Will it put your mind at ease if you do this?"

She nodded.

"Then of course! But if he gets all rowdy you tell me."

"I don't think he will. He's not at all like our father—at least I hope he isn't. But if anything happens you'll be the first to know. Then, you can ride in on your beautiful horse and save me."

"Do I get rewarded after?"

Jennifer giggled and kissed him. "Of course. You always get rewards for good deeds."

"Lady, I love the way you think."

She chuckled. "Are we still on for a little get away tonight?"

Rone nodded. "I can snag a bottle of wine from my place with a couple of glasses and we can go down to the beach, make a small fire and relax for a bit."

"Sweetheart, I would enjoy that.

Fifteen

Jennifer left him alone in the living room while she disappeared down the hall to speak with Darlene. He could hear their muffled voices and for a moment he simply stood where she left him. He didn't want to move.

What if he was in a dream, and moving would wake him?

Rone didn't want Jennifer to disappear. He didn't want her to have been just a figment of his imagination.

When he did pull enough air into his lungs to walk across the room, Rone pulled his cell phone and called Megan to check in at the station then called his father.

"You're not home yet," Raymond said.

"No. I'm going to spend some time with Jennifer then go home. Everything all right?"

"Fine. I'm heading to the diner for dinner with the gang. And why do you insist on calling her Jennifer and not Jenny?"

"I don't know. Jenny is just—"

"Do you call her Jennifer in bed?"

"Dad!"

"You're such a prude!" Raymond accused.

Rone was too shocked to have a come-back for that. The two talked for a few minutes more until Rone heard his name from down the hall.

"Dad, I have to go. I love you."

"Love you too, son. You two have a good night. Oh! Before you go. Chance called for you. Is there a reason he doesn't have your cell?"

"He does." Rone groned. "But it was off for most of the day. What did he say?"

"Said he handed in his papers. He'll call you tomorrow."

Rone rubbed his eyes. He had to call in some favours and get Chance that fire chief job. Thanking his father, he quickly hung up. Rone walked to the door and poked his head out. "Yeah baby?"

She was standing there with a bag over her shoulder.

"I'm ready."

Rone took her bag and arched a brow. "What do you have in here? Bricks?"

She laughed softly and wrapped her arm around his hip, leading him toward the door. "Nah. I have a couple towels, a blanket, a change of clothes just in case my clothes got wet at the beach, deodorant..."

He kissed her to silence her words. "Sorry I asked."

Their first stop was the local grocery store. He took her hand and walked into the building and couldn't help wondering why people were staring. Glancing down at where Jennifer was squeezing his tighter, he reached across to kiss her head. "Breathe, sweetie. You're dating me, not them. We don't care what they're thinking."

"Easy for you to say. We haven't really been out in public before."

"Why is this hard for you? Are you ashamed of me?"

Jennifer shook her head and stopped them in the breakfast aisle. She pulled her fingers from his and framed his face tenderly. "I would never be ashamed of you. Remember what I said about all this attention?"

"I do." He placed a kiss against her forehead. "But let me be your strength."

"You're too good to be true."

Rone laughed. "My father would disagree with you there."

Jennifer laughed and reached for a box of cereal. "That man thinks the sun rise and falls because of you."

Rone chuckled, took her hand again and they continued on.

By the time they made their way to the cashier, they'd picked up sandwiches, water, juice, popcorn and candy. When she snagged his cell phone and left him for the truck, Rone pulled out his wallet to pay for their loot.

"So, it is true," the cashier said.

"You got something to say, Mary?" Rone asked, desperately trying to hold onto his patience. Jumping to conclusions was the absolute wrong thing to do at that moment. Perhaps she wasn't talking about his relationship with Jennifer. He had to admit, however, the one part of Barley he never missed was the gossip. People were too busy nosing their way into everyone else's affairs rather than focusing on their own.

"Of all the women in Barley, you had to pick that one?"

"I'm not understanding how who I sleep with is any of your business."

"Of course, it's my business. My daughter is single. What about her? I mean, she waltzes into town and take up a job one of us could be doing and now one of our most eligible bachelors."

"Do you know how stupid you sound right now?" Rone inhaled in an attempt at holding on to what little control he had left on his temper. He leaned in to eye the woman. "Who I date is none of your concern. And if you dare say anything like this stupid crap to Jennifer, I will make it my mission to make you pay. Got that?"

She gasped and jerked back from him. Though she looked terrified, she nodded.

He really wasn't the one to intimidate people but when he thought of anyone doing anything to hurt Jennifer his back went up. Still, he didn't apologise, but paid for his stuff and left.

"What's wrong?" Jennifer asked, climbing into the truck with him.

"I cannot believe that woman." Rone frowned.

"R.J?"

"I have one, last, nerve left. And this town is starting to bounce on it." He exhaled loudly. "Don't worry about it. I just want to be with you tonight. Can we do that?"

"Of course. We can talk about it tomorrow."

Rone laughed. "You don't give up easily, do you?"

Jennifer beamed beautifully at him.

Rone melted.

Groaning, he reached across for a quick kiss while turning the ignition on. Their next stop was his place for some wine and a couple of glasses and then they were on their way.

The fire roared, crackling and soaring heavenward. Rone settled on the ground with his back against a large log with Jennifer sitting between his legs and resting into his chest.

He wrapped the blanket around her then pulled the edges behind his back and took a breath. Rone shivered at her closeness, clearing his throat wondering why he was so damned terrified of the feelings raging through him.

Perhaps it was too soon—too early to tell her just how she made his heart flutter leaving him feeling feeble. For the first time in a long time, he was holding a woman in his arms and didn't feel as if he wanted to run.

With Jennifer, though he was terrified at the thought of what came next, he wanted to stay.

"I'm going to tell you something, but you can't laugh or be weird about it." Jennifer broke the silence. She didn't move and for a moment Rone didn't either.

He finally kissed her head.

"All right."

"Darlene likes Chris."

"Likes Chris? My Chris?"

Jennifer shifted to look into his eyes. "Why do you say it like that?"

"Like what? I'm just surprised. She's never showed any interest what-so-ever."

Jennifer rested on him again. "I know how she feels, you know?

It's like she sees him all the time and he's so out of her reach, out of her league.

"That was how I felt about you. I still feel that way—a little bit. Can you just feel Chris out and see if he might at least be a little interested? Don't tell him why. I think she would die of embarrassment if she found out he knew."

He kissed the side of her head. "Well, I can try. But I make no promises."

She lifted her mouth to him. "That's all I can I ask."

He kissed her, snaking his hands up her body to her breasts and kneading gently. Her moaned vibrated from her, shaking his tongue making him groan. When he lifted his head, her eyes were deeper in the firelight. Rone tried kissing her again but she braced her palm into his chest and turned in his arms.

"I need to tell you." Her voice was soft and flowed over him like the rays of the sun first thing in the morning. "I didn't know all this before Michael—the beginning I mean. My father was abusive to my mother. When she found out she was pregnant with my brother, she hatched a plan to get him away from our father. When she had the baby, she had the nurses take him away and told my father he died in childbirth. She had plans in place for him Me, not so much and just to give me an added kick in the head for being born, she had to die leaving me alone with him."

"She died? How?"

"Childbirth. Dad blamed me for her death." Jennifer confessed. "So, every day, for as long as I can remember he made my life hell."

Rone held her tighter.

"I remember one day when I was ten." Her voice shook. "He beat me so bad my arm broke. When he realised I was hurt and I needed a hospital he warned me to tell them I fell. He took me to the hospital, and I told them I fell. They believed it, told me to be more careful and sent me home. Each time I tried telling someone he always had an explanation. I asked Gale to tell her mom but there was nothing she could do. So, I stayed, I suffered. And I prayed to any God who would listen to just let me die."

Rone's heart broke. "I'm sorry."

"It's not your fault, Rone. I'm just telling you because it's the logical next step. I got a letter from my father's lawyer."

"Your father's lawyer? How long has your father been dead?"

"Eleven years. Apparently, he made it so they couldn't tell me for quite a few years."

"Why would he do that?"

"He wanted to see if he'd sabotage my life enough and I'd starve to death?" Jennifer shrugged. "He never once taught me how to take care of myself, pay bills, get a job. Whatever his reason, they say they need to speak with me about his will. I didn't even know my father was ever lucid enough to make a damn will."

"What if he left what he had to charity or something?"

"They can have it. I'm just curious."

"Are you going to see what he left? Do you want someone to go with you?"

"Nah. I'll be fine going alone. He won't be there."

Rone chuckled and kissed her head. "True."

"I just—with everything I told you earlier, I want a fresh start with you." Jennifer used a nail to scratch her neck. "I don't want to walk into a relationship with you and have this—this *thing* weighing on me. You have to know where I'm coming from so you can make your decisions."

"What decisions?"

"If you want this to get more serious than we are right now."

Rone pulled back and lifted her chin. "You listen to me. No one is supposed to go through half the things you went through. And I'm not going anywhere. I'm here, as long as you want me. Understand?"

Jennifer tried looking away but he wouldn't let her.

"Tell me you understand." His voice broke and his eyes stung with unshed tears. "Don't nod. Don't hide your eyes from me. I need to hear you say it."

"I understand."

"Do you believe me, Jennifer?"

She smiled just as a tear trickled down her cheek. He brushed it away gently with his knuckle but that one was quickly followed by more.

"Ah, baby girl." He pulled her into his arms again.

Silence filled the air around them penetrated only by the soft reminder that the fire was still going and the waves still moved.

"So, now I have a brother, Rone." She pointed out. "A brother who I don't know if I can love like I should because of what my mother has done. And I can't help wondering why I wasn't important enough for her to save."

"Baby."

"Instead, she left me with him. And he took pleasure in breaking me repeatedly."

"Baby, you don't have to explain it to me. I've been a cop for long enough to know what abuse does to people and their minds and bodies—even their souls. Just know, whatever you need, I'm here."

Jennifer pushed from him and he met her gaze. He didn't know if she was trying to read him to see if he was lying, but he kept her eyes.

"Thank you. I don't know what I did to be so lucky." She caressed his cheek.

"Whenever you feel scared just remember one thing."

"What's that?" She questioned.

"I'm only a man."

Jennifer laughed softly.

"I have this overwhelming urge to feel you, Jennifer." Rone admitted.

Jennifer snaked her arms around him to pull in even closer. He sighed as her mouth traced from his jawline, down his neck to nip at his shoulder.

Rone closed his eyes and allowed his head to fall back in what he could only describe as pure bliss. His hands weakened and slipped from her body even as his back arched inward to her. She unbuttoned his shirt, kissing each bit of his skin.

In that moment, Rone realized something.

He'd always been the kind of man to take what he wanted in a woman's bed. Control had always been something he held fast to. Yet, with Jennifer, allowing her to take over, to do what she wanted to him, freed him. It was almost as if he was floating on air each time she kissed a certain part of him, or traced her fingertips over his skin.

She tasted every inch of his chest, his abs until finally she had him engulfed in her hot, wet mouth. Rone watched his control slip slowly away as he buried his fingers in her hair then yanked them back to bite his knuckles.

Jennifer licked him, sucked him, tasted him with such practise eased, his heart fluttered then raced almost painfully.

"Jennifer." He braced his hands on the ground.

His thoughts swirled around inside his head then all became of her. He wasn't sure if he wanted her to stop or carry on.

She was giving him something that threatened to make him implode.

She took him deep in her mouth with each pull. Then just when he thought she couldn't possibly make him feel any better, Jennifer Cozel rose over him and pulled him into the very centre of her. She took him into the hot, wet folds of her body.

This time when they made love every part of Rone's body pulsated. He shouted her name to the night.

From somewhere in the back of his mind, he could hear her name echo off the waves and rolled in on him.

Rone held his breath—wanting more.

Needing more.

Jennifer dug her fingers into his flesh, pulled him deeper into her body, riding him faster.

He desperately wanted to close his eyes but how could he when such beauty towered over him?

Rone watched her. He felt her. He welcomed every climax that rippled through her body. They made him bite his lip harder, forcing himself to prolong the moment.

His fight ended in a blinding explosion when she dragged a nail over one of his nipples through one of her orgasms. He was left mindless, without control and sweetly stunned.

"Damn Jen, that wasn't planned." Rone panted, pulling her into his chest and bringing the blanket back over them. "But it was— wow."

She laughed softly while snuggling into his chest. "They say those are the best kinds of giving booty."

Rone chuckled. "You said booty."

Sixteen

The diner was strangely busy. A few kids from the local high school sat in one corner playing Angry Birds on their phones while periodically dipping their hands into a fry basket.

Raymond sat with Beatrice at their usual table in deep conversation. From time-to-time Beatrice would laugh out loud leaving Jennifer to chuckle as she moved from table to table serving lunch.

A few of the other residents who came out about once or twice a month were scattered around the room, speaking softly.

"Hi Mrs. Lupowitz." Jennifer smiled in greeting.

"Jennifer! How are you?" The older woman turned from her husband and rose to hug Jennifer tightly. "It's been a while."

"I know." Jennifer accepted the hug then helped the older woman with her chair. Once Mrs. Lupowitz was sitting again, she turned to the woman's husband. "Hello Sam."

Sam Lupowitz grinned at her. "I hear you're making an honest man of our sheriff. About time a good woman snatched him up."

Jennifer blushed.

"Is he treating you well?" Andrea Lupowitz asked. "Are you happy?"

"Very well," Jennifer replied. "And yes, I'm happy."

"Good." Sam nodded. "Those are the two most important things."

Jennifer knew not to be cross with them. They had always treated her as if she was their child. "Before I forget." Jennifer leaned in. "Moses baked cheesecake today. I know you and Sam love his cheesecakes. It's Oreo crusted—so good."

Sam laughed haughtily. "We'll have that later. But when I walked in the door, I know I smelled jerk chicken."

"You did." Jennifer laughed softly. As long as she'd known the Lupowitz, Sam loved his jerk chicken, but it was never good on his body. Moses had started making a milder version, for those who couldn't handle the heat. It tasted just as good—she had to admit.

"Ha! See?" Sam smirked. "I told you, Andy."

Andrea grinned and reached across to squeeze her husband's hand. "Yes, you did honey. We'll order the mild Jerk chicken for both of us."

"Mild?" Sam exclaimed. "Hot. Hot. Hot!"

"We both know what spicy food does to your heart burn." Andrea scolded. "We're going with the mild, Jenny."

Sam muttered under his breath causing Jennifer to laugh. "I'll put in your orders and bring you something to drink while you wait. Is that okay?"

"Orange juice for me," Andrea said.

"I can't drink citrus with my diabetes medication." Andrea perused the drink menu. "How about some cranberry? The doc says it's better for me than soda."

With a nod, Jennifer patted Sam's shoulder, smiled at Andrea and hurried to put their orders in. She stopped for a brief moment to allow Moses a quick smoke break then returned to her tables.

Everything was busy—it was almost as if everyone in town chose that day to pop into the diner for lunch.

When it finally slowed, she was able to fall into one of the corner booths for something to eat. Deciding to treat herself, she ordered the avocado chicken burger, French fries with a side of mayo and a tall glass of apple juice.

The door opened just as she stuffed a fry into her mouth and Jennifer felt like sobbing. When she looked up and saw Michael, she felt physically ill. A part of her prayed he wouldn't see her, but God wasn't listening. Michael waved, hurried over and sat across from her without being invited.

"What do you want?" She asked.

"Food, that's all," Michael replied. "You look tired."

She shoved her food away and rested back into the seat. "I'm fine. I'll go get you something to eat."

When she tried getting up, he caught her hand and she yanked her hand back from him,

"Hey!" Moses hollered. He pointed a knife toward Michael. "Don't touch her."

"It's all right, Moses." Jennifer promised.

Moses didn't move right away. He stared daggers at Michael and after looking at Jennifer once more, he disappeared into the back.

Jennifer frowned at Michael.

"you are you trying to get gutted like a fish?"

"I'm sorry. I—can we just talk? I just want to talk. It kills me that you're always walking away. I don't know what else to do here."

"And what do you want to talk about?"

"You still blame me for what mom did." He frowned. "For leaving you alone with him. You blame me."

She leant forward. "Of course, I blame you! Why did she put so much thought into getting you away from him? She obviously new he was nuts! Why'd she leave me there with him? She had nine months to come up with a plan or use the same plan. That man would beat the shit out of me just because the weather changed and neither you nor mom gave a damn."

"I didn't know!"

"I know that." Jennifer tossed up a frustrated hand. "I can't wear a swimsuit because I'm covered in scars!" Tears streamed down her face then. "I…"

Michael reached for her again, but she pushed away from him. "I know. I shouldn't be angry at you, but he's gone and she's gone and you're all that's left."

"I get it."

"Do you? Do you really? Because I'm sure when you're with women you don't have to worry about them being physically ill at the sight of you."

"Rone isn't sick by the sight of you." Michael stressed. "I've only met him once and I know that. It's going to be hard, Jennifer. But you're going to have to let go and let him in. And I know you don't want to hear this right now—but you're going to have to get over yourself and this hatred or jealousy you have for me because you aren't the only person who lost something in all of this. When other guys are out there with their baby sisters, I didn't even know I had one. I've missed out on your life—can you imagine how empty that makes me feel? You're stuck with me so get used to it."

"I don't even like you!"

"Well, tough!" Michael snapped. "This isn't hard on only you! Can you imagine what it felt like to have your mother—the only mother you've ever known tell you she wasn't really your mother and not only that, but you have a sister out there they just conveniently forgot to mention?"

Jennifer gasped but the tears didn't stop coming. As she stared at Michael across from her, he became a hazy blob of white. She reached a hand over and he accepted and squeezed gently. His seat creaked under his shifting weight and soon he was pulling her into his arms. He hugged her tightly and for the first time in a long time, she sobbed.

But this cry wasn't for pity.

It was a cleansing kind of cry.

"I'm sorry for all of this, Jennifer." Michael caressed her shoulder. "Don't you think I wanted to be there for your first date, your first time bringing a boy home, the first time you had a problem that only your big brother can help you with? They robbed me of something too. At my age, I shouldn't be just falling in love with my sister."

"How old are you?" Jennifer pushed from his arms and wiped the back of her hand across her eyes."

"Thirty-two," he replied. "You?"

"Twenty-nine."

"When I think of all the things I've miss out on with you."

"You haven't missed much." She admitted, "Rone is my first, *real* boyfriend and I didn't do many of the things regular kids did. I wasn't allowed."

"Can we start over?" Michael extended a hand to her. "Hi...I'm Michael Kitchens, your brother."

Jennifer sniffled but couldn't hide the smile that broke her lips even as she used one hand to wipe her eyes again. She took his outstretched hand and shook. "Jennifer Cozel. The cute one."

Michael laughed.

"I have to get back to work," Jennifer said. "Can we talk later?"

"Like I told you before. I'll be here for as long as you need me to be. I still have more to talk to you about."

He pushed from the booth to let her out and before Jennifer went back to work, she hugged him tightly then ran off to help Moses.

"Hello beautiful." Rone's voice was soft behind her.

Grinning she stuffed her tips into her purse and turned on the stool. She rested her elbows on the counter. "Why, Sheriff. Are you hitting on me?"

"You can't ever tell my girlfriend." He inched closer, trapping her between his arms.

Jennifer tilted her head, pride filling her. "Deal."

"But since we're in public I'd settle for a kiss."

Jennifer giggled and offered her mouth to him. She pulled back and licked her lips. "You taste like chips." She whispered, positioning herself for another taste of his lips.

"Knock it off you two." Moses called from beside them. "Datsun says you're to get a room."

Rone laughed, stole another kiss and turned to shake hands with Moses. Jennifer gathered her things, removed her apron and folded it. She figured she could take it home and wash it before she had to use it again.

"I'm here to treat you tonight." Rone spoke. He cradled her against his body with a hand against her lower back. "What do you think of a nice bath, a home cooked meal, a glass of wine and some peace and quiet?"

"It all depends."

"On what?" Rone scratched his head.

"Am I cooking?"

Rone laughed, a beautifully, thunderous sound that caused Darlene to stick her head from around the back.

"Rone!" Darlene called.

"Hey Darlene. And no, Jennifer, you won't be cooking. I cooked."

"Talk dirty to me." Jennifer whispered.

Rone chuckled.

After saying their goodbyes, Jennifer allowed Rone to her to his place.

The moment they got through the door, Raymond called.

It was as though he had been waiting for them.

She kissed Rone deeply then climbed the stairs to his master bedroom. Stripping her dirty clothes off, she walked into the bathroom and ran herself a bath.

It dawned on her then that she didn' have a lot of things at his place. As a matter of fact, she needed to brush her hair up into a high ponytail and had to use his brush.

She then climbed into the bathtub and moaned.

Jennifer wasn't sure how long she was like that until she heard footsteps coming into the bathroom. Jennifer turned slightly to see Rone pulling up the stool and reaching for a large sponge hanging from the side of the tub.

Without a word, he dunked it into the water then lifted it gently over her shoulder. Tears burnt her eyes.

"Rone."

"Shhhh."

Each time he lifted the loofah over her flesh, she trembled and the more she wanted to cry. He caressed over her scars, brushing them with the loofah then with a tender fingertip. Finally, a tear toppled down her cheek.

"Baby?" Concern filled his eyes and voice.

"I'm sorry."

"Shh, no. What's wrong?"

Jennifer met his gaze then.

"One of these days, you're going to have to get used to this Jennifer." Rone dragged the material down her chest and over a very tender nipple.

She gasped.

"I love touching your skin." Rone admitted in a soft voice. "Feeling the shiver down your arm and having your body heat to my touch. Is that a bad thing?"

The old Jennifer screamed at her fruitlessly, telling her of course it was a bad thing. But he was right—the new Jennifer should get used to being a woman. She smiled at him then gripped his hand to move it lower.

She stopped its travel between her legs.

Rone smirked. "You bad, bad girl."

Jennifer licked her lips.

She looked down but Rone's hand had disappeared beneath the suds. She knew precisely where it was though for she could feel his fingers spreading her. As one of his finger trailed over her tender core, Jennifer whimpered his name and gripped his arm.

"Want me to stop, baby?" Rone eased closer to draw her earlobe between his teeth.

"Don't you dare!" Jennifer warned, grinding her hips against the digit.

Rone laughed and stopped but only to strip down.

Jennifer couldn't believe just how lucky she was.

The man towering over her, blue eyes dancing in the glow of the light was like a statue, perfectly sculpted. She could remember just how hard he was against her but how gently he could touch her.

He was hard and waiting for her.

Reaching up, she trailed a finger along the shaft of his arousal. He was watching her with his head tilted to one side and his hands folded in fists as though he was fighting something inside.

He then climbed into the tub with her, knelt between her legs and rolled her over so she was on top.

"I'm sorry this isn't more romantic, Jennifer. But I need you now."

Nodding, she braced her palms into his chest and leaned forward. She kissed him, allowing her tongue to swirl around him before sucking it into her mouth. Hearing him growl did something to her—it was almost paranormal.

For some reason she loved feeling like the sexiest woman in the world to this one man. Jennifer lifted her bum slightly, pushed back and wiggled her hips until his tip was at her entrance. When she sat back, it was to impale herself to his thickness.

Rone's eyes shot open. She clenched around him, squeezing tightly and taking his breath away. Reaching up, he cupped her breasts, kneading them, pinching the nipples as his mouth watered to taste them.

Still, his body needed release, and he drove his hips upward just to show her what he wanted.

A smile graced her lips as she tossed her head back and rode him, rolling her hips to drive him mad. Clutching her hips, he allowed her to take him as deeply as she wanted him as many times as she needed him until she climaxed around him.

Each time that happened, Rone gasped, whispered her name.

His eyes widened.

His body trembled while he fought for control. Watching her in the throes of passion was one of the most beautiful things he'd ever had the pleasure of witness. He wanted to see it over and over until he was blind with desires.

Sitting up in the tub, he wrapped his arms around her and lifted.

"I need you to turn around and grip the sides of the tub." He instructed through gritted teeth.

She kissed him but quickly did as he asked. When her rounded ass rose in the air, Rone swallowed nervously and moved in between her kneeling on the hard surface. Once more he entered her.

"Jennifer..." With this woman he couldn't help losing himself. He couldn't help calling her name and showing weakness as her body took a hold of him.

Once again, he gave over to it, allowing her to orgasm for him and taking her with him.

His body shook violently and there was nothing he could do about it.

Seventeen

Jennifer spent the night after Rone dropped her home staring at the darkened ceiling of her bedroom with Darlene breathing softly beside her.

She couldn't sleep. Perhaps it was because she hadn't wanted to leave Rone.

What she was feeling for Rone was more than fascination—having the urge to cling to his side and stand up for him sent pride through her. It left her weak, mindless and craving him, from his touch to the taste of his kisses. Everything about Rone made her happy.

Gently, Jennifer turned to her side and stared at the bedside clock. It was almost two in the morning.

"Can't sleep huh?" Darlene asked in the darkness.

Jennifer rolled to her back and looked at her friend. Darlene's dark hair was hanging into her face. Jennifer chuckled. "Nah. Keep thinking about Rone."

"I guess you did have fun on the beach and at his place," Darlene giggled.

Jennifer's cheeks heated. "Yes. I was going to tell you when the time was right. I've never had sex on a beach before. It was—naughty! But the damn sand got into everything."

Darlene burst out laughing. "Yeah—sand tend to do that. It's annoying but we still tend to do it. Honestly, there's nothing like having the waves lapping against your over-heated skin while your lover stoked the fire higher."

"You're a lush."

Darlene grinned. "In my opinion, every woman should have a chance at that feeling."

"You've done it?"

She nodded. "Yup. It's been a while. I think there are cobwebs down there."

"Well, it can't be that bad." Jennifer shifted to sit then curl her legs before her. "I told Rone about how you feel about Chris."

"Oh man! This is not going to end well."

"No. Listen. Rone says he's going to put feelers out there to see if Chris would be interested and let me know. I figured once we knew how he felt, then you can make your move?"

"My move?" Darlene scoffed. "If I had moves I wouldn't be watching him outside glass windows like some damn stalker."

Darlene climbed from the bed and stormed from the room. Jennifer called after her but her friend didn't stop to even look back. Slapping her forehead, Jennifer took a deep breath. "I'm sorry!" she shouted to the empty room.

Jennifer definitely thought she was helping.

Then again, she wasn't sure why she thought that would be helpful. When Raymond was playing Cupid, she couldn't have been more displeased. Then why did she think meddling into Darlene's love life or lack there-of would be a good idea? She listened to the toilet flush and turned her head in time to see the light in the hall go off before Darlene appeared at the bedroom door.

Jennifer climbed off the bed and stood in front of her friend. "Look, I'm sorry, okay? I really thought I was helping. But all I did was make it worse. I'll tell Rone not to say anything to Chris. That way he doesn't have to know. Can you not be angry at me anymore?"

"I know you were trying to help Jenny. I don't feel I deserve a good man right now."

"Oh don't be silly! If I deserve a good man, why not you?"

"I live with my best friend! My father tried to kill me!" Darlene reminded her. "Hell, my father is in jail at sixty five years old! I can't bring that much drama into a man's life!"

Jennifer took Darlene's arms and shook. "You listen to me. Your Rone is out there. I mean sure he hasn't said he loved me or promised me forever but if he's it for me if he walks away I'll be happy to have had that happiness. You can't give up because your father lost it."

She hugged Darlene tightly. "Now, in the morning I'll call Rone off"

"No. I would like to know if Chris could be interested in me. Somehow it means something to me."

Jennifer stepped back to look into Darlene's eyes. "If you're sure. Can we go back to bed now, please? I'm exhausted and we have work in the morning."

When they were settled in the bed again, Jennifer rested her head against Darlene's shoulder and closed her eyes.

The shrill ring of the telephone pulled Rone from his sleep. He groaned and reached over to cuddle with Jennifer but his hands only hit empty bed.

It was a constant thing for he always forgot when Jennifer didn't spend the night. Grunting, he looked out the window. It was barely light outside. Being the Sheriff had its downside.

Shaking his head, Rone reached for the phone.

"Yeah?"

"Sheriff, you have to head into lock up."

"Megan what's going on?"

"It's Martin. You have to get down here. The paramedics are trying to revive him right now but it doesn't look good."

"Shit."

Dropping the phone, he quickly hauled on some clothes, grabbed his gun and badge and as he rushed out the door, he picked up his hat. He couldn't help thinking he was being punished. He'd barely put his head down and already the phone was ringing.

And of course, it was bad news.

To make matters worse, Megan hadn't given him much information, but trying to revive someone seemed bad.

When he arrived, the paramedics were loading Martin onto the bus. Rushing over, he tapped one on the shoulder.

"What's going on?"

The Paramedic turned to glance at him then refocused on his work. "He had a heart attack. We've managed to revive him, but we have to get him to the hospital soon."

"Go," Rone said.

He watched the ambulance speed from the lot and turned in time to see Megan jogging over to him. "What in the hell?" Rone questioned resting a hand on his hips. "It's one thing after another."

"Yeah."

"Anyone called Darlene?"

"No. Not yet. We thought maybe you wanted to do the job since she's staying with Jennifer. But if you want me to do it..."

Rone shook his head and took a breath. "No. I'll head over there. You go to the hospital. We don't want him waking up alone. I'll get Darlene there as soon as I can."

Megan patted him on the shoulder and rushed to her squad card.

Rone looked around one last time and climbed back into his truck.

How was he going to explain this to Darlene?

She'd already been through so much. At the building he still didn't have an easy way to say it but he had to. Knocking, he waited until Jennifer answered, pulling her robe around her body.

"Rone?" She asked. "You're here late—what's going on?"

"Is Darlene back?"

"Yeah she's in the bedroom. What's going on?"

"Her father had a heart attack."

"Oh Lord..." Jennifer gasped before running back toward the bedroom. He closed the door and followed in time to see her leaning over Darlene and speaking softly.

He knew the moment Jennifer delivered the news for Darlene let out a cry that shattered Rone's heart. He'd seen a lot of horrible things in his life but watching a woman weep so openly did things to him he couldn't explain.

Wanting to turn away, he forced himself to stand still until Darlene climbed from the bed and began rushing around the room gathering things. He assumed she was getting dressed so he left the room.

"Rone, I need a favor." Jennifer spoke, keeping her eyes on her friend.

"Anything. You know that."

"I'm going to need you to pick Gale up at the airport. I can't leave Darlene now."

"I don't know what she looks like."

"Hold on." Jennifer hurried back into the room then returned. She pressed something into Rone's hand. "Here you go. This is the last picture I have of her. Her plane comes in at eight in the morning."

Rone gave her a quick kiss then turned to look at Darlene. "Darlene, I'm sorry."

Darlene nodded and she walked by him with eyes that were dead. He pushed some air out his mouth and turned to hug Jennifer tightly against him.

"Babe you have to let go." Jennifer told him. "I have to get dressed."

"I'm sorry. I'll get your friend and bring her back here for you," Rone promised.

With another kiss, he released Jennifer and walked into the living room to where Darlene was sitting. She looked so tired he sat down beside her and pulled her into his arms. With her head cradled beneath his chin, he rubbed her back not knowing what else to do.

"Martin is strong, Darlene." He encouraged her. "He'll pull through this."

"He's an unhealthy man, Rone," Darlene sobbed. "His heart is broken, and this is only proof. What if he doesn't want to get better?"

"I'm sorry to say then there's nothing anyone can do for him." Rone explained. "The doctors can only do so much."

Darlene nodded.

"Don't jump to any conclusions yet. Jennifer is going to take you to him."

Cowboy Lullaby

Eighteen

Jennifer hugged Gale tightly and after stepping back from her she turned to Rone. He looked troubled but she figured it was just because of what was happening to Darlene. He reached for her and Jennifer thought it would be a quick kiss.

When Rone wrapped an arm around her hips and took her lips, she sighed into him.

He moaned and released her.

"I'm heading to the office." He reported to her. "If you need me that's where I'll be. I'll stop by your place tonight if you're home."

"Rone told me what's happening with your friend." Gale pointed out. "Now is not the best time for a visit."

"But I'm glad you're here." Jennifer squeezed her friend's hand. "Really. And Rone thank you for this."

He smiled tightly at her. "Want me to take Gale to your place?"

Jennifer nodded.

"I'm fine staying here with you, Jenny," Gale told her.

"Nah. You're tired. Besides, you never liked hospitals, remember? Get some sleep and I'll be home soon. There's plenty of food in the fridge."

"All right. I'll sleep until you get there." Gale conceded. "If I can't I'll just make some calls and get some work done."

"Thanks. It's just Darlene doesn't have anyone else and I don't want to leave her alone right now."

"I understand," Gale replied.

"Rone, I'll see you later?" Jennifer wanted to know.

Rone took her hand and walked her out of earshot of Gale.

He took her hips in his hands and turned her to face him. When he stepped in close, Jennifer trembled, closed her eyes and inhaled.

When she looked up, his green eyes were studying her from beneath the brim of his black Stetson. Each time he wore that thing she just wanted to strip out of her clothes for him.

Licking her lips, Jennifer pushed to her tip\toes and kissed him. When she eased back to her feet, she rested her forehead against his chest.

"You're tired." He whispered. "I don't like seeing you like this."

"I know. But I still have to work a double at the diner to cover Darlene's shift."

"Datsun will understand if you called in sick."

"I know, but Darlene and I have bills. We can't just not work. And besides, if we called in sick he has no one to cover."

"Jennifer I..." he stopped.

Rone sighed and she looked into his face. His facial hair had grown in a little thicker, making him sexy rugged. She saw the way his jaws were set tightly and pressed a kiss to his chin. "I'll be fine. You'll just have to give me a little extra TLC later, that's all."

That got a smile to spread his beautiful lips right before his tongue flowed over them. "All right. But I'm checking in on you every chance I get. Understand?"

"You promise?"

"Now you're just teasing me."

She chuckled. "I'll see you later."

"Sure, baby. Later."

But he didn't release her until after he curled her toes again with another searing kiss.

Trembling, Jennifer watched them leave and she sighed. Why was everything going so absolutely wrong?

Her legs were stiff as she entered again. Each time she entered one she remembered the day she went into the morgue to see her father's body.

The same smell of disinfectant mixed with death overwhelmed her by slowly seeping beneath her skin and choking her.

She coughed, rubbing her neck before glancing both ways down the hall to remember where Martin's room was. Glancing over at the signs on the wall, she found the cardiac unit and made her way back to Martin's room.

Darlene sat by her father's bedside.

His eyes were closed and though he was barely breathing, the hospital had him attached to a ventilation machine.

Jennifer stood by the door, not knowing if she should feel sad for a man who terrorized his own daughter.

But when she looked at her friend her heart broke and she realized it didn't matter if she was sad for Martin, all that mattered was her friend was miserable and she should be able to help her. Taking a breath, Jennifer walked in and pulled up the extra chair.

"Did Rone get Gale?" Darlene wanted to know.

"Yeah. He's taking her to my place right now. I told her to take a nap and I'll get home soon. Something happened."

"What do you mean, something happened?"

Jennifer rolled her shoulders then looked down to where she was clenching her fingers tightly together. "He gets this look in his eyes when he's in serious thought. When he's trying to make up his mind about something and he doesn't want me to worry he gets this—this—fighter's look."

"Fighter's look?"

"I don't know how else to explain it." Jennifer offered a helpless shrug.

"You should have gone home with him. You're tired."

Jennifer shrugged but she said nothing to that. As much as she would love to be home sipping on a beer while cuddled in Rone's arms and talking to Gale, she wasn't about to leave Darlene when she didn't have to.

"How's he doing?" Jennifer asked.

"They say if he made it till morning, they'd be surprise." Darlene replied around a sniff. "His heart is really weak. This is his second heat-attack and they told him he should get a pacemaker a year ago, but he refused. Now this."

"Wait, you mean he was warned?"

Darlene nodded. "But you know him. No one knows more than he does. And he'd make you regret saying otherwise."

Jennifer was about to tell Darlene her father had a death wish but kept her thoughts to herself. Instead she rested her head on Darlene's shoulder.

"Did anyone call Paul and Jared?" Jennifer tried changing the subject.

Darlene sniffed and wiped the back of her hand against her nose. "Paul is on his way in. Jared said he would come just to make sure I was alright."

"That's good, right? They should be here soon."

Darlene nodded. She kissed her father's hand and Jennifer watched her shoulders rise and fall. "He's going to be sleeping a while. I should get ready for work."

"No. You stay with him. I'll cover you."

"And who's going to cover you? Jenny, I know you hate doubles."

Jennifer smiled. "Look, I don't want you leaving your father. I know if something was to happen when you're at work you'd never forgive yourself."

"You mean him dying."

Jennifer lifted her head from Darlene's shoulder but didn't reply to her friend's implication. That was precisely what she meant but didn't want to say it out loud. "Don't worry about the shift," Jennifer said instead. "It'll be okay."

"But I need the money."

"I'll put your name so Datsun pays you." Jennifer promised. "Stay with your father."

Darlene looked at her then. "You'd do that for me?"

"What kind of question is that?" Jennifer asked. "Of course. You'd do it for me. Now, I have to go if I'm going to make the shift. I'll come back as soon as I can."

Darlene hugged her tightly. And Jennifer stayed with her until Darlene released her before rising and walking out the door. She stood there a moment, watching Darlene before turning away hoping it would stop the burning in her eyes.

But it didn't until tears flowed down her face.

Hurrying out the door, she glanced at the clock, frowned and sped from the parking lot. She had just enough time to get home, shower, change and head back to work. She was sure Moses wouldn't mind if she was a few minutes late but she hated being late for anything.

Work was a pain. People kept asking her about Darlene and each time she thought she was strong enough to handle it she had to fight not to break down.

Moses let her take a few extra breaks just to gather herself. Halfway through Darlene's evening shift, Paul showed up and she took her final break to speak with him. He hugged her tightly after kissing her cheek then cradled her face.

"You've been crying and you look exhausted."

Jennifer smiled. "I'll be fine. I'm more angry than depressed."

"Why angry?"

"Darlene is in so much pain, Paul. I-I don't know how to help her. I'm hoping you and Jared will be able to."

"Well, Jared should be on his way. I wanted to stop in and talk to you first, see how you're doing." He leaned back to study her features. "After I see Darlene you're going to have to tell me about you and our good Sheriff."

Jennifer blushed. "I'll tell you everything, just go to Darlene."

"I didn't mean to leave her." Paul offered. "I thought if we Jared and I left he would be kinder to her because she'd be all he had left. But we were so wrong. This is all my fault."

Jennifer reached forward and cradled his face gently. "Don't do that. Darlene isn't blaming you. She just needs her brothers right now. This is no one's fault but a stubborn man who didn't want to listen to doctors."

"Darlene told you about that?"

"Yes. His heart is too weak. The doctors won't operate on him."

"I figured." Paul kissed her cheek again. "I'll see you later. Stay strong."

Jennifer smiled sadly.

"You too."

Nineteen

It'd been two days since the incident with Darlene's father. Two days since he'd kissed Jennifer or held her. People were always around from Jared and Paul to Darlene and Gale.

Each time he wanted to take her into his arms Gale would interrupt and it took everything inside him not to snap.

He missed Jennifer.

Her scent was still fresh on his sheets so he didn't change them. The irrational fear he would lose her charged through him every moment he thought of putting fresh sheets on the bed.

He also had a secret he had to tell her and Rone wasn't sure how that would affect their relationship.

Rone paced Jennifer's living room, waiting for her to get back from taking Gale to the diner.

It was the closest place around with wifi and Gale was complaining about having to check in with the office and some emails for a business proposal.

He spent time thinking about what he was about to do and the more he thought about it the more he had to say something. He spoke to Megan about it and his father then Chris and Justin and they all said the same thing—he had to say something to Jennifer.

Finally, he heard the keys in the door and his heart jerked him around.

Taking a breath, he walked out into the hall to meet her. Gale wasn't with her.

"Rone! I didn't think you were coming over today."

"I wanted to talk to you when Gale and Darlene weren't here. Come, sit."

"Rone?"

"Please. This is hard enough. Just—give me a little room?"

She looked into his eyes for a moment then allowed him to lead her into the living room. When she sat, he took his place before her, sitting on the centre table. He took a deep breath and straightened his back. The troubling look in her eyes made him want to cry but he had to.

"You're breaking up with me." Her lips trembled slightly.

"No. I'm not going anywhere unless that's what you want."

"Then what? Rone, you're killing me here."

"It's about Gale...you asked me to pick her up at the airport."

Jennifer nodded. "I remember."

"—Jenny—baby...she tried hitting on me."

Jennifer blinked a few times then chuckled. "You probably read it wrong. She'd never do something like that to me. She's been my friend since we were kids. She knows how much you mean to me."

"Jennifer."

"No. No! I will not believe that. And if you do then—then I can't talk to you right now." She jerked from the seat and pushed by him. "I'm going to go out now and you should be gone when I get back."

"Jennifer!"

Instead of answering, she lifted her hand and stormed back out the door. That didn't go as well as he hoped. Rone, dragged a frustrated hand through his hair. It was either that or punch a hole in the wall. He couldn't believe it. All he wanted to do was be honest with her. If another man had made a pass at her he'd want to know. Wouldn't he?

He didn't know what else to do but he knew when he'd been dumped. Rone took a breath and figured he'd give her a couple of days to deal then try speaking with her again.

Letting himself out of the apartment he jogged down the stairs to his car. He drove past the sheriff's department and toward his house.

But even after he got there, stripped down to a pair of jeans and a beer, he still couldn't get his mind off Jennifer and how she'd reacted.

She actually thought he made it up to hurt her.

He took another sip from the beer, but it was doing nothing for the burn and anger he felt inside.

Making his way into the kitchen, he eyed the bottle of whiskey sitting on the shelf.

The bottle of Johnnie Walker called to him. It would be so easy to simply reach for it, wrung the cap off and turn it to his head. The burn the liquid would cause would be worth it.

He reached for it and the thought of Martin flashed through his head. Dropping the bottle into the sink, he walked from the room and turned the light off.

Rone ignored the stairs but instead walked into his den and called the only person he knew would understand.

"You told her?" Chance asked after Rone explained.

"I didn't have a choice. She deserved to know what kind of person her best friend was. I just didn't think she'd freak out so much."

"What did you think was going to happen? From what you told me, her father was an ass, and this girl was the only person in the world who hadn't tried to hurt her. I understand where she's coming from. Rone, do you love this woman?"

Rone said nothing. He pushed his fingers through his hair and groaned. "I should have called dad."

"Rone, you don't have to answer me, but I know you're asking yourself the same question. It's either that or you already found the answer."

"It doesn't matter how I feel about her." Rone grumbled. "I can't be in a relationship on my own."

"Now you're not making any sense—I'm coming sweetie!—look, Anne is calling for me. It may do Anne well to hear from you and I think you need it too."

"Chance I can't talk to..."

"Uncle Rone?"

Rone smiled, pushing the hurt and confusion he was feeling down deep and took a breath. "Hey there princess. Isn't it past your bedtime?"

"I couldn't sleep. Dad told me we're gonna come see you soon."

"That you are."

"Can we go get ice-cream?"

"Sure, we can. Now, you go to sleep for daddy, okay? And I'll see you soon?"

"Okay. I love you."

Rone's heart did a beautiful, little flip and he laughed softly. "I love you too, Anne. Now give daddy the phone."

"Okay."

There was a shuffle on the other end, soft murmurs from Chance to his daughter until Chance finally came back on the line. "Listen, Rone. You're a smart guy. You can't just let one woman come between you and the only woman who I see you go to pieces over. Talk to Justin and Chris, they'll tell you the same thing. I'm sure of it."

Rone rubbed his eyes. He couldn't stay seated anymore. His butt was suddenly burning in the seat and his legs felt as though he had pins and needles in them.

Rising, he walked to the window and peered out into the darkness.

"And what if I said I loved her?"

"It would mean nothing to me, my friend. This is all about you."

"Can I ask you something?" Jennifer curled her legs beneath her bum and cradled her warm mug. "I had a conversation with Rone and I haven't had time to actually speak with you about it because of Darlene and her dad."

"What conversation is that?" Gale wanted to know. She didn't turn from the window she'd been staring out.

"He told me you hit on him."

Gale said nothing.

"Did you do it?"

"Yes."

Gale's answer was soft with no hint of guilt or regret. The cold, distance in those three words worried Jennifer. She uncurled herself and placed her mug down.

A sharp pain shot through her chest causing her arms to go numb. She rose and walked over to where Gale stood.

"You're lying."

"Why would both of us be lying to you, Jennifer. God, you cannot be that naive!"

"Why? Why would you do that?"

"He has to be gay." Gale muttered as though Jennifer hadn't even spoken. "Those gay men who want to hide it and marry a woman. He has to be one."

"Gale!"

"That has to be the only reason why he didn't go for it. There is no other reason."

"I cannot believe this!" Jennifer grabbed Gale's arm tightly and tugged, sending Gale spinning to face her. "You of all people would do this to me? You! Who knows what I've been through, would do this to me. You're my friend."

"Is that what you think? You think I'm your friend?"

"All these years, Gale, you've been there for me." Jennifer cocked her head to one side. "Why would you then throw it all away just when I can take care of myself enough to actually be something to you?"

Gale didn't speak but the change in her eyes told Jennifer all she needed to know. Jennifer's eyes burned dangerously, and she knew she would cry. But she was stronger than that.

"I get it." Jennifer muttered. "As long as I'm miserable and you're happy the world is perfect. As long as I'm depending on you, you would pretend to be my friend. But the moment I find someone who cares for me and you see I'm happy you want to take it away from me."

Gale tried leaving but Jennifer wasn't about to have that. She was pissed off as hell and Gale was going to stand there and feel her wrath!

She stepped before Gale and shoved her roughly in the chest. "You pretended all these years to care for me to satisfy some perverse need you have to see me suffer! What did you offer Rone, sex?"

"We're not having this conversation, Jenny."

"You don't get to call me Jenny!" Jennifer snapped. "Not anymore. Only my friends call me that, people who love me. You have *no* right! What did you say to him?"

"I told him you were a fat pig! Happy now?" Gale spat. "That's right. It was all about figuring out what he saw in you. I tried showing the moron I would be a better woman for him. We both know I'd look better on his arm, in his bed. But the braindead man couldn't see that. I don't get it. I hit the gym, fight to look the way I do and you—you probably don't even know what a treadmill is, and you get the sexy, cowboy sheriff?"

"Wow." Suddenly, Jennifer wasn't mad anymore. All she could feel for Gale was pity.

She was proud of Rone. He'd stood up for her and decline Gale's offers. He'd walked away from her seduction and chose Jennifer. Rone was a sculpted Adonis who was so damn sexy with his badge and gun at his side. How could she possibly feel self-conscious of her body after that?

"If there was any justice in the world." Jennifer growled. "I'd be able to strangle your backstabbing-ass and not wind up in prison."

"Are you threatening me?"

"Sweetie, you know better. I don't make threats. But test my patience and find out."

"I'm still better for him." Gale pushed. "If you were any kind of real woman you'd see it too."

"You pathetic, pathetic woman." Jennifer scoffed. "The old me would cry at your words and feel angry about it. Then, the me after my father died would punch you in the face for being such a bitch and not feel an ounce of guilt about it. But you know something? Rone saw you for what you are and that makes me love him even more. All I feel for you right no wis pity."

"Save your pity."

Jennifer smiled. "You see, Rone has my heart. God owns my soul. Pity is all I have left for you. Now, you will get your shit and get out."

She stepped aside, lifted her chin and watched her ex-best friend leave the room. And though she'd lost someone she thought had her back, Jennifer smiled, grabbed her keys and exited the house.

By the time she pulled up in front of the Sheriff's department she was so happy, Jennifer thought she could burst. She hurried into the office.

"Jennifer! I've been meaning to talk to you!" Megan called.

Jennifer waved her arm. "Can we talk later? I have to see Rone first."

"Okay."

Jennifer opened Rone's office door and he looked up at her. She smiled and closed the door behind her.

He closed the file he was scribbling in and eased back into his chair. He was so handsome—his dark hair raked backward, his green eyes pursuing her with intense curiosity. It showed he hadn't shaved in a while too for his facial hair looked dark and thick.

His arms lay atop the desk, fingers laced while his shoulders looked tense.

Hugging herself, Jennifer walked closer and closer to his desk until her thighs were bracing to it. She swallowed the nervous lump in her throat as her knees shook. "You chose me."

"Say what now?" Rone asked.

"You rejected someone who looked like Gale—so perfect, and you chose me."

"You may not look like a doll, Jennifer, but you have something else. You have something I've been searching for that Gale could never give to me."

"Um…"

"You are real to me." Rone explained. "Can you understand that?"

Jennifer nodded.

"When I first saw you, Jennifer, I knew I wanted you and the moment it was clear to me how desperate you made me, it was you and only you. I don't believe in straying. I will never give away what belongs to you to another woman. I need to know you believe me and you trust me."

"What belongs to me?"

He smiled. "My love. My heart. My—my body."

Jennifer hurried around the desk to kneel beside him. She looked up into his eyes and braced her hands against his thigh. "I do. I believe you and I do trust you. I just never expected Gale to do what she did. I feel like such a moron. I'm sorry I hurt you."

Rone smiled sadly. She saw the exhaustion in his eyes. He caressed the side of her face before bowing his head to take her lips.

This kiss was different from all the others—this time he was soothing himself from her so she tossed herself into it, giving him everything she could.

"I'd like to spend some time with you today if that's alright," Rone explained. "I say we pack a basket and just head down to the beach."

"You just want to see me in a swimsuit."

Rone laughed and helped her to stand. "Is my ploy working?"

She giggled. He pulled her into his chest and wrapped his arms around her to tap her lightly on the bum. She tangled her arms around his neck and looked up into his face with such happiness she was overwhelmed with it. "Maybe."

"What can I do to see you in a swimsuit today?"

"Well, Sheriff." Jennifer took a breath and sidled up closer to her man. "You only have to ask me nicely—or does your door lock?"

Rone smirked but released her to lock the door.

"What did you have in mind?"

"Sit." Jennifer pointed.

Rone sat in the leather seat and Jennifer climbed astride his thighs. He gripped her hips and lifted her to the desk to face him. She held onto the sides of the chair and pulled him between her legs.

"You now have to pay the toll." She joked. "What are you going to do about that?"

He grinned at her while easing her dress up. He was leaning forward when there was a loud knock on the door.

"Sheriff?"

Rone growled.

Jennifer frowned. Her body had been anticipating his touch, the feel of his wonderful lips on her. She cradled his face and kissed his lips gently. His hands were still against her flesh, warming her body and making her tingle. "We can finish this later."

"Count on it."

"Sheriff?"

"Megan, give me a minute!" Rone hollered.

Jennifer climbed off the desk with his help and adjusted her clothes. Blowing him a kiss she unlocked the door. "I'll pack our lunch and wait for you."

Rone nodded and she opened the door. Megan hurried by her with a folder and she continued out the door.

Twenty

Rone took a breath and dragged his fingers through his hair. So many little things were getting in the way of growing with Jennifer.

Now, she lost what was supposed to be her best friend and he still wasn't sure he believed the bravado she was putting on about it. Still. he wouldn't push. If she had an issue he would just leave himself open for the conversation to come up again.

After his meeting with Megan about what to do about Darlene's father and a few break and entries at the old warehouse, he stopped off at Raymond's.

"You look like dirt." His father pointed out. "Haven't you been sleeping?"

"Barely. I almost lost Jennifer."

Raymond sipped from his beer and eyed Rone. " "The whole gale thing?"

Rone nodded. "But everything is okay now."

"What's changed?"

"She had a talk with Gale". It didn't end well."

The two men sat in comforted silence. Rone took a moment to grab himself a beer before sitting and stretching his legs out before him. "I don't have much time to sit with you. I promised Jennifer I'd spend the day with her. She's been going through a lot."

"I figured. From what you told me she has a brother." Raymond recalled. "Then the whole Darlene double shift thing. Then add to that losing Gale."

"Tell me about it." Rone dragged a hand over his head. "I got the rest of the sordid details behind her long lost brother and I hate it."

"What do you mean?" Raymond questioned.

Rone took a moment to explain the whole Michael situation. When he was finished, he was physically exhausted.

"So why did she leave Jennifer with this jerk?"

Rone shrugged. "She died in childbirth. I want to believe she just didn't have a chance to make other arrangements. Jennifer is thinking her mother didn't love her enough to make the plans since she was left alone with this man. I don't know what she's going to do now."

Raymond took a breath. "All you can do is love her through it. When she starts getting irritable and confused, hold her. When she gets angry about it, you make love to her."

Rone blushed. "Aww dad!"

"Don't aww dad me. I'm an old man. Your mother and I had those days. Sometimes the days and people in those days just get to you so bad all you want to do is go home, take her into the bedroom and just lock yourselves in."

Rone pushed off the embarrassment and nodded to his father's words. Though he may feel it was a little too much information, Raymond was right. When the world is conspiring against them, Rone should know enough to let what he was feeling for Jennifer take charge.

He hugged his father quickly. "I gatta run dad. I'll see you either tonight or tomorrow."

"Give her a hug for me, you hear?"

"Yes, dad."

Jennifer watched the spot in the water where Rone went under the large waves.

When he rose again, he was like Poseidon himself. It hypnotized her, seeing water flaring upward, then falling over his body like rain. He pushed his fingers through his hair and walked toward her in the corniest slow motion she'd ever seen.

She smiled and lifted her hands to him. Rone pulled her up in one quick movement sending her crashing into his chest.

She whimpered.

He nuzzled her neck, before focusing on dropping feather light kisses on her nose, forehead then lips.

His wet body was hard and muscular beneath her.

"How are you feeling?" Rone wanted to know.

"I'm happy for us, sad for Darlene."

"That's not what I meant." Rone took her hand and led her back to the air mattress and sat her down. "I mean with Gale. You two have been friends for a very long time and I feel kind of bad it ended the way it did. I just had to tell you because I thought it was the right thing to do. I didn't want you to lose a friend."

"You did do the right thing. And if she did what she did then what kind of friend is that?"

"I'm sorry. I just—I don't like causing you pain."

"Are you saying I should talk to her?"

Rone shook his head and stepped away from her to grab an apple from their basket. Wiping the fruit against his chest, he bit into it. "No. That's not what I'm saying at all. I'm saying she shouldn't have done what she did but I know losing her hurts you."

Jennifer licked her lips, leaned in and bit the other side of his apple.

"Get your own apple, Moocher."

Jennifer smirked as she chewed.

"What fun would that be?" She bit his apple again before curling her legs before her. "As for Gale. She was never my friend—she pretended to be. If she was, then she would never have done what she did. It kills me that she was happy I was miserable and the one time she saw me truly happy she tried stealing that away from me. I really don't want a friend like that."

"I feel like this is somehow my fault."

"This is not your fault. Your father has been more of a friend to me than Gale. Even though she pretended to have my best interest at heart, I think she just wanted to keep me around because my life falling apart made her life look so much better. It just...I think what hurts the most is all these years I shared everything with her. I told this woman things I've never told anyone. I told her my deepest fears and she tried to break me."

Rone held her then, cradling her face against his wide, warm shoulder. "I understand. We don't have to talk about her anymore."

"What did she say to you anyways?"

He eased back and met her gaze. "Jen..."

"I want to know."

Jennifer watched the tense way Rone ground his teeth. His shoulders fell as a long breath seeped from his mouth. "Jennifer, I don't think that's a good idea. Just the thought of her hitting on me caused you pain and you don't even know what she said to me."

"Rone."

He sighed. "She asked what I was doing with you. Asked if it was a part of a practical joke right before she..."

Jennifer turned her head away.

"See? Jennifer, please. Don't make me say this to you. It's hurting you even more. Today is supposed to be our day alone together. No talks about Darlene or Gale or even Megan and her crush. Today is for us."

Leaning forward, Jennifer kissed his neck, then his chin. "You're right. We haven't really had time for each other and I'm sorry about that."

"Yeah, well, that only means we have to make up for lost time."

She looked up to see Rone was grinning at her, his silvery-blue eyes shimmering beautifully. She had to laugh and hit him playfully against the thigh.

"Let's talk about something else—like the letter I got from my father's lawyer."

The two sat together beneath their umbrella and cuddled. "They want me to come see them."

"Well, you should go. See what it's all about."

"I *am* curious."

Rone chuckled. "Then go. Your father is dead there isn't much he can do to you now. This is just to get closure and then you come home to me."

Rone's rationale made sense to her. Jennifer kept wondering what her father could have possibly owned to leave for her. Then again, he was always a very stingy man. Even if he did have money or property she wouldn't have known about it. It could wait awhile while she enjoyed Rone.

Still, going to this lawyer and getting it out of the way would be good.

With her decision made, she rolled over and climbed astride him. She braced her palms into his chest and looked down at him. He caressed her arms up to her shoulders and down again before smiling up at her.

"You're so beautiful." His voice cracked.

"You think so?" She dragged a hand over her hair. It'd been a while since she'd bought any weave or the like for it. She chemically straightened it herself and it was beginning to grow out. "I really want to look nice for you, but I don't have that kind of money to go the salon."

"Darling, don't you know, you could be wearing rags and barefooted and I'd still want you?"

Tears slid down her cheeks then even though she didn't mean for them to.

He was tender with her then, wrapping his arms around her and sitting up to hug her tightly. She allowed him to hold her—allowed him to sooth her with soft whispers of his love.

Those whispers turned to kisses and touching.

Jennifer felt as if for the first time in a long time she was loved. Her body trembled with her inhalation and when Rone rested on the towel again beneath the umbrella, it was to hold her securely against his chest.

Cowboy Lullaby

Twenty-One

For a while after the sun rose, Jennifer sat in her car staring at it. The warm rays floated over her face, skimming her skin like Rone's touch.

The heat traveled the length of her spine all the way down her body to curl her toes. Moaning, Jennifer clenched the wheel and opened her eyes to look around. Her lower back throbbed with exhaustion.

She was so tired it took a bit of time for her to pull herself together in order to force her brain to co-operate.

It was two days later and still Jennifer hadn't had a chance to get much sleep.

From Rone's side to Darlene's and Martin's she was running full speed on empty. She left Darlene with her brothers and decided to spend her break with her own.

It was still strange to call Michael her brother, but he was right. She had to get over the uncomfortable feelings.

After she explained to him what her issue was, he insisted on coming down to the diner to talk to her—right after she fed him of course.

Smiling, she pushed from the car, dragging her purse with her.

"Jenny!" Raymond called. "Didn't think you'd be in this morning."

"I have bills to pay, my darling." She kissed his cheek and patted his shoulder.

"You look really tired, Jenny." Beatrice spoke up. "Has Rone Jennings been keeping you up at nights? I tell you, that boy must be as insatiable as his father."

Raymond sputtered around his juice. "Listen, woman. Don't be starting rumors about my boy."

Jennifer was shocked. "Um..."

"Rumors?" Beatrice chortled. "Bah! You just have to look at that boy and you can tell he's some kind of wonderful. Am I right, Jenny?"

"Um..." Jennifer sputtered.

"Leave the child alone." Raymond shushed. "I doubt she wants to talk to you about my son's virility."

"And that's my cue!" Jennifer shook her head and ran to get her apron on. She stopped behind the counter to hug Datsun tightly. "Thank you so much for being understanding."

"Are you kidding? You and Darlene has been nothing good for this place." Datsun grinned. "So, take as much time as you need off now. You've been pulling a lot of doubles. The last thing I need is Rone coming in here and demanding to know why I'm making his girl work so hard."

Jennifer giggled at the title of *Rone's girl*. She batted a wrist. "It's fine. Darlene and I have bills to pay. Rone may not like it but he understands. But I am going to need a day off next week. I have to head into Ohand."

"After the hell you've been through in that place, you want to go back?" Datsun asked, turning away from the French fries he was staring into when she walked into the kitchen. "Why do you want to go back?"

"Something I have to deal with." She patted his shoulder. "I'll be fine. I probably won't go alone."

"Oh right. This about the brother popping in out of thing air?"

"You know about that?"

Datsun laughed just as the fryer began beeping. He lifted the cooker out and dumped the fries into a clean and salted bowl then proceeded to toss the fries, mixing them to get the salt even. "You live in a small town, darling. I hear everything. Are you sure this guy's for real? I mean how much do you know about him?"

"I don't know much." Jennifer admitted. "I've been running around crazy for a few days now. And the other times I was trying to run interference between him and Rone."

"Ah, that little in-your-face dealie they had in here."

"Yeah. See, Michael said something that made Rone think that Michael and I were—you know. Rone got mad and I believe his words were *I'll kill him.*"

Datsun laughed. "Yeah. Sounds like the Jennings men struck again."

"Yeah well." Jennifer nodded and took the bowl from him. She picked up a pair of tongs and served some of the fresh fries into a plate. She handed it to Datsun to add the other food items. "He looks just like my father, Dat. Just like him. His eyes, his mouth, his ears—the only thing is, Michael is kinder. When he found out what was happening to me he got this tender, almost sickening look in his eyes as if he wanted to throw up. I've never seen those eyes with anything but hate and evil before."

"I can understand that."

"He is my brother. There is no doubt in my mind about that. I mean, if he's not he has to be the world's worse con-man because I have nothing he could possibly want."

Datsun nodded and gave her a plate piled with hash browns and sausages. "This is for Raymond. Listen—don't rush into anything. Take everything with stride because if this guy hurts you, Rone will kill him before I get a chance to. And Rone wouldn't do well in prison."

She chuckled and kissed Datsun's cheek. "Thank you."

He nodded.

When she made her way into the dining area and fed Raymond, Michael walked through the door. After a quick hug she got him some coffee.

"What do you want to eat?"

Michael shrugged, falling into his seat. "Surprise me."

"You look like a scrambled eggs kind of guy."

He smirked at her. It was a strange expression coming from that face. He looked so much like their father and Jennifer couldn't remember a day he smiled. All she recalled was evil.

Jennifer left him to put in his order, checked on the other patrons then carried his food back to him. Jennifer refilled Michael's coffee cup and sat across from him. He shovelled some scrambled eggs into his mouth then pointed his fork at her.

"I think you should go." Michael suggested. "I can tell it would be closure for you—as corny as that may sounds."

"It doesn't at all. Rone suggested the same thing. I've been meaning to get a dinner set up for all of us but with everything happening—I just haven't had a chance."

"Don't worry about it. I'm not Rone's favorite person at the moment. The longer I get to stay away from him, the better. Besides, some stuff came up for my business I had to tackle."

"What do you do?"

"I own my own software company. I should give you the grand tour sometime."

"A company? Wow."

"It's not as exciting as it sounds." Michael told her. "When is your birthday?"

"In two weeks. June eighteenth."

"Really? I didn't even bring you a present."

Jennifer shook her head. "Don't worry about it. You didn't know. I've never really gotten a present for my birthday. I mean, Gale used to take me to dinner but no presents."

"Not cool."

Jennifer left him so early that morning it was still dark outside. There had to be a way to get her not to work so much. When she was leaving, he tried getting her to stay, to rest a little longer. But she only kissed him and rushed out the door.

He watched her car disappear down the street and for the life of him, he couldn't fall asleep again.

Instead, with his day off, he decided to do some work around the ranch. He spent most of the time unpacking some things for Chance then turned his focus to his horses.

He fed then, mucked out the stalls and re-shoed Kicker. He was on his knees at the front porch, replacing the bottom step when a sound came from behind him. He turned to see a car and wondered how he didn't hear it coming from down the street.

One of the back doors opened and Anne came charging toward him. "Uncle Rone!"

Without standing, he caught her to his chest and hugged her tightly. The moment her tiny body was against him he realized just how desperately he'd missed her.

He kissed the side of her head and walked to where Chance was climbing from the car. Chance bent backward moaning and rubbing his lower back.

Rone smiled. "I know that feeling."

"I feel like I got worked over by a two by four." Chance groaned.

The two men bumped fists then hugged with Anne's body between them. The little girl giggled.

"You're squishing me!" She called, wrapping her arms around both their necks.

"I'm sorry darling." Rone kissed her head.

"We would've been here sooner, but we stopped for ice-cream," Chance said. "At a diner in town. That place is amazing. And their home-made Grape-nut ice-cream is to die for."

"I know, right? Jennifer came up with that idea. It was only supposed to be a one-time deal but the people in this town fell in love and it stuck. Did you meet Jennifer? She works there."

Chance shook his head. "No. We did meet Datsun."

Rone nodded. "He owns the joint. You two must be tired. Why don't I take you into the house so you can shower and get something to eat and maybe take a nap?"

"Did our stuff make it here okay?" Chance questioned.

Rone nodded, leading them to the guesthouse. "Yeah. I spent the morning unpacking the kitchen and Anne's room. Figured you wanted it set up for her when she got here."

"Can we see your horsies?" Anne questioned.

"In a bit sweetie," Chance replied. "First, food and nap."

"Okie," she replied but Rone knew she was not impressed by the answer.

But she was out like a light before her head was on the pillow. She fell asleep on the walk from the living room to the bedroom. He laid her on the bed, covering her and kissing her forehead. He didn't leave her.

Even as he pushed some hair from her little face he knew she would be as close as he'd ever come to a child of his own. Though he hadn't brought the subject up with Jennifer he just had the feeling. Besides, it was too soon to start talking children with Jennifer they needed more time. Taking a breath, he rose.

"Uncle Rone?"

Rone turned. "Yeah sweetie?"

"Daddy says we're going to live here now. Does that make you happy?"

He rubbed his palms on his thighs. The thought of having her close made him happier than he ever thought he could or had a right to be. "I thought you were sleeping."

"I was."

"And yes. I'm happy you and daddy are here."

"I get to see you every day, huh?"

He chuckled and touched her cheek gently. "Yep, you sure do."

"Daddy says you have a girlfriend. He didn't want to tell me. He says I shouldn't worry cuz you will always love me."

"And he's right about my girlfriend and about me always loving you. No matter what happens in my life or if I have children, you're my girl. I'll be here for you when you need me, especially to scare away the boys."

She giggled. "Uncle Rone—boys are yuckie."

Rone grinned and kissed her head. "Just know I love you and nothing will change that. You never have to worry about me leaving you—okay?"

"You promise?"

"I promise. Now, get some sleep."

She hugged him and snuggled into the pillows again. Rone left her, closing the door quietly behind him. When he met up with Chance on the front porch, the ex-cop was just sipping from a beer and pushing himself.

"I love that little girl like you can never believe," Rone spoke.

Chance looked up and tilted his head. "I know. You'd make a great father, you know? You should work on that."

Rone felt his heart sink then. Not everyone was meant to have children. It was as simple and complicated as that. "Did she ask you about my girlfriend?"

Chance nodded. "She heard me talking to you about Jennifer a while back and wanted to know who that was. I didn't want to lie to her, but I told her she wasn't to worry because she is your baby and you'll always love her. I think she was worried about that. Did she talk to you about it?"

Rone sat beside his friend and took a breath. "Yeah. She seemed a little worried. I don't think I ever thanked you for naming me her God-father."

"You don't have to thank me. There were no other logical choices."

He smiled. "Yeah. You don't understand how much this means."

"I do. But there isn't anything to really understand. What I do know is I don't think you could love her anymore if she was your own. How are things with you and Jennifer? How did she react to the whole *her best friend hitting on you* think?"

"The same way you told me she would. Still, it almost broke my heart when she walked away."

"And?"

Rone took Chance's beer for a couple swallows before giving it back. "We worked things out—rather she confronted this woman who admitted to it. She was crushed."

"Bummer." Chance sounded genuinely sad. "I just can't believe this woman would throw away such a long friendship over a man—no offence."

"None taken. I know precisely what you mean. That friendship should have been able to withstand anything but how do you go back after that line is crossed?"

"Did you talk to Jennifer about children?"

"Where did that come from?" Rone asked.

"Sorry. I've been meaning to ask you that for a while and I kept forgetting so now that I remember...."

"You thought you would give me whiplash?"

Chance chuckled. "Did you?"

"No. Why?"

"I know you, Rone. You want kids and if this woman doesn't you shouldn't be investing in this relationship especially at your age."

Rone winced.

"It hurts. I get that. But Rone, you know I'm right."

"I know. Don't you think it's too soon to be asking her that? We just started dating and with everything that's been happening around us lately we haven't even had time to go on a second real date."

"When did you want to have that discussion? Two years into the relationship when you've invested enough time to be considered a legally married couple?"

"Damn. When you put it that way. But I love her, Chance. I love this woman more than I ever thought I would. I think, even if she didn't want children I'd still want her."

"I never thought of you with a woman like Jennifer. From what you told me she's unlike any woman you've ever been with."

"You mean she's black."

Chance shook his head. "Colour has nothing to do with it. You're happy Rone. I can tell. "I have some good news."

"Whiplash from the change of topics. Let's hear your good news."

"I applied for that fire captain position here. I was shocked when they called me back that same day. Did you have anything to do with it?"

Rone shrugged. "No. I haven't even had a chance to scratch my butt. Why? Did something happen?"

"I got it."

"That's fantastic! When do you start?"

Chance drained his beer. "In a week. I have to get Anne enrolled in school then I can focus on the job. This place is so peaceful. I can see why you like it here."

"There's that and the fact this is home."

"When do I meet this Jennifer woman?"

Rone chuckled. "I was supposed to see her later tonight."

"For a booty call?"

Rone laughed out loud then shook his head. "Maybe. But dinner first. She'll love Anne."

Chance nodded and went inside. Rone sat by himself a while longer thinking of the conversation about children. He knew then he could be happy without any of his own as long as it was with Jennifer. But he couldn't just assume she didn't want any.

That was a conversation he just had to have with her once things settled down.

Twenty-Two

Rone stood with his arms folded and shoulder against the window of the hospital room. He and Jennifer had finally talked Darlene into going home to at least shower and come back.

\She hadn't really slept in days and Jared volunteered to drive her home and bring her back once she was ready. Paul sat by the bed silently looking as if his world was ending.

"Should you get some rest too, Paul?" Jennifer questioned.

"I can't leave. This is my fault."

"I don't see how. These things happen, especially at his age and with the alcohol."

"But I should have been here," Paul insisted. "I should have..."

"You can say you shoulda done this." Rone added. "Or you coulda done that. No matter what, you can't change the past. That would be like un-ticking a clock."

"I didn't think I wanted to come back here for him," Paul spoke softly. "That's the part that will kill me if he dies. I shouldn't feel guilty—I mean, after all the things he's done to us. All the times he scared us with that shot-gun left me terrified. Darlene had a little bit more tolerance. We always thought he'd never do anything to hurt her. But I guess the joke was on us."

"This is not your fault, Paul," Jennifer said. "Darlene knew going in this was the way he was. She did it because she thought the same thing you did—he'd never turn on her, but you can't make deals with the devil and expect heavenly results."

Paul hauled in a noisy breath and nodded. "I know. What do we do now? I mean he's here and we have no idea what's going to happen. My life is falling apart right now I don't need this."

Jennifer looked up at Rone and he nodded.

"Paul, come with me," Rone said.

"What? Where?"

"Just take a breather. We're going to the vending machine and get you something to eat."

He stopped to press a kiss to Jennifer's head before leading Paul out the door and silently down the corridor to the machine. He dug around in his pocket for some coins and bought two cups of coffee and a couple chocolate bars. He shared his loot with Paul. and they sat in the waiting room. "When you said your life was falling apart, what did you mean?"

"I mean, my girlfriend left me and stole my car," Paul replied, sipping from his coffee. "I filed a report with the Colon County PD, but I don't think it's going to amount to anything. I loved her, Rone. I really, really did. Who am I kidding? I still love her now."

"Listen to me. There are no guarantees you're going to get your car back—hell there's no guarantees in love. But a human heart can only tackle one catastrophe at a time. Forget about this woman for a second and focus on your sister. She's here and when the world implodes, she'll be here at your side. Right now, she's falling apart. All that other stuff—not important. Got it?"

"But I..."

"No. Think about it all—what is more important to you? Some woman you met who doesn't return your love or the one woman who's always been there for you even when you do some stupid stuff—and trust me, you and Jared did some *stupid* stuff."

Paul turned to look at him. "One catastrophe at a time?"

"One catastrophe at a time."

The two men remained seated where they were for a while. Rone watched Paul and when he thought Paul was breathing like a regular person again, he suggested they head back. By the time they returned, Jennifer was sleeping in one of the chairs with her legs stretched out in front of her. He covered her gently with a blanket from the extra bed in the room and sat on the windowsill between two small flowerpots.

"I have to ask." Paul sipped from his cup. "Things between you and Jenny are serious?."

Rone watched her. Her face was so peaceful. She shifted, moaned and snuggled back into sleeping. "Yeah. I never thought I could love a woman like I love her, but it was just so damn easy."

"And she feels the same way?"

Rone nodded. "I think so. When she looks at me with those big, brown eyes, I melt.

I don't have to question how she feels about me. And you know, she never once asked me how much I made or how much I have in the bank."

Paul chuckled bitterly. "Mine asked me a week after we started dating. I don't make that much. I work overnight security and I guess that wasn't enough for her."

"Some women are just like that. When it comes to love you have to wander through the frogs of them to find the best of them."

"And you think you've found your best?"

"Yes." Rone didn't have to think about it. The answer was simple.

Darlene and Jared walked through the door then and Rone rose. "I'm glad you guys are back. I'm going to take sleeping beauty here home and make some dinner. You guys need anything?"

"No. You've done more than enough," Darlene replied and hugged him. "Thank you."

"I don't want to wake her but her back is going to kill her if she doesn't get into a bed for that nap."

Jared smiled. "You take your lady home. We'll call if anything changes."

Rone knelt in front of Jennifer. "Baby?" He called. Pushing up slightly, he kissed her lips, her bare shoulder and then her nose. "Baby? I want to take you home now."

"Rone?" She yawned. "Excuse me."

She covered her mouth and Rone smiled.

"Yes?"

"Did Darlene come back?"

"I'm right here, Jenny." Darlene told her. "Go home and sleep. Datsun told me you've been working both our shifts so you need the rest."

Jennifer sat up and smiled, rubbing her eyes. "It was nothing."

With their final goodbyes, Rone led Jennifer to his truck. "Chance and Anne are here."

"Oh! I forgot they were coming!" She touched her cheek. "Did they get settled? Do you know if Chance needed anything for the little girl? I have a few little things at my place—like toothbrushes and the like. I know moving to a new place is hard..."

"Nah, he's good. Think you would be up to a small dinner with us tonight?"

Jennifer nodded.

"Of course. This man means a lot to you.I should get some sleep first though. My muscles are starting to get sore from the lack of sleep."

Rone smiled and reached for her hand while keeping the other on the wheel. He kissed her fingers as he took the scenic route from the hospital to his place.

When they finally arrived at the ranch, Chance was playing with Anne in the front yard. The little girl was hopping along on her hopscotch. For a moment he simply stood there watching her but it wasn't for long. She turned and saw him then this bright, big smile spread her face. She walked from where she was playing to him and looked from him to Jennifer.

"Heya. Uncle Rone!" Anne waved. "Is this your girlfriend?"

"Yup." Rone scooped her up to kiss her. "Anne, meet Jennifer."

Anne extended a hand to Jennifer. "Nice to meet you."

"It's nice to meet you too." Jennifer smiled. "You're very pretty."

Anne giggled.

Rone knew then, Jennifer had made a friend for life.

"And this is Chance Efron." Rone motioned to his friend.

"Jennifer." Chance accepted her hand. "It's good to finally meet you."

"Same here. We should go inside." Jennifer motioned. "I don't mean to be rude, but I have to take a nap and Rone is going to make us dinner."

"Yeah. I taught him well—you know, not to burn down the joint!" Chance exclaimed.

Jennifer laughed.

"And don't worry about being rude. Rone filled me in on what's been happening around here. I have to say, lady you deserve a nap. Hell, you need a vacation." Chance pointed out.

She chuckled.

"Jenny, you're supposed to be on my side." Rone pouted.

Jennifer kissed his cheek and left them outside. Rone shook his head and carried Anne into the house with Chance close on his heels.

In the kitchen he placed Anne down over some cookies and milk. He then excused himself to talk to Jennifer before she had a chance to fall into the bed. When he made it to the bedroom, she was in the bathroom. He knocked on the door.

"Rone?" She answered.

"Can I come in?"

"Of course," Jennifer replied around a yawn.

In the bathroom she was standing by the shower with her clothes in a pile on the ground. "Want me to throw these in the washing machine for you? The last time you were here you left a pair of panties and a dress. They're in my drawer."

"I did? Sorry." She stepped into the tub and closed the door. "I didn't remember."

"It's all good. I washed them."

She giggled, opening the door to stick her head out and he laughed. "You washed my panties? Aww Rone Jennings you are the perfect man."

He bowed his head to hide his smile and slid the shower door wider to watch the water flow over her dark skin. He wanted to climb in with her but knew he shouldn't. Anne was downstairs, and he promised to make dinner. Still, he reached in and caressed a hand down her spine, over the curve of her bum and down her thighs. The water was warm, perfectly set to caress him as well as her.

"Don't start anything you can't finish, Mr. Jennings."

"I so can." Rone moaned. He rose, leaned forward and dropped a kiss to the center of her wet back. When she whispered his name and arched, he smiled. "Still, you're right. I should leave but I wanted to see you before you slept."

She turned off the water and faced him then. It was hard for Rone to meet her gaze and not stare at her beautiful breasts. While his hands skimmed her body, he inhaled deeply. "Sweet dreams?"

"Of course. They'll be of you."

His heart did a wonderful flip at her words, he just had to kiss her. There was no way he could walk from that room and not kiss her. The helplessness he felt sent a tremble through his being. Taking a breath, he pulled back and with a final smile, he exited the room leaving her to finish up and go to bed.

In the kitchen he began dinner of roast beef, baked potatoes and gravy with a side of vegetables.

"Where's Anne?"

"Sleeping. She's been running around all day. I took her riding and if I let her she'd stay out there all day. I had to tell her the horse needed a rest."

"Good. I can talk to you."

"Now I see what you see in her," Chance said. He rose, picked up the knife and cleaned and sliced some onions. "She has the same sense of humor you have."

Rone laughed. "Yeah, something like that."

"And she's beautiful," Chance added.

"Yes, she is."

Twenty-Three

Jennifer rolled over in the bed and sat up. It was getting dark outside and she hoped it wasn't too late. Rone had guests and she really didn't want to seem as if she was ignoring them. That would just be rude.

She found her clothes dried and folded on the loveseat so she quickly got dressed, used Rone's brush to do her hair as best she could. She was inspecting her handiwork when her stomach did a slight flip.

"No, no, no!" She muttered rushing into the bathroom.

Her body heaved and when she finally righted herself, it felt as though she'd thrown up everything she'd ever eaten. Rinsing her mouth, she wondered why that'd happened. Maybe it was the clam chowder she had earlier. She loved the stuff but it was never kind to her stomach.

Then again throwing up had been happening for a few days. That would mean, it couldn't be the chowder.

After rinsing her mouth a second time, Jennifer managed to take take a steadying breath before making her way downstairs.

"Rone?" Jennifer stuck her head into the kitchen. When she found no one there, she made her way into the living room where she found Chance watching a movie with Anne.

"Hi." She tugged her dress down a little.

"Jennifer!" Chance greeted happily. "Come on, join us through *Home Alone.*"

"I don't want to impose on your father daughter time." Jennifer waved at Anne who returned the greeting. "You seem so peaceful. Where's Rone?"

"He went into town for a bit." Chance explained. "And it's not an imposition. Come on, sit."

"You two want some popcorn?" Jennifer wanted to know.

"Yay! Popcorn!" Anne cheered. "Can I help you make it?"

Jennifer laughed. "Sure. If it's okay with your dad."

"Well, yes." Chance replied. "As long as you share."

"Yay!" Anne hugged him then scooted off the sofa. "Can you pause it daddy?"

"Sure baby." Chance paused the movie.

Jennifer took Anne's hand and walked her into the kitchen. Jennifer searched the cupboards and soon came up with a bag of corn to make the popcorn. She added a pot to the stove, added some butter and waited until it was hot. While she waited she placed Anne to sit on the counter.

"Okay, I want you to fill this bowl with corn." Jennifer instructed.

"This isn't how we make popcorn," Anne said. "Where's the bag from the store? All you have to do is put it in the microwave and then wait."

Jennifer laughed. "Well sweetie, this is how you make it from the corn. It's going to be delicious. You'll see."

Anne nodded but she didn't look convinced. So together they worked until Jennifer poured the corn into the pot and quickly covered it. When it began popping Anne flailed and giggled. Jennifer laughed at the child's happiness of each pop.

"How do we know it's finished?" Anne questioned.

"When we no longer hear the popping, it's all done!" Jennifer announced. "While that is going, we're going to need butter for the popcorn, right?"

"Right."

Jennifer scooped some butter into a small bowl and placed some salt in Anne's hand.

The little one poured the salt onto the butter and Jennifer put it into the microwave. By the time it was all melted the popcorn was finished. She dumped the popcorn into a large bowl, then showed Anne how to spread the butter over it.

With a little shake, it was ready. She dumped some in a smaller bowl, covered it and showed Anne how to shake it.

"Hi you two."

Jennifer looked up to see Rone standing there. She grinned.

"Uncle Rone, we made popcorn!" Anne pointed out.

"Awesome. I'll get some in a bit. In the meantime could you take some to your dad?"

"Sure."

Jennifer lifted Anne from the counter and placed her on the floor with the small bowl filled with popcorn. She walked gingerly from the room calling for her dad.

Suddenly Jennifer felt self-conscious as Rone stared at her with a smile.

Rubbing the back of her neck, she grabbed a handful of popcorn and shoved some into her mouth. It was a way to occupy herself, so she didn't say or do something stupid.

"You know I love you, right?"

She chuckled even as her heart did a strange flip. Her stomach didn't take too well to the smell of the popcorn either. She swallowed the lump in her throat hoping to settle her stomach, but her skin broke out into a cold sweat. "I know. Are you up to something Rone Jennings? This is how the confessions always start on the *Maury* Show."

"Er..." Rone laughed. "No, I'm not about to tell you I cheated and my baby may not be yours."

Jennifer giggled. "All right. Good. Go on."

"And anything I do for you it's not because I have to but because I want to—because I want to be a good man for you and because I love seeing you smile."

"Rone. What's wrong?"

He took a breath and stepped forward. In his hand was a small, white bag. He placed it on the counter and pushed it forward. Jennifer couldn't understand how she didn't see it before.

"What's in the bag?"

He tapped it with a large finger. "I know your birthday is in a few days and everyone else will be doting over you. I just wanted to—well...Open it."

His smile reassured her and she reached for the dainty bag. With a deep breath both to steady her racing heart and to quell the upheaval within her stomach, she pulled the light blue tissue paper from the bag.

Those she discarded carelessly behind her. She reached into the bag and pulled out a red, velvet box.

Her hand shook as she retrieved the box and lifted it to nose level. Slowly, she lifted the cover and she felt it the moment the ring took her breath away. It was silver with two pearl stones and an orange stone in the center she didn't recognize.

"It's not an engagement ring," Rone explained. "It's a promise ring."

"It's beautiful. What's this orange stone?"

"Alexandrite. It's your birthstone—your semi precious stone. Do you like it?"

Jennifer's eyes glazed with tears as she nodded her head furiously. Perhaps it was the emotions surging through her, but her stomach did another little lurch. She pushed the box at him and darted from the room.

"Jen? Jennifer!"

In the bathroom she slipped to her knees in time for her body to heave again as she threw up. When he finally caught up to her, she was panting and frowning as her throat burned.

"That wasn't the reaction I was looking for." Rone admitted.

"No. The ring is beautiful. I haven't been feeling well. Can you help me up?"

He took her arm and lifted her from the floor. While she rinsed her mouth, he flushed then turned to her.

"How long have you been feeling like this?"

"I'm not sure." Her body heaved again but when she doubled over the sink, nothing happened. "I mean, I thought it was the fact I hadn't been sleeping. At the hospital, I was a tad queasy but I just figured it was because I was, you know, at the hospital. . It happened earlier but I had some clam chowder today—it shouldn't still be bothering me, right?"

"We should go see Doc Sheppard?"

"Rone, sweetie. I think it's just my allergic reaction to the clam chowder or food poisoning. Nothing a good cup of tea and a good night's rest won't cure. Don't worry."

"I do worry. I love you. I'm supposed to worry." Rone pushed. "And it couldn't be the chowder if it happened before the hospital."

"Would it make you feel better if I go see Doc Sheppard tomorrow?"

Rone nodded.

Jennifer smiled and hugged him tightly. He kissed the side of her head and Jennifer never thought she could feel so loved by anyone. For a long while she allowed him to hold her. He never once complained or tried to get her away from him.

When she finally stepped back, it was to accept his kiss to her nose then her lips.

"I didn't put the ring on you yet."

She giggled. "I'll go get it."

"No need." He pulled the box from his pocket and she watched with baited breath as he extricated the ring from the velvet folds and picked up her hand. He slid it onto her ring finger then kissed it.

But hours later, Jennifer still wasn't feeling well. She tried eating supper but her stomach was not happy about it. Rone pampered her, put her into bed and turned on a movie so she could watch. 4+

Anne snuggled against her chest to watch the movie with her. Jennifer was so tired she didn't remember even falling asleep.

Rone stood by the door and watched two of the four people he loved most in the world sleep. The movie had long since ended and the television was playing static.

Though he didn't want to disturb them, it was getting close to Anne's bedtime and he wanted to spend some time with Jennifer in his arms. He carried Anne across the yard to the guesthouse and put her in her father's arms with a kiss to the forehead.

"Wait," Chance told him. "Let me put her down."

"Sure."

Chance left him alone and he stood by the window staring across the yard to the main house where Jennifer was asleep in his bed. He remembered the first time she slept over—the first time they'd made love. The bed smelled of her perfume for days afterward.

She was ill. There was something wrong and though she told him not to worry, how could he not? He loved her so desperately. Seeing her in any form of discomfort broke his heart.

"How is she feeling?"

Rone inhaled then turned. "She's sleeping now, but she's been throwing up. After sipping some hot water she settled down some."

"Since you're not thinking it, I'm going to say it."

Rone arched a brow and folded his arms across his chest. "Say what?"

"Down boy."

"Sorry. Didn't mean to sound all big-bad-wolfie just then. But say what?"

Chance laughed. "Are we sure she's not pregnant?"

"There's no way she's pregnant." Ronen chuckled. "She would know—wouldn't she?"

"Come on, Rone. I don't have to explain the bird and the bees to you right? You two have been—you know? Active?"

"Um...what are you six?" He rubbed the back of his neck as heat passed over his face. "Come on, you can say it."

"Don't make me!"

Rone laughed. "Jackass. Of course. But she's not pregnant. If she was the sickness would be in the morning."

"That's what you think. It differs with each woman, especially those going through the first trimester." Chance explained. "Anne's mother had both."

Rone's heart did a strange little twist and he walked by Chance to fall into the sofa. Resting his head back he groaned. "I didn't think about that. Okay—I'm not going to get ahead of myself. We're going to see Doc Sheppard tomorrow so we'll find out for sure."

"It's just a thought."

"Yeah, a very scary thought."

Chance sat beside him and Rone felt like he was going to cry. He'd wanted to have the baby conversation with Jennifer earlier but things didn't really work out as planned. He'd always wanted to be a father but now there was a possibility he was going to be one.

All of a sudden, he was terrified of the kind of father he would be. How could he be responsible for raising another human being? That certainly cannot end well—could it?

Cannot end well indeed.

"Don't put so much thought into it," Chance reassured him. "You would be a great father. I've seen you with Anne and I don't worry when I leave her with you. Well, actually, the only thing I worry about is you hyping her up on sugar then leaving me to deal with her."

Rone laughed. "That's what a God-father is supposed to do. Didn't you know?"

Chance muttered under his breath.

"Still, it's not the same." Rone huffed. "My own child I have to do the whole discipline thing and all that. I don't know if I can do that."

"Don't worry about that now. First you need to find out if she is pregnant. If not then you'd just be ripping your hair out for nothing. If she's pregnant then we can cross that bridge when we get to it."

"When did you become the voice of reason in this friendship?"

Chance chuckled. "Scary, huh?"

Rone laughed. "I need to head back. I want to be there when she wakes up."

Twenty-Four

Rone didn't sleep all night. He spent it holding Jennifer all through the night.

When she whimpered his name and snuffled into his body, he smiled and brushed is lips against her forehead. A couple of times during the night she woke up and he swore his heart would jump from his chest. But she hadn't thrown up—just used the bathroom and crawled back into his arms.

Morning couldn't come fast enough. The moment light began pushing its rays through the windows he was out of the bed calling Doc Sheppard.

"Good morning, darling," Jennifer whispered.

Rone bowed his head and smiled. "How are you feeling?"

"A little queasy. But I'm fine."

"I called Doc Sheppard. He should be here in an hour."

"Oh. I should get up and get washed. I don't want him coming and I'm funky."

Rone laughed. "Funky...okay then."

She pushed from the bed and when she stood, Rone saw it. She wavered on her feet. He rushed forward, catching her into his chest and helping her back to the bed. "Yeah. I'll help you with that wash up. Stay here."

Quickly, he rushed to the kitchen and grabbed one of the large bowls. He then proceeded to the bathroom and filled it with water.

Dumping some body-wash into it, he grabbed a wash-rag and made his way back to her side.

He dipped the rag into the water, wrung it out and proceeded to wipe Jennifer's body. He started at her neck, down between her wonderful breasts and over her stomach.

By the time he was through, his body was tense with arousal. But he simply kissed her lips, dressed her and pulled the sheets up to her neck.

He left her to make some tea for her and coffee for himself and when he was starting up the stairs again the doorbell rang. He turned back to let Doc Sheppard in and led the older man up the stairs.

"Jenny," Doc Sheppard greeted her.

"Hi, Doc."

"How are you feeling? Rone tells me you've been throwing up." He placed his medical bag by the bed and sat beside her.

Jennifer grinned up at the doctor. "Rone is just over-reacting. I think it was something I ate."

"And I told her it was better to be safe than sorry." Rone reiterated. "Once Doc gives you a clean bill of health or tell you it's just something you ate, then we'll stop worrying."

"He thinks I'm fragile." Jennifer frowned.

Doc Sheppard pressed a palm to her forehead then reached for his stethoscope. "It's a guy thing." He said, easing her top out of the way to press the stethoscope to her body. "Inhale deeply for me."

Rone stood by the window, arms folded across his chest holding his breath. He watched the doctor give Jennifer the once over before handing her a pregnancy test with a small container and pointed her to the bathroom. When he stepped forward to help her, Jennifer simply flashed him a look that simply told him to back off.

When she closed herself in the bathroom, Rone sat on the bed and faced Doc Sheppard. "So? What do you think?"

"It wasn't something she ate," Doc Sheppard said simply, packing up his bag. "She's pregnant."

"She's what?"

"You know? With child?" Doc Sheppard faced him and inhaled. "Rone, Jennifer is pregnant...why do you look like you've seen a ghost?"

"But I thought she can only have morning sickness. She's sick at nights too."

"Some women get it during the night, others in the mornings, others both. It all depends on the woman. I've been a doctor for thirty-two years. I know the signs."

"So why did you get her to take the test?"

"To confirm. Of course, I still have to run the test at the hospital."

Rone swallowed the lump in his throat and held his breath. It was a useless attempt to calm his racing heart.

Jennifer did the test and filled the container. She rinsed her hands and sat on the toilet seat staring at the test. What was she going to do?

It hadn't even occurred to her she was pregnant. Her and Rone loved each other but they hadn't once discussed children. She knew he loved Anne but what if that little girl was the only child he wanted?

There was no way she could saddle him with a child—he didn't deserve that. She had no money and barely had a roof over her head and a job.

If she was pregnant, she had to get a new place with what money?

Taking a breath, her eyes burned fiercely. She pressed her eyes closed. If she spun her savings just right she would be able to get a new place closer to the center of town and the schools.

She could get a few extra shifts at the diner, maybe pick up a second job somewhere. She'd have to make it work.

"Wait a second, Jennifer. Don't start freaking out. You're not pregnant. You can't be pregnant."

When she finally looked at the pregnancy test, her heart sank. The two blue lines contradicted her mantra.

She screamed.

"Jennifer?" Rone's shouted then barged in the door.

He slipped to his knees in front of her and cradled her face. "Baby?"

"What am I going to do?"

"What? What's wrong?"

"I'm pregnant."

"And my work here is done," Doc Sheppard said, reaching past Rone for the container. He tested the cork and dropped it into his bag. "I will have the results in a couple a days. Congratulations."

"Thanks Doc." Rone replied. "Thanks for coming."

Jennifer was still so shocked. She felt her body shaking even as Rone hugged her but she couldn't stop it. She held her breath, counted to ten silently, closed her eyes but nothing stopped it. "I'm sorry. I'm so sorry."

"Why are you sorry?"

"I didn't ask if you wanted a child. I should have been more careful."

"Baby, listen to me. I've always wanted to be a father. And protection falls to both of us. It was both our responsibility. I meant to talk to you about having a child, seeing where your mind was but things just kept coming up. I want children."

"You're not just saying that?"

Rone laughed. "No. I'm not just saying that. I'm thirty six, Jen. I said love you—and I mean it. Children kind of comes with that."

Her heart soared. She leant forward and pressed her forehead on his shoulder. "I'm so glad you said that. I was terrified you wouldn't want children or me."

"Not want you? Jennifer, how could I not want you? I've wanted you ever since I first laid eyes on you that day leaning on your car in the parking lot. Now I just need you."

She fell into his chest, wrapped her arms around his body and held on tight. The ring he'd slipped to her finger caught her eyes and she laughed softly, kissing the side of his head. "You promised."

"Yes, I did. But my heart outweighs all promises made. My heart wants you, Jennifer Cozel. And this baby is going to be the most beautiful, most loved, most perfect child."

"There's still a chance I'm not—the doc could be wrong."

Rone lifted his head and rose. Taking her hand, he helped her from the toilet seat and walked her back into the bedroom. "But he's not. I know he's not."

She chuckled. "And just to be sure—you're ready to be a father."

"More ready than you'll know. Now, stop worrying so much. Are you hungry?"

Jennifer giggled. "Breathe. I am not fragile—remember?"

He kissed her hand. "I'll try to remember that."

"Do you have any cornmeal?"

"Um..." Rone arched a brow. "Cornmeal?"

Jennifer nodded.

"No, why?"

"I'm craving some porridge."

"Says no one ever." Rone groaned.

Jennifer crinkled her nose. "Is it possible for you to get some for me? I will come with you and you can drop me off at the hospital to see the guys while you do that."

She noticed Rone's bows knitted together and knew he wanted to protest but when she set her lips in a thin line, he nodded.

"All right." He relented.

Twenty-Five

It took a while for her to climb out of Rone's truck because Rone wouldn't let her hand go. One kiss led to a second kiss then a third and a forth—

"Rone. You have to..."

"I know. I don't want to let you go—ever."

"I'm not leaving forever, darling. I'm just going to check on Darlene. Besides, someone has to tell your father he's about to be a grandfather."

Rone laughed. "He would love that, but are you sure you want to tell him already? I know women are kind of superstitious about telling anyone before the second trimester."

"Don't you want him to know?"

"Of course. I want it to shout it through a bullhorn while driving down Main Street." Rone grinned impishly. "Are you comfortable with me telling dad now?"

Jennifer grinned. She leaned in and kissed him quickly. "Yes. He's your father. And we both know Doc Sheppard isn't known for secrecy. It's better it comes from you."

"That is true."

They slipped into an easy silence once more while Rone caressed her hand.

Jennifer shivered. "Baby."

"Mm, I know." His voice cracked.

Rone dropped a final kiss to her hand then her lips. She watched him drive away before ducking into the hospital.

The smell of the place instantly made her want to throw up. It was the same nauseating scent she remembered well from the day she identified her father's body.

Now it was stronger, nastier to her.

Frowning, she stopped at the gift shop and got a pack of gum. She quickly shoved one into her mouth, bought it and some flowers and headed up to Martin's room.

The doctor was exiting when she arrived, so she stopped to ask him a few questions. Jennifer wasn't sure what she expected him to tell her, but the news wasn't good.

Lifting her chin, she walked into the room and hugged Paul, Jared then Darlene before handing the flowers to Paul.

"I spoke with the doctor." Jennifer sat in Jared's lap and wrapped an arm around his shoulder. She was feeling a little green around the gills but she tried to hide it. "Most of what he told me I didn't get but I think I have the basic jest of it."

"He got worse," Jared replied for Darlene. "He's not breathing on his own anymore and his organs, are slowly shutting down. Me now have to make a decision."

"I'm sorry." Jennifer pressed a kiss to the side of Jared's head.

"Jenny, it's like I just can't catch a break." Darlene whispered.

"I'm sure that's not true." Jennifer tried to pick her friend up. "Your dad drank all his life and smoked—none of this is your fault. Dee, this has nothing to do with breaks or luck."

"You know the sad thing?" Paul turned from the window and rested his back against the glass. "I don't feel bad letting him go. They say his brain is gone."

"I keep looking at his chest and seeing it rise and fall and have to constantly remind myself the machines are doing that." Darlene sobbed. "If he wasn't on them in the first place he'd be dead."

Rising, Jennifer sat on the arm of Darlene's chair and pulled her into a hug. It was always hard losing a loved one, even if they were horrid.

Darlene's father wasn't as bad as her own but it was still a loss. Her news of a baby seemed almost inconsequential in the grand scheme of things. She kept her news to herself and just be there for her friends. She looked at Jared and Paul then with new eyes. She saw the confused fear in their eyes and knew no matter what Martin had done to them—they loved him.

"I feel like I'm intruding. I should leave you guys alone."

"No," Darlene said. "I'm glad you're here. You said you had news."

"Yes, but it can wait," Jennifer replied. "I can tell you when you're not so worried."

"Are you sure?"

Jennifer cradled her friend's face. "I'm sure, my darling." She kissed her cheeks. "Now, I will be right outside that door until Rone comes and kidnaps me. I will be at his place or mine. Either way I'll be here for you. Now, you and your brothers have a decision to make and I'm going to let you make it."

"What if we make the wrong decision?" Darlene cried softly.

Her tears dripped hot against Jennifer's palms. "You won't. Just trust yourself and rely on your brothers. That's why they have those wide shoulders."

Jared laughed softly. "Thanks Jenny."

"You're welcome...I'll see you guys later?"

Darlene nodded but Paul and Jared rose to hug her. The hugs lasted a little longer than normal. But she didn't mind. At the end of each she cradled their faces. Stopping she dropped a kiss to Darlene's nose and excused herself. Outside the room she pushed air out her mouth trying desperately not to cry. It was as though she was losing a father all over again. It wasn't because Martin was good to her but because Darlene's heart was breaking and Darlene had been more than good to her. Darlene was the sister she never had.

"Jen?" Rone tilted his head.

"Rone..."

"What's wrong?"

"The doctor says Martin is gone. They have to make a decision to take him off the machines and it's killing them."

Rone held her tightly. "I'm sorry darling. I'm so very sorry."

"I'm fine. I'll be perfectly fine. Can you take me home?"

"Your home or mine?"

She smiled. "Mine. I still have to grab clothes and I really would like to cook some food for Darlene and the boys."

"All right. I'll drop you at your place." He conceded. "Then run into the station while you do that but if you need me, for anything, *anything* at all, all you have to do is call. You know that."

"I know."

Long after Rone left her, Jennifer sat on her bed, legs curled up before her hugging a pillow. For that moment, alone in her first home, she tried wrapping her mind around everything. She took the silence to breathe and pray.

"Come on Jennifer. You've grown leaps and bounds." She lectured herself. "You can take this and be happy. This man loves you. He will love your baby."

Pushing air out her mouth, she uncurled herself and walked to the mirror. She looked at herself, really looked. Finally, she settled on the thought she wasn't ugly. In fact, she was beautiful. She kept seeing Rone just lying beside her, staring at her.

"What?" she asked, his fingers trailing lazy circles around her belly button.

"You're so damn beautiful," Rone replied.

She blushed but lifted her chin. Turning one way, then the other she embraced her curves for the first time in her whole life. She even grabbed the pillow from the bed, folded it in half and stuck it beneath her shirt. It protruded horribly and looked nothing like a pregnant belly. Bursting into laughter, she pulled it out and chucked it back to the bed.

Whatever happened in the coming months, Jennifer knew she was loved. She was beautiful and both her and her baby were precious.

Justin and Chris were late, as usual, but Raymond was on time and sitting across from Rone in his office. Rone signed his last report and after he closed the folder, he realised his father was staring at him. Arching a brow, he took a breath, eased back in his seat and laced his fingers. "What?"

"Where's our Jenny?"

Rone made a face. "She's at her place. She's cooking—I think."

"Okay. So why this meeting?"

Rone took a breath. He rose and walked to the station on the far side of the office and poured himself some coffee. After he'd taken a drink he rested his bum to the counter and crossed his ankles. "I wanted to wait until Chris and Justin got here but I figure I should tell you first."

Raymond pushed forward in the chair, resting his elbows to his knees. "Tell me what?"

"You're going to be a grandpa."

Raymond went stiff in the chair. It was then Rone realized he probably should have eased into it.

"Dad...say something."

"I..."

"Dad. I just told you the woman I love is pregnant and all you can do is sit there and stare at me? Please. Say something."

"I..." Raymond cleared his throat. "I mean…"

"Damn it to hell." Rone muttered under his breath and turned for the door.

"Are you sure she's pregnant?"

"Yes." He turned to look at Raymond.

Another brief moment of silence followed before his dad jumped to his feet to do a little jig. Rone arched a brow and rubbed the back of his neck.

"Ah...dad?"

"Yeah son?"

"You're dancing." Rone laughed. "You haven't danced in years."

"I know." Raymond twirled around the room. "This is the best news I could get in my old age."

Rone laughed. "So, you're happy? You're okay with this—with Jennifer and me?"

"Of course, I am." Raymond paused to stare at Rone. "I've been trying to nudge you two together for a while."

Rone groaned.

"Now, you just have to make an honest woman out of her."

"I gave her a ring."

Raymond's eyes lit up. "Did she say yes?"

"Um—it was a promise ring." Rone replied.

"A promise ring?"

"Dad, what are you trying to say?" Rone asked.

"You young kids these days worry me." Raymond laughed. He sat. "A promise ring? Back in my day when you see a woman and you love this woman you give her two rings. Sometimes not even two—you just take her down to the old courthouse and *voila!"*

Rone sat. "Things were different back then. These days it's a lot more complicated."

"Oh please. Vector calculus is complicated." Raymond muttered.

"What does that even mean?"

"I mean." Raymond leaned forward. "There's nothing complicated about lobr. I saw your eyes at the diner when you saw her. I knew if you didn't sit on your hands and screw it up you could be happy together."

Taking another drink he stretched his legs out in front of him. "I'm thinking of asking her to move in with me. I just—I'm terrified she'll think I'm only doing it for the baby."

"Aren't you?"

"I'm not going to lie and say the baby isn't a part of it." Rone dragged a hand over his head. "When her face is the first one I see in the mornings, my day is unshakeable. I guess that's a selfish reason to want her to give up her apartment, her freedom."

"Son—you worry too much. You get that from your mother. If it's one thing I've learned from all my years with your mother, it's this. Women aren't complicated. All you have to say is *you're right* and when she tells you to take out the garbage, take out the garbage."

Rone grinned. "What if she's not right?"

"Say it anyways."

Rone said nothing. He merely sat back in his seat, sipping from his coffee.

"I have to run."

"But dad, you just got here."

"Yes. But I'm an old man. I like my routines." Raymond walked over to press a kiss to Rone's forehead before giving him a hug and headed out the door.

Rone finished his coffee and was grabbing his coat to leave for his patrol rounds when the phone on his desk rang. He pushed his hair back, silently debating if he should get a haircut then stuffed his head into his hat. Reaching for the door to exit leaving the phone ringing, he remembered Darlene and Jennifer and rushed back.

"Sheriff's department. Rone Jennings here."

"Rone...."

That drawl.

There was only one man alive who ever said his name with that prolonged *oh* and that short *N.*

He never thought he'd hear from that man again and he'd resigned himself to not having to face him.

That man broke Rone in ways he swore never to let anyone break him again.

"It's Matt."

Rone's hand shook fiercely.

"Rone?"

He swallowed the lump in his throat and bowed his head trying desperately to push the pain he was feeling away.

"Rone, please."

"What do you want from me?"

"I just want to come home."

"Matt, didn't you hear?" Rone asked. "You can't go home again."

Silence.

"I was hoping they were wrong."

Licking his lips, Rone stumbled around the desk to fall into his seat. He wrenched the hat form his head and hurled it to the desk. "It's a free country. Do whatever the hell you want."

"I can't come home unless I know you will welcome me." Matt's voice shook. "I know it's hard to believe but I—I know I haven't really been there for you and I know I've been a horrible person. But please Rone. Say you will be there."

"What happened Matt? The real world isn't being nice to you? I thought that was your home?"

"I deserved that. Some things have happened. I know you don't follow the news—you never have."

"What do you want me to say, huh Matt?"

"Say we can at least try."

"Fine—but I promise nothing."

Hanging up the phone before Matt could say anything else. Rone buried his face in his hand wondering where in the hell Beatrice was and why the call wasn't screen. He had enough crap on his plate, and he really didn't need to deal with Matt on top of it all. He was finally happy—finally with the woman of his dreams, a baby on the way and all the happiness he could ever crave.

Matt, your timing sucks—as usual.

Taking a breath, he grabbed his hat. He'd promised Anne a swim and some ice-cream, now he had to hurry through his rounds.

Twenty-Six

The news of Martin's death came just after lunch on Jennifer's birthday. She didn't feel much like celebrating. She stayed with Rone, allowing him to dote on her for a little before having to go do what a sheriff had to do.

Rone was at the hospital and had sent *the boys*—Chance, Justin and Chris over to sit with her until he could get home. She buried her face into Chance's chest happy Anne wasn't there to see what was happening.

Justin and Chris volunteered to take the little girl on a ride while the adults dealt with the news. Darlene sounded shaken on the phone as though she couldn't believe her father was really gone.

Though Jennifer wanted to rush to her friend's side, another round of nausea made it almost impossible to go very far from a place with a toilet.

The scent in the hospital would only make it worse. Instead, she waited patiently while the day dragged on and on.

As the Sheriff, Rone had work to do when someone died in his town and she understood that. It didn't keep her from missing him terribly.

When he finally got home, she curled up on the sofa in his arms. Neither of them spoke much—just stayed where they were, holding each other.

Life was definitely too short.

Morning came with a flurry of activities; from Rone's squad car breaking down and had to be towed, to Darlene waking up screaming for her father.

Still, Jennifer managed to keep it together and help everyone get on their way. Once she was finally alone, she sipped on some unsweetened Peppermint until her stomach settled down before facing her own day.

She then spent most of the day running around town picking up ingredients and the like for the dinner she wanted to cook for Darlene and her brothers.

She wanted to invite her own brother, but truth be told he was a stranger. They were going to have a nice dinner, sit down and relax before the hectic rush of planning a funeral began.

Hurrying down the stairs, as the elevator was out again, she walked into Mosley's office.

"Jennifer! How are you?"

She grinned. "I'm good. I'm having a dinner tonight in my place can I borrow some chairs?"

"Sweetie, of course. How many people?"

"Well." Jennifer stopped to list people off on her fingers. "Rone, Darlene and her two brothers, Chance and Anne, me, of course..."

"Why don't you use our party room?"

She eyed him. "We have a party room?"

Mosely laughed and grabbed some keys from the hook by his desk. "Come on. I'll show you."

She followed him down a corridor, past the laundry and down a couple steps. He opened a large door leading into a room that was a pretty decent size. It wasn't the Ritz but it looked good. "How much is this going to cost me?"

"Don't be a complete goon, Jenny. As long as you cook your own food and you clean up after yourselves, you can have it for free for tonight. It's not booked anyways so it was only going to sit here."

Jennifer hugged him tightly. "Thank you! Wait...how am I going to get all the food from my place down here? The elevator isn't working!"

"Don't fret *mon Cherie.*" He grinned at her. "The tech is coming in about...." There was a loud holler from the front and Mosely grinned. "There he is. We'll have the elevator fixed in a jiff!"

"Good. That's very good because if Rone ever finds out I'm lugging stuff around, he's liable to blow a gasket."

"Why is that?"

"I'm pregnant."

"Oh!" Mosely cheered. "That's wonderful news! Congratulations!"

Jennifer laughed and accepted his happy hug.

"All the more reason to celebrate!" Mosely beamed.

"It's not really a celebration. Martin died yesterday so I just wanted to cook the family something. Nothing's better than a nice home cooked meal, right?"

"Right. I heard about that..."

The tech shouted from the front again.

"I'm comin! Keep your panties on!" Mosely yelled. "Some people are so impatient."

"I have two other calls behind you so if you're not going to hurry up I can go and come back!"

"No!" Jennifer flailed. "No. Go I'll lock up and bring you the key. Hey, if you're not doing anything tonight—you wanna come by?"

"I sure will. I'll see you later, sweet'ums."

Nodding, Jennifer watched him leave then turned to inspect the room a little more closely. When she was fully alone, she checked, she did a flail, a happy twirl and tried to kick up her heels. She only succeeded with a sense of wanting to be sick.

"Oh no!" She locked the door then motored into the laundry room. She doubled over the sink and heaved. "I swear, you'd better be a perfect child." She rubbed her stomach, inhaled and turned on the tap to flush the sink out. Once it was clean, she rinsed her mouth and made her way, slowly, back to her apartment.

It'd been a while since she'd cooked for a group of people. But it was like riding a bike.

Soon she had the chicken for Anne frying nicely, the rice and peas simmering, the jerk chicken in the oven seasoned to perfection and ready to go, the juice cooling, the wine chilling and some beer in a cooler on ice.

The first person, Jared, showed up early with a bottle of wine and together they carried things down to the party room on the first floor. True to his word, the elevator was working and by the time Paul and Darlene showed up, they had the party room decorated, food set out, tables set and music playing softly.

When Rone and Chance arrived with Anne, Rone quickly had her sitting down while he hurried back to the apartment to grab the last of the things.

"How are you?" Jennifer asked.

"Not sure," Darlene replied. "I feel like something huge is off my shoulder because now he's not suffering anymore. Is it bad that I think he just gave up?"

Jennifer hugged her friend tightly. "No. I don't think so. But you can't fault him. The woman he loved was gone and he hadn't been the same since then."

"He blamed himself, you know?" Darlene explained. "I told him it wasn't his fault but he said he should have made more out of his life so he could afford all the best treatments for her. I get his logic I just don't understand it."

"Tonight, is for family." Jennifer nodded. "We're going to sit around and take a break from all the bad things and all the drama and the unrequited loves..."

"Unrequited loves?" Darlene asked.

Jennifer laughed. "Not me. Not anymore. Rone loves me dearly and was very happy when he found out I was pregnant."

Darlene's eyes widened. "Pregnant? You?" She then dove into Jennifer's arms, hugging tightly. "Oh lord! Congratulations!"

Jennifer laughed harder, holding her friend in her arms.

"Congratulations?" Jared questioned. "What happened?"

All eyes were on her now as Rone walked through the door then. Jennifer giggled and waved to him. Rone walked to stand beside her.

"I take it we're telling them?" Rone questioned.

"What? Tell us what?" Chance and Paul chorused.

"We're having a baby." Jennifer explained.

The room erupted in a big cheer that Anne covered her ears, Rone picked her up and Jennifer wondered how this news would affect her. She hadn't thought of it before but Anne and Rone were close.

Damn it.

But Anne said nothing, and Jennifer made a mental note to talk to the little girl later. It was important she didn't think the new baby would take Rone away from her.

"Well, this calls for a toast!" Darlene said, wiping her eyes.

"Orange juice for me!" Jennifer reminded them.

Rone ate while everyone else talked. Though he tried not to let Matt's call bother him, he just couldn't help it. For a moment all he could think of was the day Matt left and the hurtful things he'd said.

That was until Jennifer touched his thigh gently and kissed his lips. He had to take a breath and pull himself together. It was good to have a dinner like this one to take their minds off the hard days he knew were coming.

The funeral wasn't going to be easy, especially for Darlene and he really didn't want Jennifer stressed out.

"You okay?" Jennifer asked when dinner was over and they all sat around playing dominos. There weren't enough room at the table for Rone to play in the first round so he was waiting until someone lost before he joined in. He pulled Jennifer into his lap and wrapped his arms around her. He kissed the side of her head, her nose then finally took her lips.

"Yeah. I'm fine. Something happened at work but we can talk about it later."

"It's obviously bothering. Let's talk."

He kissed her nose. "No. Not yet."

Anne walked over to them then and Jennifer picked her up to sit in her lap. Rone felt his heart soar so high then it was almost as if he was flying. He reached forward to brush his lips against Anne's forehead.

"Uncle Rone?"

"Yeah, baby?"

"You're having a lil' baby of your own, huh?" Anne asked.

"Yes. How do you feel about that?"

"Can I play with the baby?"

"Not for a while." Rone smiled. "When the baby comes, he or she will be really tiny."

"Oh." She said sadly.

"But when the baby is older, they're going to need a big sister." Rone explained to her. "What do you say?"

"When the baby is older?"

Rone nodded. "Yes, but in the meantime, you can visit the baby and help us feed the baby. Would you like that?"

"OooOooo!" She dragged out. "Yes, please."

Rone laughed softly.

"Can we still get ice-cream?" Anne wanted to know.

"Of course, Peanut. Of course."

Rone hugged her and moaned in disappointment when Jennifer climbed off his lap.

"Anne, how would you like some alone time with Uncle Rone?" She questioned.

"You mean it?" Anne asked.

Jennifer nodded.

Anne beamed. "Yes, please."

"I tell you what. If you go with Uncle Rone, there's some ice-cream in the fridge. It was my favorite as a child. It's butterscotch."

"I've never had it," Anne said, tilting her head.

"That's okay. You can try it. If you don't like it, there's also chocolate."

"Okay! Come on, Uncle Rone!"

Anne was tugging at him, but he took a moment to mouth, "thank you" to Jennifer.

She smiled and blew him a kiss.

He allowed Anne to drag him toward the fridge.

Cowboy Lullaby

Twenty-Seven

The days blended into one. From burying Martin to having a dinner so Rone could meet Michael, it was a good time. Darlene was back at work and Jennifer's tummy was getting larger. One night she laid in Rone's arms, shirtless and eyeing her stomach.

"What's wrong?" Rone asked.

"It's like there's nothing in there. But there is a little person growing in there."

"That's a good thing, right?"

"A very good thing. It's just so—it makes me feel so insignificant."

"But it is more than significant. Jennifer, you're about to have a baby—to be a mother. Do you know how beautiful that makes you to me?"

Soon two months had passed, and life was beginning to take on some normalcy. Jennifer worked as much as she could to Rone's horror. He would stop by the diner a few times during her shift to check in on her. At first she found it cute but after a while she wanted to strangle him. When he finally left, Raymond showed up.

"You know. I love you and your son dearly but I'm not fragile," she explained. *"I'm pregnant. There's a difference."*

"We know that—I mean I know that. Sit with me for a second."

"Raymond."

"Please?"

Pushing some air out her mouth, she sat in the seat. Only the booth was squeezing her stomach some. She turned her body slightly and rested her elbow on the table. "Okay, I'm sitting."

"Okay. Rone worries about you because he's a man. When the woman we love is carrying another life we love, we try desperately to make sure everything is perfect. Yes, I know women don't want us doing that all the time but it's in our nature."

"And you're babying me because you're a soon to be grandfather."

Raymond nodded. "Sorry. This will be my first grand-child and I'm a little excited."

"Don't be sorry. I understand."

Jennifer pulled her mind from that conversation and tried focusing on what was happening at that moment. The drive to Ohand was a strangely long one. It was longer than it really should have been but Jennifer had to pee so often. "I'm sorry but I have to go again," she whispered to Rone.

He chuckled.

"It's not funny."

"Yes, it is—not the fact you have to go again but the adorable look on your face when you say it." Rone pulled the car into a gas station and was leaning over but Jennifer bolted from the car and dashed into the diner beside it.

"Can I use your bathroom?" she asked.

The pimple face kid behind the counter frowned at her. "The bathroom is for paying customers."

"Look kid." Jennifer leaned against the counter and peer at him. She really didn't have time to argue because she really had to go. "I'm pregnant. I only asked to be polite."

She glanced around and found the sign for the bathroom and turned for it.

"You can't go back there!"

"Call the cops!" She shouted over her shoulders.

Who did he think he was? Hurrying, she used the bathroom and washed her hands. After a quick glance at her reflection and a second to fuss over her hair, she made her way back out to the front.

"This punk didn't tell you to buy something because I used the bathroom, did he?" She glared at the kid who took a step back.

"Nah. I was craving chocolate."

Jennifer grinned. "I thought I was the pregnant one?"

Rone kissed the side of her head then accepted his change. "Here, I thought you were a caramel and chocolate kind of woman."

He handed her a chocolate bar. After wishing the kid a good morning, she allowed Rone to lead her from the diner by resting a hand against the small of her back. Once they were settled in the truck once more, she rolled down her window and stuck one hand out while the other shove sweet chocolate and caramel into her mouth.

"I wanted to talk to you about a part of my life I swore I'd never think about again," Rone spoke.

Jennifer blinked, retracted her arm and wound the window up. "Okay."

"I told you about Matt," Rone said.

Jennifer nodded.

"Growing up we swore we'd be the next country stars. I mean, we were going to be the next Brooks and Dunn—take over the world. We would play anywhere they'd would let us. And of course we were under aged so not many places would let us. One night we were playing at the diner—before Datsun bought the place. We were too young to actually play clubs. There was a record producer there and he wanted to talk to us. I had to make curfew. Matt promised he'd talk to the agent and let me know what's happening."

"Sounds right."

"He spoke to the producer alright. He told him he was responsible for everything—even the songs I wrote. Because of that the producer wanted to develop him as a single act not as a duo. He was a year older than I was and I was seventeen at the time, so it was easier for them to wait for Matt rather than both of us."

"I'm sorry, sweetie."

"Yeah. Matt skipped town, made it Nashville and never turned to see how I was doing. I went off to become a cop. I mean if that was indicative of what the music business was like I didn't want anything to do with it. He started calling me recently."

"Who?"

"Matt."

"What does he want?"

"I don't know. He said he wanted to come home."

"What does that have to do with you?" Jennifer asked. "You don't own the town."

Rone smiled. "Apparently, he needs me to forgive him before he can set food back in town."

"Um…"

"I don't think I get it either." Rone sighed. "He stole a dream from me. How can I get pass that?"

"Baby, pull over."

She watched Rone checked his mirrors and pulled to the shoulder of the road. Jennifer turned in her seat as much as her seatbelt would allow. She took his hand and kissed the back.

"Listen," she said, softly. "I know what it feels like to have someone steal a dream. And since I've met you, I've learned to let it go and build new ones. I realized that I couldn't hold on to that hate and love you—do you understand?"

"I think so."

"I couldn't do both. The hate I felt for my father would have killed any light your love gave me and that scared me. Hate is a horrible thing. It swallows you and spreads throughout your core and it eats you alive."

"Is this your round-about way of telling me I have to get over it?"

Jennifer tilted her head and dropped a chaste kiss to his lips. "Baby, look how much its eating you up. What would it hurt letting him come home and seeing if you can get that friendship back? Besides, he's probably in pain why he wants to come home. Just don't do anymore business with him."

Rone smiled. "You are so smart."

Jennifer flipped her hair. "Well, you know." She laughed softly. "I'll think about it and let you know, okay?"

She nodded.

Rone sat beside Jennifer in the lawyer's office and waited. She hadn't said so much as a word since they were seated to await the lawyer's arrival. Though she clutched his hand, and he could feel her tremble, he respected her need for silence.

Finally, there was a click behind them, and the door opened to admit a man.

Barry Lowe was a slender man who wore suits that were at least two sizes too big over his skinny frame. There was a slight hunch to his back, and he walked, lifting one foot and somewhat dragging the other.

His sunken in, dim eyes were shaded by wire-rimmed glasses worn over a long nose. His hairline had receded so far back all he had was a slight line of hair around the sides and back of his head with liver-spots on the exposed flesh at the top.

"I'm sorry to keep you waiting." His voice was raspy as he closed the door behind him and made his way around the desk. "But it seems every fire that could be started here today has been."

He placed the folder he'd been clutching under his arm on the desk before taking his seat and opening the file. He peered at Jennifer then at Rone. "I have to ask you Ms. Cozel if you are giving permission for this gentleman to be here with you at this time."

"Yes," Jennifer replied without hesitation, squeezing Rone's hand.

Rone lifted the hand to his lips and brushed his lips against the soft flesh.

"Your name is?" Brian questioned.

"Rone Jennings."

"Sheriff, Rone Jennings." Jennifer corrected.

Rone smiled.

Barry scribbled on a notepad in the file and took a breath. He laced his fingers then leant in slightly to eye both of them like a lawyer—with beady, tired eyes.

"Your father retained us to handle some funds he came into when his wife died. Since she died of natural causes, the law stated he was to get two hundred thousand dollars from her life insurance with an added one third of the rest. What is left over after should have been divided equally amongst her children. I am not sure what your father was doing with the funds from the time of your mother's death until he retained us but upon his death he's asked the following."

Brain consulted a piece of paper in the file, cleared his throat then pushed the glasses so he could look through them. "Your mother's life insurance paid out the sum of three hundred and seventy-five thousand dollars. Your father has not taken his share and since he is deceased what is left is yours."

"What?" Jennifer asked. "That's can't be right. Are you sure we're talking about the same man here? The same man who would get upset if I ate anything in the fridge?"

Brian pulled his glasses down to the bridge of his nose once more. "He was a son of a bitch, wasn't he? I've dealt with him since the day of your mother's death and he hadn't been easy to deal with. Still, even if he didn't state this in his will, the money would legally be yours. You are his child. I guess what I am asking is, do you wish to have this money, or do you wish me to sign it over to the state?"

Rone could hardly believe what he was hearing. When Jennifer looked at him questioningly, he waited for her question. But it never came. Instead, he saw her square her shoulders and lifted her chin.

"I'm pregnant, Mr. Lowe." She told him, pride in her voice. "While I won't be taking care of this child alone, raising said child will be pricey. I'd like to go back to school and set aside a little fund for the baby. I'll not put pride before that dream. I guess what I'm trying to say is, with the hell he's put me through it's the least he can do."

"Very good." Brad cleared his throat. "I will need you to sign some papers and once those are finished we will cut you a certified check for your funds."

Rone left Jennifer alone then and waited for her in the waiting room. His mind was still going a mile a minute with what just happened. Jennifer was three hundred thousand dollars richer. But that wasn't what made him float on air—he didn't need the money.

What made him absolutely gush was the fact she knew he'd be by her side for the baby. She believed him and trusted him to keep his word.

At that moment she was so sexy to him, so unbelievably a woman, it took everything in him not to kiss her right in the office.

But before he could do that, he had a phone call to make. He'd been sitting in the waiting room clutching his cell phone in his hands trying to think of happy things rather than what he was about to do.

Still, he had to get it done before Jennifer came out. He didn't think he'd be able to hold it together and he didn't want her to see him break.

He searched through his phone for the number and dialed it. A part of him didn't expect an answer. But on the second ring, Matt did pick up.

"It's Rone."

"Hi."

"You can come home, Matt." Rone told him. "There are a few more people in my life right now but you can stay at my place."

"Do you mean that?"

"Why is this so important to you? Why after all these years?"

Matt cleared his throat. "Would it be enough to say I've missed you?"

"And I'd say you're full of shit."

"I've learned the hard way that not all who say they are my friends truly are. You were my friend Rone, and I hurt you in the worst possible way. I just want to try making up for that."

"Let me know when you get here. I'll pick you up at the airport."

"Thank you."

"Don't thank me. When you meet my girlfriend, you thank her."

He hung up then and hung his head.

"Rone?"

Shoving the phone into his pocket, he stood to see Jennifer approaching. A smile he conjured from somewhere deep spread his lips and he wrapped an arm around her hips. They made their way out the door into the Ohand County sunlight before he said anything.

"How do you feel about this?"

"I think in a perfect world, I would tell the lawyer to bury this money with my father. But if I'm to be a mother, I have to start putting my child ahead of myself."

"Our child."

"Yes...I'm sorry. *Our* child." She amended. "This money will make a way. I don't want to depend on you for my life and I've always wanted to go back to school. Molly over by the high school said I'd make a great teacher."

"Yes, you would. There's hope in your voice, Jennifer. I love hearing it."

She beamed at him. "Me too." Stepping closer, she snuggled into his chest, tucking her head beneath his chin.

"Anything else you wanted to do while you're here."

She remained silent as though thinking about his question then stood back to kiss his chin. "Can we have lunch together? Just you, me and maybe the sunlight somewhere. I don't want to go home yet."

"Are you feeling up to it? I know you've been feeling better lately but I don't want to push it."

She squeezed his hand. "I'm fine. All I need right now is to be with you."

"Of course, Sweetie. We'll stay here as long as you need."

She kissed him but he wasn't satisfied. Wrapping his arms around her back, he brought her into his chest and kissed her soundly.

When she moaned, he pulled back.

"Any place you recommend?" Rone asked.

"Yes. There's this restaurant on the water." She explained as he opened her door. She gripped his shoulder and climbed into the truck. "It's beautiful there."

Rone smiled at her and closed the door. By the time he climbed into the truck he was feeling lighter and less worried about what was coming. He reached over and tangled the fingers of his free hand with one of hers and listened to her directions as to where to go.

Twenty-Eight

It didn't take long to find La Cabeza. Jennifer remembered the way as if it was drawn on her brain. At the door, she stopped, her heart raced inside her chest. Rone's gentle hand against her lower back caused her to look up.

He caressed the area gently.

"We don't have to do this," Rone said, softly against her ear.

She lifted a hand and caressed the side of his face with a smile. "I know. But I'm tired of being afraid. And this is the last step to complete freedom."

"All right, my darling." He kissed her head, wrapped an arm around her hips and stood by her side. "When you're ready."

Feeling his strength, she took her first step into La Cabeza.

The restaurant on the inside was just as beautiful as she imagined. Hardwood floors, chairs with gold trimmings and potted plants adorned the room. Soft music played and the sounds of cutlery moving across plates made her feel as if she was at home.

She didn't want to stay inside though—she wanted to sit on the patio.

"Table for two?" The host questioned.

"Can we have a table on the patio?" Jennifer spoke up.

"Of course. Right this way."

Her knees were water as she followed. She knew if she fell back Rone would be right there.

His strong hand had moved from the small of her back and upward, close to her neck. He helped her with her chair before sitting. Jennifer sat across from Rone on the patio and took a breath.

Ever since she was a little girl she would walk by the restaurant and watched the young women sitting on the patio.

They were so stylish as they chatted away. Sometimes they would spare her a look leaving her feeling useless and alone. She always wanted to sit on the patio just to see what it would feel like from the other side.

As she sat there and looked over at Rone, it all seemed so insignificant. She'd gotten so much better having him as well as his friends who'd welcomed her with open arms. She smiled.

Their orders were taken, and she sipped on a chilled glass of fruit juice.

Her stomach didn't feel as hinky as it did before, and she'd gone through the last few days without throwing up. She even managed to work a few short shifts at the diner. Datsun fussed over her, something about Rone's wrath if he didn't take care of her.

Looking over at Rone, she was the luckiest woman in the world. He was beautiful and so kind. "You want to know what I think?"

"What's that?" Rone asked.

"You're my reward for the hell I went through as a child."

"You think I'm good enough to be your gift?"

She chuckled softly. "I think, Rone Jennings—you are the most wonderful gift."

He caressed the side of her face. "I love you."

Jennifer felt the warmth of those words flow through her to her core. "You love me..." she whispered.

"With all my heart."

"Sometimes I lie awake beside you while you sleep, and I reach out to make sure you're breathing. Other times I would poke you and close my eyes, count to ten and open them again to see if...if..."

"I'll disappear."

"I love you."

His hand left her face when the waitress arrived with their meals. She didn't touch her food though but watched him. For the first time in forever she could relax fully. The man across from her loved her and she no longer had to worry about it.

Each time he thought someone would hurt her he was right there, holding her hand and making sure she wasn't in any pain.

Each time he touched her or smiled at her or stared at her all was right with the world again.

"Rone?"

"Hmm?" He set his glass back on the table.

"Marry me."

Rone choked.

"I'm sorry. I didn't mean to just throw that out there." Jennifer used her napkin to dry his lips as he coughed.

"What did you say?" He sputtered.

"I didn't mean to just..."

He gripped her hand. "No, no, before that."

"Marry me."

"Don't ask me that if you don't mean it." Rone warned her. "Those aren't words I take easily."

"I'm serious."

"Then say it again—ask me again." Rone eased forward.

"Will you marry me?"

Rone smiled. "Of course."

"Are you sure? You didn't think about it. You just said yes."

Rone moved around the table to frame her face. "Think about it? Are you insane woman? When a beautiful, talented woman who loves you beyond reason ask you to marry her—you don't think about it. Only a fool would and I'm no fool."

She didn't mean to be cry but the tears toppled hot down her cheeks. He caught them on his large fingertips then kissed her. She allowed her body to fall into his chest and wrapped her arms around his neck. "I don't want to be scared anymore and you make me stronger than I've ever been. You love me, Rone and it feels so damn good to be loved by you."

"You've just made me happier than I ever thought I could be—do you understand that?"

Jennifer had no words. She lifted her face to the ceiling in her attempt at quelling her happiness so she would stop crying. People in the office were beginning to stare so she beamed happily. "He said yes!" She cheered. "I asked him to marry me and he said yes!"

Applause filled the room. Rone pulled her into his arms, hugging her until she squealed happily.

Finally, they could settle into eating. There were no rings exchanged because who ever heard of an engagement ring for a man? She grinned at the thought and shoved a piece of chicken into her mouth.

"I have an idea," Rone said.

"Okay. I thought I smelled fire."

Rone chuckled. "Smart ass."

"You know you love my ass, so stop playin'," She teased.

The smirk he gave her took her breath away and she shivered. "What's your idea?" Jennifer questioned.

"We passed a bed and breakfast on our way here. Why don't we spend the night?"

"Are you doing this because you think I am tired and shouldn't sit through the ride home?"

Rone shook his head. "No. I just want to do something wonderful. Besides, I'm tired and don't think I'll survive the ride home. I haven't been sleeping at nights."

"Why is that? Why didn't you say something?"

"Well, I spend the nights staring at the ceiling wondering if I'm cut out to be a father—no I'm not having second thoughts. I'm just scared I'm going to mess this kid up."

"You're not going to mess this kid up." Jennifer whispered. "You will be an amazing father. Now, we both can't be sleep deprived."

"Yes ma'am."

The bed and breakfast seemed to do Jennifer well. For the first time in a long while she relaxed and wasn't worried about anything. During her sleep she would whisper Darlene's name but other than that, she didn't seem overly exhausted as she was before.

That night before bed, he climbed into the tub with Jennifer, holding her into his chest and caressing her stomach. It was hard to believe there was a whole person growing in there.

Back in town, reality swarmed in on them again. Still, Jennifer spent some time with Rone at his place. When she left them, he sat back with his father, sipping a beer.

"Didn't think you were coming back," Raymond said. "You were supposed to go there for the day. It's two days later."

"Jennifer and I needed some time to ourselves." Rone replied. "She's been overdoing it and with the stress of her father's will and all that—I wanted to spend a little time with her—just her."

"I hear that." Raymond leaned back in the chair until it creaked then stared out across the vast front yard. Chance was busy chasing Anne around with the hose. The little girl was giggling. "She's just a beautiful child."

Rone couldn't disagree with that at all. He was trying to spend as much time with her as he could and so far, she seemed to understand the new baby wouldn't replace her. He lifted his legs to the porch railing while sipping from the bottle.

"Where is Jennifer?"

"She went over to Darlene's," Rone replied. "I still can't believe Darlene is going to live in that place. But she's strong."

"Strength nothing." Raymond murmured. The truth is, she needs a place to live. She can't really stay at Jennifer's old place forever and its now up to her to make good memories in the house. Besides, its paid for—no mortgage."

Rone wasn't sure that was even possible. "How many times were you called to that place when you were sheriff? Then give me a rough estimate of how many times you thought Sawyer was called out there."

"Too many to count."

"And since I've started here before Martin died." Rone pushed. "I was called there eighteen times. Megan was called four. That place needs an exorcism."

"It's not all bad—I'm sure it wasn't all bad. All she has to do now is focus on the good times she had there."

Like that's possible.

He didn't voice his disagreement. Rone merely turned his head to look at his father. "Dad, you were right about her."

"Her?"

"Jen."

"So, it's Jen now?" Raymond smirked. "Don't like Jenny, huh?"

Rone groaned. "Would you grow up?"

Raymond laughed. "I can read people, son. You don't work as a cop for as long as I did and not pick up a few things. I'm just glad you put yourself out there with her."

"It took some work, let me tell you."

"What have I always told you?" Raymond asked. "Nothing worth having comes easy."

"Right." Rone nodded. "Something happened while we were in Ohand."

"Sounds serious."

"It kind of is." Rone thought of the enormity of being someone's husband—of being someone's father. He shivered in anticipation but couldn't help the smile to pass over his lips.

"Um…you gonna sit there smiling like a fool or are you going to tell me?"

"She asked me to marry her."

Raymond's eyes widened.

"I know. I should have asked her because it's not manly to have..."

"Rone Jennings did I not teach you anything?" Raymond demanded. "Manly has nothing to do with it. She just beat you to the punch, that's all.

"Yeah."

"And you said?"

"I'm no fool." Rone chuckled. "I said yes. I'll never be able to find another woman like Jennifer and I'm not about lose that because I'm scared of this next step. She's about to be the mother of my child."

"How do you feel about that?" Raymond cleared his throat. "We haven't had a chance to sit down and talk since it happened."

"How do you think I feel?" Rone took a breath and tried stopping the smile creeping to his lips. He failed. "I'm ecstatic. Sometimes I get scared but its expected."

"When your mother told me she was pregnant with you I almost freaked." Raymond admitted. "I mean, I didn't know the first thing about being a father. Both my parents were already gone. I didn't have anyone to help me there and your mother's family—well they thought she could do better."

"I'm sorry."

"Ah." Raymond batted a wrist at Rone. "She could you know?"

"She could what?"

"Do better."

"Dad..."

Raymond held up a hand to stop Rone's speaking. "I knew she could. But she loved me. It didn't matter what her family thought or wanted."

"Luckily, I don't have the family issue with Jennifer. I know she loves me though. Aside from the fact she tells me I can tell whenever she gives me that look. It's a look that fills me with warmth."

"I know that look very well. I miss it from your mother."

Rone shifted so he could hug his father. "She's here. I promise."

"I know, son. I'm going to make us some dinner."

"I have to head into the..." He stopped as the phone began ringing. His father stressed his dinner comment by rising and Rone followed him into the house. While Raymond headed for the kitchen, Rone picked up his cell phone from where it was sitting on the charger.

"Sheriff Jennings."

"Rone—it's Matt. Can I trouble you for a pickup at the airport?"

"You're here already?"

"Yes."

"All right. I'll be there. Gimme half an hour." Hanging up he grabbed his keys and entered the kitchen. "Dad, I have to go pick up Matt at the airport."

"Whoa!" Raymond exclaimed. "Which Matt?"

"How many Matts do I know?"

"Rone. Matt Sheppard?"

"The one and only."

"Something I should know?"

"I'm not sure what he wants." Rone admitted. "Not really. But Jennifer said I should face this with an open mind just not to trust him with business again."

"Smart woman. Was I right about her or was I right about her?"

Rone laughed and after a quick mock salute to his father, he hurried out the door wondering what in the world he was thinking offering Matt to stay at his place. He stopped to scoop a soaking wet Anne into his arms and hugged her until she squealed and kissed his cheek.

"Where ya going?" She wanted to know.

"I have to go pick up a friend at the airport. You be good, 'kay?"

"Kay," she nodded.

"I'm taking her into town for dinner." Chance walked over, also soaking wet. "I promised her daddy daughter date."

"Were you two playing with the hose again?" Rose chuckled.

"Maybe." Chance winked at Anne who giggled behind her hand. "

"I look forward to my daddy daughter or daddy son dates." Rone sighed.

Chance grinned. "I'll see you later tonight."

Rone nodded and lowered Anne to the ground. While he climbed into his truck he called Jennifer.

The phone rang a few times and her voicemail picked up. His brain began freaking out as he pulled over to the side of the road and called her again. This time she picked up on the second ring and he suddenly felt foolish. Like she kept telling him, she was *pregnant not fragile.*

"Hey, baby. I'm heading to the airport to pick Matt up."

"Oh, you need some company?" Jennifer wanted to know.

"Is the company a devilishly sexy, goddess who drives me crazy?"

She giggled. "You cheating on me, Sheriff Jennings?"

He laughed, resting his head against the headrest. "Darling you weren't supposed to find out."

"Well, I'll come with you to the airport if you come and pick me up at Darlene's. She's trying to feed me some line about needing rest."

"She's right you know."

"I know." Jennifer admitted. "But some alone time with you is exactly what I need right now."

"All right sweetie. I'll grab some apple juice at the dinner and those little chocolate things you love so much lately and then come get you."

"My hero," she told him with a soft laugh.

Jennifer rested her hand atop Rone's on the gearshift. He hadn't said anything since they climbed into his truck to head back to the airport.

The last time he did that in recent weeks was to pick up Gale who tried ruining Jennifer's life and Rone all in one step.

And now it was to pick up a long-time friend who'd hurt him far more than Gale ever could. She squeezed his hand and he glanced at her quickly then pulled over to the side of the road. There was something in his eyes that terrified her.

It wasn't a kind of stare she'd seen before on him—a haunting, scared stare.

Without speaking, he removed his Stetson and tossed it into the back seat. He eased from the seat and walked around the vehicle. She watched him with her heart racing. Finally, he pulled her door opened, helped her from the truck and pulled her into his arms.

Rone held onto her then, pressing his face to her neck. She could feel his lips tremble on her flesh.

Wrapping her arms around him, she pulled him closer to her body as her belly would allow and kissed the side of his head. She wasn't sure how long they stood like that but from time to time a car would come by, they would stop to see if Rone and Jennifer needed any help.

"No, thank you for stopping though." Jennifer replied and the man or woman would drive on by with a honk and a wave.

Still, she stood there, holding her man, feeling his chest rise against her with his breath and feeling his body tremble, caressing his back. Eventually he lifted his head, and she pushed his fallen hair from his face.

"Tell me where it hurts?" Jennifer whispered.

"Everywhere."

"What can I do?"

"You're doing it, Jen." His voice husky, raw. "I'm supposed to be stronger than this."

"Than what?" Jennifer asked. "Look, I'm supposed to be your safe place. When you have to be macho for everyone else, I'm your woman. And if you need to breakdown, I'm that place."

Rone sighed. "I'm not cut out for this—for being the bigger man. Matt hurt me and now I'm supposed to forgive and forget. A few years ago, I wouldn't care. But now, I have you and this baby, how can I teach this baby to turn the other cheek and forgive if I can't?"

"There's a difference between turning the other cheek and being a coward, Rone." Jennifer explained. "There's no shame in wanting peace, wanting to end this. Don't do this for him—do it for you, because *you* want to. Just don't put anything you hold dear in his hands until he's earned that honour."

"But..."

"This sucks. I get it. Just know, I'm only on board with this because it will be helpful for you." Jennifer told him. "If he acts the fool, I'll kick his ass myself."

Rone laughed then, a soft heated sound before he leaned in and pressed his lips to hers. Jennifer spread her lips, allowing him entrance and moaning. Inhaling deeply, she pulled back and noticed his stare had changed.

She smirked at him.

"Rone Jennings. We are on the side of the road."

He moaned his disappointment but still reached down to gently pinched one of her clothed nipples. "You're right. Let's go."

They made it to the airport and Matt's jet was still not there. According to the agents, it should be arriving in a little under an hour.

"Can I treat you to an ice-cream cone?" Rone asked. "A chocolate ice-cream cone?"

Jennifer giggled. "You can treat me to anything you want." She stressed her words by wiggling her brows at him suggestively.

"You are bad." Rone laughed. "We both know we can't until the baby is born."

"Says who? There are no rules that we can't fool around." She pouted at him. He dropped a kissed to her raised lips. "After ice-cream we totally should--like high school kids."

"You're going to make an amazing wife, Jennifer Cozel."

She looped her arm with his and allowed him to lead her away from the entrance of the airport and down the street a little. "Aren't you scared?"

"About?"

"I didn't have a mother. I don't have a clue of how to be a wife."

"Yet *you* proposed to *me.*" Rone reminded her. "I don't have a clue of how to be a husband. Sure, I learned from my dad, but different relationships call for different things. My father has no idea how to work in an interracial relationship—that's what we have here, you know."

"You don't say." Jennifer smiled.

Rone smiled. "I love you."

"Say it again."

"I—love—you."

Jennifer moaned happily. "I love you.?

Epilogue

Jennifer opened her eyes to the wonderful smell of sea air. Smiling, she reached for Rone, but her hand hit empty bed. She rolled over to see Rone standing by the window with their one year old daughter in his arms.

Though the doctor cleared them to fly, she refused to bring Rayne on a plane until she was at least two or three years old. The way ears popped while on a plane would definitely be painful for the little girl.

Jennifer eased to her back and listened to Rone's soft words to their daughter and shook her head, smiling.

"You know, she is way too young to be talking about dating," Jennifer spoke.

"Maybe." Rone turned with a grin on his face. "She'll be strong enough to handle the dating thing—it's me I'm worried about."

Pushing her feet from the bed, Jennifer knew why he was freaking out already. The moment he laid eyes on little Rayne, she had him wrapped around her tiny fingers. She walked across the room to kiss to her daughter's cheek and accepted Rone's lips in a brief kiss.

"The loves of my life want breakfast?" she questioned.

Rone pouted beautiful and nodded. Rayne seemed as though she was trying to imitate her father and that left Jennifer laughing. "Okay, my darlings, come on. One bottle and room service, coming right up."

"See that, Ray?" Rone bounced Rayne gently on his arm. "All you have to do with mommy is pout."

Jennifer laughed. "Stop teaching my baby bad habits."

"My bad," Rone said for her ears then whispered something to Rayne.

The three of them made their way into the kitchen and after Jennifer made Rayne a bottle, she handed it to Rone who fed his daughter quietly.

She did as she was promised and ordered some room service for the adults and while they waited, Rone burped Rayne who fell asleep in her father's arms.

Jennifer took over, placing her daughter on the large bed, and set large pillows around her so she wouldn't roll off.

By the time their food had arrived, Jennifer had changed Rayne's diaper, took a quick shower with Rone and was busy trying to hook her bra behind her back.

"Let me." Rone accepted the straps.

She kissed his cheek then turned to let him hook her in. Once he was finished, she rewarded him with a kiss then pulled on a sun dress.

"This came for me right as we were leaving," Rone said, dropping an envelope on the table. He picked up his fork to get a bite of eggs.

Jennifer arched a brow at the way he simply picked up his fork and went back to eating. She rested her fork on the plate and picked up the white envelope. It was addressed to him from *Black Turbo Records* and her heart did a crazy little leap. There was something hard inside it, and that further drew her curiosity.

"Did you send them your song?" Jennifer asked.

"My song—you mean the one I haven't been able to finish?" Rone asked. "No."

Jennifer ripped into the paper and when she finally got into it, she pulled out the CD and something fell to the ground. Ignoring the CD for a bit she bent and grabbed the paper.

It was a check.

"Ah, Baby?" Her hands shook.

"What's wrong?"

Jennifer coughed. "Day-um."

"Jen?"

"That's a lot of zeros."

"What are you talking about?" Rone reached for it and read the check. "Is this a joke? We should call Matt. They probably sent this by mistake."

"Maybe." Jennifer turned the over in her hand. She blinked at the credits and noticed Rone's name listed on two of the twelve songs. "No. I think it's back royalties."

"Back royalties for what?"

"For the two songs you wrote for Matt. See here?" She leaned in to point to all the spots his name showed up on the cover. "You're given a credit as writer."

"He didn't have to do this."

"But remember what he said? He said he wants to make things right. This is a way to start. I guess he was serious about getting your trust back."

"He can't buy it, Jen."

"Sweetie, I don't think that's what he's doing." She pleaded. "If you'd gone on the road together you would have been paid for your work, right?"

Rone nodded. He tapped her nose gently with his finger and she grinned lovingly at him.

"I'm sure he thinks he knows that. But let him. We can put it away for Rayne's college tuition."

Rone laughed. He extended his hand to her and Jennifer walked into his arms. He pulled her into his lap and kissed her neck. "Remember that day a while ago when I almost lost it on our way to pick Matt up from the airport?"

Jennifer nodded.

"I never thanked you for what you did for me."

"And what did I do for you, Rone?"

"Everything." He told her. "I'm sorry it's taken me so long to tell you this, but that day I couldn't believe how desperately I loved you because of that."

"But you loved me before, right?"

Rone chuckled and framed her face. "I've loved you since the day I saw you standing against your car looking up at the sky."

"Sweet talker.'

His words seeped through to her core, sending a shiver down her spine, but she couldn't let him go.

She clung to him, caressing his face, feeling his day-old beard rough against her palms. Her thumbs traced his cheeks until she lifted her right hand and dragged her index finger over his full lips. She whispered her love to him feeling as if her life had finally found where it was supposed to be.

She was a teacher with a child and a husband who looked at her as if the sun rose and set on her.

"I love you more than I thought possible. And I'm so proud of what we've done in the year we've lived together. I still get nervous and wake up with a start just to make sure it wasn't a dream. Then I see you beside me and it's all perfect again."

"Why do you get nervous?"

"Michael said it best." Jennifer shrugged. "After so long of having the bad, now I have the good, I'm terrified it'll go away."

"Don't worry about it. I love you very much and I'm not going anywhere."

Jennifer stared into Rone's eyes, tangling her fingers in his long, dark hair.

She saw a glimmer of something there, something which sent her heart racing and her body burning. Smiling, she kissed her husband.

The kiss soothed her and brought her to a place she never thought she could go with a man. His arms tightened around her and as he pulled his lips back and whispered her name, the baby monitor buzzed on.

Rayne made sounds of being awake from the bedroom.

"I just needed a little while longer with you," Rone whispered.

"Don't worry." She promised. "When we go home, grandpa, Chance and Michael can baby-sit, and you and I can steal some time away."

Rone moaned. "I love you." He nodded, releasing her.

Jennifer took her husband's hand and led him into the bedroom where Rayne sitting up as best she could. Her mop of soft, dark hair stood in kinky curls at the top of her head. Rayne had her father's eyes. The thought sent tears to Jennifer's eyes but she stepped forward and sat on the bed. Reaching for her baby, she pushed the pillows back against the headboard. Rayne climbed on her and Rone lay on the other side of the bed.

"I'm so thankful." Jennifer kissed Rayne's head. "And I'm going to teach this little one to be too."

The day drifted by, leaving a lasting impression on Jennifer's heart.

Her daughter saw the beach for the first time and came back to the hotel with sand everywhere. After she was fed, washed and put down for the night, Jennifer cuddled with her husband.

In the silence of their room, she listened to his breathing, felt his chest rise and fall against her.

Splaying her fingers on his abs, she enjoyed the warmth of his body, the tightness of the muscles and slipped closer.

She whispered her love for this cop who loved her despite her faults, closed her eyes and slipped into a peaceful sleep.

Find Kadian on the web!

https://kadiantracey.wix.com/romancenorth
Twitter: @kendramechailyn